THE BACHELORS

THE BACHELORS tells the story of two poverty stricken members of the French provincial aristocracy, the baron de Coëtquidan and his nephew the comte de Coantré, who live in the suburbs of Paris, each pursuing an eccentric, decaying existence cut off from the pressures of the twentieth century. This is a story of family intrigues and physical and mental disintegration. Neglected and humiliated by society each lives in his private world of near madness. Finally one is helped by a rich relative whilst the other dies of neglect. Montherlant portrays with a mixture of irony and sympathy and a terrifying realism the strange twilight world inhabited by these two characters.

Also by HENRY DE MONTHERLANT
and uniform with this edition:

SELECTED ESSAYS edited by Peter Quennell

THE BACHELORS

by

HENRY DE MONTHERLANT

Translated from the French by
Terence Kilmartin

with an introduction by
PETER QUENNELL

THE MACMILLAN COMPANY
New York
1960

c. 4

M. Elie de Coctquidan and his nephew,
the Comte de Coantre, are the relics and
the dependents of an aristocratic family.
Called Gog and Magog by their family, they
struggle in pathetic futility for some sort
of dignity in existence.

IT IS NOT very often that an English visitor to France finds himself being entertained in one of the households of the French provincial aristocracy; and, should he happen to enjoy this privilege, the experience will probably strike him as somewhat odd and disconcerting. He may have imagined, for example, that most French citizens, wherever they lived, were more or less enamoured of the idea of Paris—only to learn from the middle-aged lady, modestly swathed in *broderie anglaise*, sitting next to him at dinner, that she rarely visits the capital, except now and then to buy a new dress at the *Printemps* or the *Bon Marché*, and that when she enters the Parisian Babylon she feels completely at a loss. From a foreign point of view, she and her husband may bear a certain resemblance to an English 'county family'; yet their name and title suggest the history of the Crusades and the chronicles of Villehardouin.

Such a family, poor and proud and isolated, provides the subject matter of the present novel. True, the Coëtquidans and the Coantrés have been uprooted from their native province. But in the charmed circle of family acquaintances—'*nos familles*'—to whom they are related either by birth or by marriage, they lead a circumscribed and largely provincial existence. The baron de Coëtquidan and his nephew, the comte de Coantré, have transferred the atmosphere of a remote provincial château to their commonplace and dilapidated little house off the boulevard Arago; and behind its garden fence they pursue their separate manias undisturbed by the pressure of the twentieth century. Both are unmarried; both are born eccentrics. Each wears a patchwork costume of old and ill-assorted clothes; and M. de Coëtquidan has developed an uncontrollable passion for collecting miscellaneous odds and ends—used stamps, pieces of string, scraps of bread and dusty lumps of sugar. Although they are poor and steadily losing money—the kitchen-table at which they eat, however, is always very well served—neither of them is capable of turning his talents to any form of remunerative work.

According to a recent biographer, Henry de Montherlant, when he composed *Les Célibataires*, now more than twenty-five years ago, took some hints from a pair of eccentric relations who once inhabited his parents' house; but no doubt as in all his novels—and, indeed, in every novel that possesses genuine imaginative quality—the auto-biographical element has undergone a far-reaching literary transformation. Whereas the gifted journalist merely reports, the imaginative artist transfigures his subject; and then, besides portraying his queer protagonists with a blend of irony and poetic sympathy, Montherlant establishes their relationship to the larger world around them. On modern society they have chosen to turn their backs; and society, in revenge, dooms them to neglect and humiliation. They are grotesque failures, laughable anachronisms. But is the way of life in which they decline to participate after all so sane and dignified? Mademoiselle de Bauret, their emancipated young kinswoman, is a foolish, restless, unattractive girl, a slightly raffish blue-stocking, the victim of her own spurious intellectual catchwords—'*la pauvre fille était une proie désignée pour les charlatans de la palette et de la plume*'; while their rich and respectable relation, the baron Octave de Coëtquidan, professedly a modern man—'*l'homme moderne avec la nuance "genre américain"*'—who flatters himself on having come to terms with 'real life', cultivates the illusions and superstitions of his age as eagerly as the two ridiculous bachelors cherish their inherited follies. Naturally, it is the twentieth century that wins—Léon de Coantré loses the remnants of his fortune and dies alone in a gloomy gamekeeper's cottage: he is swept away into the rubbish of the Past. But the question remains whether the victorious Present can afford to stand a very close scrutiny.

First published in 1934, *Les Célibataires* has often been considered Henry de Montherlant's most rewarding novel; and certainly nowhere else does he display so wide a range of qualities. The effect that the narrative produces is by turns tragic, comic and poetic; and, as in life itself, the tragedy, the comedy, the poetry are all details of the same pattern, and we pass from one to the other without any sense of making an artificial change. Montherlant's comic gifts, I think, have frequently been under-valued: like Henry James, he is usually admired for a very different set of attributes. But what could be more felicitous than the portrait he gives us of that 'advanced' plutocrat the baron Octave, a minute rosette of the Legion of Honour in the buttonhole of his American-cut suit, diligently keeping abreast of the times with the help of his favourite English newspaper?

> *Le baron Octave de Coëtquidan . . . était assis dans un rocking-chair, et il lisait le* Daily Mail. '*Lisait*' *est une façon de parler, car il ne savait pas l'anglais. Allons, n'exagérons pas: il en savait quelques mots. Mais le baron professait qu'on ne connaît rien de la politique française si on ne lit pas les journaux anglais ou americains.*

The comte de Coantré, on the other hand, is an undeniably tragic personage. At least, he acquires a tragic dignity, once the sufferings of his lonely last days have laid the essentials of his character bare. Then the forlorn eccentric becomes assimilated into the surrounding world of nature. As his loneliness increases and mankind grows more and more unfriendly, he hears, overhead in the dusk, the sounds of a skein of wild geese travelling south towards the sun and freedom:

> *Le volier avait la forme d'un long ruban naviguant très bas . . . onduleux et tout d'une pièce comme un tapis volant des Mille et une Nuits, ou comme quelque monstrueux serpent de l'air. Les oies volaient—une cinquantaine—bec au vent, d'un vol sans passion, sans chiqué, vigoureux et tranquille. . . . M. de Coantré, immobile, les regarda jusqu'à ce qu'elles eussent disparu. . . . Et il restait songeur, frappé par cette impression de volonté, de cohésion, de mystère, d'apport lointain que le volier laissait derrière lui, comme une trainée de rêve à travers le ciel vide.*

Even in his most poetic passages, Henry de Montherlant is a notably restrained and economical writer, who uses words with the utmost precision and care, and never introduces a decorative digression purely for its own sake. He is not a novelist who often pauses to describe at length the natural background of his story—an exception, however, is provided by *Le Songe*, his prentice novel about the First World War; but when he does so in one of his more mature books, in *Les Célibataires* and, earlier, in *La Rose de Sable*, it is always with the purpose of enlarging and deepening our appreciation of his human actors. Released from the miserable triviality of existence at the boulevard Arago, Léon de Coantré drifts towards death under the spell of the sleeping ice-bound forest:

Dehors continuait la nuit sans histoire. Toute la forêt craquelait sous le vent et le froid. Les crapauds endormis battaient au fond du feuillard, secoués par leur coeur trop fort. Les renards dormaient dans leurs tanières, le museau sur l'échine l'un de l'autre, ravis par leur puanteur; et les sangliers dans leurs bauges, rêvant à la glace étoilée qu'ils avaient léchée à la lumière du soir. Dans les souillats récents l'eau se congelait à nouveau, et la boue durcissait, alentour, sur les troncs d'arbres où les biches et les cerfs s'étaient frottés. Mais au fond du ciel clair, au-dessus des immobilités tapies, les oies sauvages passaient toujours, les pattes collées au ventre, soutenues par le vent, parmi les myriades d'insectes des hauteurs, le long de la grande route migratrice, semblable aux routes invisibles qu'il y a sur la mer pour les vaisseaux, ou à celles que suivent les astres.

Among much else, it is his mastery of the language that recommends Montherlant to French critics; and the passage quoted above, with its short sentences, its easy harmonious rhythm, its frieze of simple yet vivid images unfolding as the period develops, has a music that will certainly appear to any well-trained English ear. As in all good writing, English or French, the author's prose style is not a form of external ornament, but the proper expression both of his individual point of view and of his attitude towards his subject. From whatever angle we approach it, *Les Célibataires* is a singularly complete achievement, which leaves the reader little to say that the novelist, in more expressive terms, has not already said before him. Montherlant himself has told us how, after turning the last page of one of Colette's most successful novels, he was moved not to comment upon its separate literary virtues, but to exclaim simply: '*C'est cela!*'— that's that; that is exactly the way it must have happened. The same sentence seems an appropriate tribute to this beautifully balanced and admirably rounded book.

Peter Quennell

I

ABOUT seven o'clock on a cold February night in 1924, a man apparently well in his sixties, with a rough beard of indeterminate grey, was standing on one leg in front of a shop in the Rue de la Glacière, not far from the Boulevard Arago, reading a newspaper by the light of the window with the help of one of those large rectangular magnifying glasses used by stamp-collectors. He was wearing a shabby black greatcoat which reached well below his knees and a dark peaked cap of a style introduced around 1885, with a chinstrap of which the double flaps were now fastened over the top. Anyone who examined him at close quarters would have noted that every detail of his get-up was 'like nobody else'. His cap was thirty years out of date; his greatcoat was fastened at the collar by two safety-pins linked together in a short chain; the collar of his starched white shirt was frayed like lace so that the lining showed through, and his tie was not so much a tie as a cord barely covered here and there by some worn black material; his baggy trousers hung at least six inches below what tailors call 'the fork'; and one of his boots (which were enormous) was laced with a piece of string which someone had *meant* to blacken with ink.

If he had pushed his indiscretion even further, the observer would have noticed that a stout piece of string was also doing duty for our hero's belt, and that he wore no underpants. His inner garments were held together by an armoury of safety-pins, like those of an Arab. On each foot he wore two woollen socks, one on top of the other (whence, no doubt, the size of his boots). Turning out the pockets, the observer would have discovered the following items of note: an old crust of bread, two lumps of sugar, a sordid mixture of shreds of black tobacco and solidified bread crumbs, and a solid gold watch, which would have arrested his attention. It was an old, flat

9

watch, stamped all over with the beauty of priceless craftsmanship, and its case was almost entirely concealed by the loops and tendrils of an elaborate coat of arms (lion, pennons, the whole shoot), crowned with a baron's coronet. Rounding off his investigation with the wallet—a tattered wallet with the pencil missing from its socket—the observer would have come across, on the one side a hundred francs, and on the other a card advertising the establishment of 'Jenny, Theatrical Make-Up, etc', and three visiting cards which must have been there a good ten years, for they were so faded as to be almost brown at the edges. They bore the following inscription, printed in a vulgar type: *Elie de Coëtquidan, 11, Rue de Lisbonne*. And—a practice nowadays confined to the provinces, and perhaps exclusively to Brittany—the inscription was surmounted by a baron's coronet.

M. Elie de Coëtquidan, propped up on one leg, jostled by passers-by, but imperturbable, read his paper from cover to cover by the light of this barber's shop, in front of which he had been reading it every night at the same hour—although several nearby shops were better lit—for the past nine years. The contents of what he read drew from him now and then a sort of growl, a very characteristic 'Hrr. . . .' or sometimes an exclamation: 'Swine!', 'Trash!', 'Hrr, that's the young all over!' Eventually, holding the newspaper unfolded by one corner, he shuffled off towards the Boulevard Arago. From time to time he would slow down in order to poke with his cane at some bit of paper or refuse on the pavement, with the age-old gesture of the ragman.

In the Boulevard Arago he stopped in front of an iron gate, behind which, in the darkness, it was possible to make out first a small garden and then a commonplace little villa, the front of which was unlit as though the house were uninhabited. M. de Coëtquidan took out a bunch of keys, which, like his trousers and his boot, were also tied together with a piece of string, frayed and fluffy with long use, and opened the gate. Then, pulling a leaf from a bush and stuffing the stem between his teeth, he walked round the house and into the only room which was lit, the kitchen, where a tall, bony, ageing woman with a face like a hen was busy at the stove.

'Ah! So you're back!' said the woman. And by the high-pitched tone of her voice as well as what she said—Mélanie usually spoke to him in the third person—M. de Coëtquidan knew she had been at the bottle.

With a grandiose gesture, arm outstretched, and an air of lordly condescension like a ham actor in provincial rep., he offered Mélanie the newspaper, unfolded, crumpled and stained with his fingermarks, which were always somehow sticky and unclean.

'Take it. It is yours!'

His gesture, and his 'It is yours!' could hardly have been more grandiloquent if he had been offering her a diamond tiara. But suddenly, his eyes darting round the kitchen with a look of almost frantic anxiety, M. de Coëtquidan said:

'Minine not here? Where's Minine?'

'Minine? Oh, yes, he's out on the tiles. But the grey one was here just now. What's more, she made a mess there, just where you're standing. It still smells.'

'No, it *doesn't* smell,' said M. de Coëtquidan in an unanswerable tone of voice.

'Well! You ought to have been here just now! Those cats! To think that we've had them for four years, and they still make messes everywhere!'

'They don't in *my* room,' said the old man in the same categorical tone. But suddenly his face lit up, became as it were transfigured, and with a cry of 'Ah! There's Minine!' he rushed across the kitchen, nearly knocking over Mélanie, and opened the door to a small cat which glided in, leapt on to a chair and then on to M. de Coëtquidan's shoulder, and began to rub itself against him.

M. de Coëtquidan was extremely popular with cats. He knew just how to stroke them at the base of the tail, between the paws, etc, a whole technique of fondling cats which is a speciality of bachelors. He drove them wild with excitement.

'Well, no dinner tonight?' he asked suddenly, in an arrogant tone of voice.

'I'm waiting for M. de Coantré. He's been to the lawyer's, and only just got back. He's upstairs changing.'

Without saying a word, the old man snatched up a bell, opened the door leading to the rest of the house, and shook it violently, with a sort of senile frenzy and an expression of great determination, as though he were giving the signal for an armed attack or shouting 'All hands on deck!' He still had the leaf in his mouth, like an old goat. A voice called: 'Coming! I'm coming!'

The kitchen was spacious and well kept; it was in fact the only well-kept room in the house. Two rows of copper saucepans glowed there like so many suns. In the middle, on the kitchen table, which was covered with a fine linen tablecloth, two places were laid, with crystal glasses and decanters: on very cold days, meals were served in the kitchen in order to avoid lighting a fire in the dining-room, where the warmth from the big stove which heated the house did not penetrate sufficiently. Silver, tablecloth and napkins all bore the coronet of a count. A piece of string was tied round the back of one of the chairs. M. de Coëtquidan and his string again! Strange that it did not appear on his coat of arms! For this was *his* chair. Of the ten dining-room chairs there was only one, it seemed, which did not wobble at all, and M. de Coëtquidan had appropriated it; if Mélanie made a mistake and put another one in his place, there was hell to pay. Today, as usual before sitting down, and even though he had seen the string, M. Elie tested the stability of his chair. Whereupon a little man came in and said rather breathlessly:

'I haven't kept you waiting, have I, Uncle? I don't think it's more than half past seven. What time do you make it, Madame Mélanie?'

(He always said 'Madame Mélanie', whereas M. de Coëtquidan called her simply 'Mélanie'.)

'No, monsieur, it's exactly half past seven. But M. de Coëtquidan was in a hurry!'

'I've just come from the lawyer's,' said the little man, adding in a low voice, 'I'll tell you about it after dinner.' He sat down, and the two gentlemen, having tucked their napkins into their collars like farmhands, began their meal.

The Comte de Coantré was a man who might have been taken

for about forty-eight years old, although in fact he was fifty-three: he was fairly full in the face, with a moustache and a short beard untinged with grey, and close-cropped hair. He wore an indoor jacket so threadbare in front that the lining showed through, and a workman's shirt of rough khaki flannel, with a greasy collar. His felt slippers both had holes in them, and his trousers were of precisely the same awkward cut as M. de Coëtquidan's—the regulation six inches below the fork. While M. Elie's hands, though crisscrossed with scratches from the cats, were delicate, almost feminine (he was proud of them, as he was proud of his sensitive feet, which obliged him to wear two pairs of socks all the year round), M. de Coantré's were rough and calloused, especially at the tips of the fingers, which were cracked and wrinkled and grey with encrusted dirt—the hands of a labourer.

During the meal, the two gentlemen churned out the most priceless collection of conversational inanities one could possibly imagine. M. de Coëtquidan recited what he had read in his newspaper, M. de Coantré what he had learnt at school. The inanity lay not so much in what they said, which contained a certain number of truths, as in the fact that they had no idea what they were talking about. And both with such passion. The name of Briand, which cropped up occasionally, drew lightning from their eyes. The Huguenots impaled by Montluc were impaled once more by M. Elie. Everything they said was categorical: men, events, opinions were judged in a phrase, almost invariably condemned, with no appeal. There were, however, two glimmers of light—one, when M. de Coëtquidan described the buttons on the uniforms of the Gardes-Françaises, and everything he said about them was correct; the other when M. de Coantré explained a device he had invented to prevent the rats from eating the food of two hens which lived in an enclosure at the bottom of the garden. During these passages the two gentlemen, each on his special subject, were interesting.

At length they rose from the table. M. de Coantré lit an oil lamp (alone, probably, in the whole of the Boulevard Arago in 1924, the house had no electricity, through fear of novelty as well as expense), and saying to his uncle, 'Excuse me, I'm going in front because of the lamp,' he went out of the kitchen. The house was in total darkness, and the lamp threw a faint light on a narrow staircase, the steps of which were covered with a worn carpet. A large stove heated the house by way of the staircase well. M. de Coantré went up first, holding the lamp. Half-way up, noticing that M. de Coët-quidan was not following him, he stopped.

'Aren't you coming up, Uncle?'

'No, I'm warming myself,' the old man answered from beside the stove. And seeing the other hesitate, he added in a patronizing voice, 'Make yourself at home in my room. I'll be up in a moment.'

M. de Coantré went up to the first floor and into his uncle's room. It was pervaded by a smell at once strong and insipid, like the smell of ill-kept babies, the basis of which was a sort of cheap brilliantine the old man put on his hair. On the table, which was littered with stained and yellowing books and reviews, only a small corner was comparatively free, and even this was occupied by an assortment of those objects, peculiar to M. Elie, which are already old acquaintances to us: lumps of sugar, crusts of bread, shreds of tobacco and, needless to say, bits of string. Most of the objects to be seen on the table—books, cigarette packets, matchboxes, medicaments—had old used stamps stuck to them; for M. de Coëtquidan could not see a stamp on a letter (every night he poked about in the garbage bin with his stick to see if he could find one) without unsticking it, with great artistry, and resticking it, with spit, on some object in his room.

In the shadows against the walls one could vaguely distinguish a profusion of frames, imitation bronze statuettes, military outfits with sabres and straps, a crucifix above the bed, and a bookcase. Seeing all these military trimmings, our observer would have decided at once: 'He's an old retired Zouave major. Of course, the beard is typical.' But M. de Coëtquidan had never done even a week's military service. 'Well then, you won't deny he's a sportsman,' our friend would have rejoined, spotting a gun and a game-bag in a corner and three copies of the *Almanach du Chasseur français* on the table, respectively four, seven and eleven years old—but M. de Coëtquidan did not even know how to load a gun, and the bag had never contained more than a few packets of cheap tobacco. But if our observer had opened the bookcase and discovered on the lower shelves (those hidden by the woodwork) the *Claudine* series, albums of Willette and Léandre, post-cards of 'artistic nudes', books by Maizeroy and Champsaur, he would have announced triumphantly: 'I've got it! He's an old lecher.' Only M. de Coëtquidan, at the age of sixty-four, was a virgin.

M. de Coantré placed the lamp on the table, then hesitated once more. Naturally he found it rather off-hand of 'Uncle' to stay below warming himself and keeping him waiting when he had told him that he had serious matters to discuss with him. But he was so used to being deferential that it did not occur to him to be shocked. He could have sat down and waited in the only armchair, which was placed in front of the table; but the idea never crossed his mind, for it was 'Uncle's chair'! The only other chair in the room was loaded with several years' supply of copies of *La Sabretache,* as though to indicate that it was not meant to be sat in and that etiquette required of M. de Coëtquidan's visitors that they should remain standing while M. de Coëtquidan naturally occupied his own armchair. Threatened with a long wait, M. de Coantré, not without going through an inward debate that one could have read on his face, eventually decided to remove the *Sabretaches,* which he stacked clumsily on the table. Then, taking a piece of paper from his pocket and placing it too on the table, he sat down and waited.

He could hear, downstairs, the spitting noise of M. de Coëtquidan's pipe: the old man was in the habit of dribbling into it until it contained such a quantity of liquid that he was often to be seen emptying the bowl in the garden, letting out a stream of blackish juice on the gravel. Then M. de Coantré heard another characteristic noise, and his face stiffened with annoyance.

This noise was made by M. de Coëtquidan turning the handle of the stove in order to make it burn more strongly and give out more heat. This gesture of his—a ritual gesture, like so many gestures and words in this house—had always been the cause of dramas—also ritual, of course. During the time when the house was run by the Comtesse de Coantré, mother of M. de Coantré and sister of M. de

Coëtquidan (this time was not long past: she had been dead only six months), M. de Coëtquidan paid his sister a rent of five hundred francs a month, which he now paid to her son. The surreptitious twists the old man gave to the handle of the stove increased the consumption of coal: *inde irae*. It was not uncommon for Mme de Coantré to scold her younger brother like a naughty boy.

'Elie, you've been at the stove!'

'No!'

'Don't tell lies! I heard you.'

'I tell you I didn't! So there!'

The handle of the stove was nowadays one of the things that induced a constant state of anxiety in the poor count's feeble brain. He lived in dread of hearing the fatal noise and then having either to accept this waste of coal, or admonish his uncle, a contingency which assumed agonizing proportions in his mind. After lunch he would watch for the old man to go out and, as soon as he heard the front door close behind him, would go down two floors to turn the stove down. At night, on the point of going to sleep, he would wake up with a start, thinking he had heard someone at it.

At last M. de Coëtquidan came laboriously up the stairs, gripping the banisters so hard that it sounded as if he might uproot them: they shook from top to bottom of the house. M. de Coantré went out to light the way for him, and M. de Coëtquidan entered his room.

'Uncle, I'm going to have to talk business to you for the first time . . .'

M. de Coantré stopped short. His uncle's eyes had alighted on the chair: the *Sabretaches* were no longer there! And immediately the old man's glance leapt round the room with the same frenzied gleam that had crossed it when, casting a circular look round the kitchen, he had asked: 'Where's Minine?'

'There they are,' said M. de Coantré, pointing to the table.

M. Elie fumbled through the reviews with nervous fingers. And M. de Coantré, though long accustomed to his uncle's behaviour, was stupefied by his action: the old man was counting the reviews as though he were afraid his nephew had stolen one of them. Then he sat down and grunted: 'Hrrr . . .' These 'Hrrr's', resembling the grunts with which certain species of monkeys punctuate everything they do, were always heavy with significance, usually of a threatening kind.

A troubled look came over M. de Coantré's face, and blinking rapidly, he said:

'Uncle, ever since Mama's death I haven't bothered you with business matters. With her example always in mind, I wanted above all to avoid worrying you in any way.'

'You did right, my boy,' said M. de Coëtquidan, with a cynicism to which both he and his nephew remained oblivious.

'Nevertheless the time must come when one has to face realities. In this life of ours,' the count went on sententiously, 'we must be realistic.' (This word 'realistic' was fashionable in the newspapers of the day. When the reader gets to know M. de Coantré better, he will realize that on his lips it had a very special savour.) 'I saw Bourdillon again today' (this was the chief clerk in the office of Lebeau the solicitor), 'and the time has come to put you in the picture.

'When Mama died, her assets, according to Lebeau's evaluation, amounted,' here he glanced at the paper he had put on the table, 'to seventy thousand francs excluding personal effects. Add to that the two thousand francs we found in her desk, and we get seventy-two thousand francs. The girl (his niece, Simone de Bauret) and I agreed to accept the estate conditionally. However, as soon as probate had begun, Antoni put in a claim for a capital sum of thirty thousand francs—forty thousand with the interest.'

'Your mother borrowed thirty thousand francs from Antoni?' asked M. de Coëtquidan, his eyes widening to show in full his pale blue pupils.

'Yes, between 1909 and 1914, three thousand here, five thousand there. . . .'

'And what did she do with this money?' asked M. Elie, with a strange glint in his eye.

'Come, Uncle Elie, you know perfectly well. It was to tidy up the past.' (Of course M. de Coëtquidan knew, or rather suspected: these sums had been borrowed by Mme de Coantré to pay her late

17

husband's debts. But the opportunity of reminding the count of his father's misdeeds had seemed too good to miss.)

'Now,' M. de Coantré continued, 'a new debt has come to light. Mme de Saint-Huberty has put in a claim for sixteen thousand francs which her father, M. d'Aumagne, lent Mama in 1912, plus four thousand francs interest. I've found among Mama's papers a letter from M. d'Aumagne in 1916 in which he says: "Let's forget it." But apparently that's not legally valid. We paid off Antoni in full by selling some shares. With Mme de Saint-Huberty we compromised, and she waived the interest: we sold some more and paid her. That makes a disbursement of fifty-six thousand out of the seventy-two—leaving sixteen thousand. You follow me?'

'Hrrr . . .' said M. de Coëtquidan, to whom everything precise was obscure.

'Out of these sixteen thousand I've spent, since Mama's death, on the house, the funeral, etc, about eight thousand francs. Then there will be Lebeau's fees and expenses, which I evaluate at two thousand francs. Which leaves six thousand provided no further creditors turn up. Your nephew's entire fortune amounts, at best, to six thousand francs, apart from your monthly five hundred francs for board and lodging. Plus the four pieces of furniture in my room. I'm giving the girl my share of Mama's furniture. It takes up a lot of room, but you know what it is—old-fashioned, broken-down stuff. She can do what she likes with it, keep whatever might be useful when she marries, and sell the rest.'

M. de Coantré stopped, and there was a silence. M. de Coëtquidan's only comment was 'Hrrr . . .'

A simple-minded person might have been impressed by the technical words scattered throughout the elementary statement the count had just made with his eyes continually glued to his notes: 'put in a claim', 'capital sum', 'disbursement', not to mention his 'I evaluate', which suggests the man who is sure of his ground. A shrewder man would have seen that it was a mask under which M. de Coantré concealed his profound ignorance and incomprehension of everything to do with money and business.

He went on: 'You understand, Uncle, that when one has on the one hand six thousand francs all told, and on the other the six thousand a year which you give me for your keep, one cannot afford a rent of five thousand francs. We are therefore faced with the absolute necessity of leaving the Boulevard Arago when the lease expires, that is on October 15th, and then each of us shifting for himself. In the next eight months we'll have plenty of time to look around.'

There was another silence. Then M. de Coëtquidan said in a low voice:

'I'll just starve to death.'

'Come, come, Uncle! *Sursum corda!* I don't know what your income is, and it isn't my business. But after all, you have something. You're not someone who has a maximum of six thousand francs to look forward to, and when that's gone, literally nothing. And anyhow you know Uncle Octave will never desert you.'

'My brother! He'd send me to the workhouse sooner than put me up himself.'

'We'll find you a good boarding-house. You have money. Perhaps by buying an annuity you could . . .'

M. de Coantré stopped. His uncle had given a 'Hrrr' which meant: 'Now, my boy, you're beginning to meddle in something that is none of your business.'

'My six thousand francs, and the three thousand five hundred you give me between now and October 15th—those are my sole assets until we leave. Two thousand for Lebeau, and two thousand five hundred for the two quarters' rent: that leaves five thousand to keep the place going for eight months.'

'And what will you do on October 15th?'

'I'll have to work, of course. I shall start looking for something tomorrow. I don't know . . . a hospital job perhaps . . .'

'Hrrr . . .' growled M. de Coëtquidan, his finger wedged in his nose.

M. de Coantré failed to grasp the meaning of this grunt, which was: 'Work, you! You won't find a job, because you're a good-for-nothing. And you'll fall back on my brother Octave, and whatever he has to do for you will mean so much less for me.'

19

'As for me,' said the old man sourly, 'I shall ask Octave to take me on as night-watchman at his bank . . .' He paused, '. . . and he'll throw me out.'

His eyes widened, and filled with a moisture that was close to tears. They were bachelor's tears, tears of self-commiseration.

M. de Coantré saw this film of tears, and immediately tears came to his own eyes; but they were not bachelor's tears: he was moved not for himself but for his uncle. Impulsively he rose on his short legs.

'Courage, Uncle! I don't know how I can be of use to you, but for me you are now mother's representative on earth. Whatever happens, I shall never desert you.'

'Quite right, my boy,' said M. de Coëtquidan.

'Allow me to embrace you, Uncle,' said M. de Coantré.

He brought his face close to the old man's, and placed his lips on the verge of the shaggy beard. M. de Coëtquidan's mouth formed in space the outline of a vague and noiseless kiss.

Suddenly, M. de Coantré's emotion changed to a little, jerky laugh, and it was in a jovial tone that he said:

'So that's the end of Arago! Well, it's none too soon. You'll see, Uncle, leaving this confounded shack will bring us luck. I tell you, October 15th 1924 will be the start of a new life for us!'

They said good-bye, and M. de Coantré, lighting a small lamp on the table on the landing, began climbing the stairs to his room, which was on the next floor. 'You can't see a thing. Shall I give you some light?' the old man shouted after him, and he placed his own lamp on the landing table. M. de Coantré felt a sort of inner gush of joy. Already this conversation had brought him immense relief. He had been dreading it. He had been afraid his uncle might reproach him or fly into a rage and declare, 'I'm not going, so there!' And now everything had gone so well that the old boy was offering to light the stairs for him! M. de Coantré was overcome with gratitude.

In his room, the lamp lit up stale sheets and a bed on which a travelling rug was doing duty for a bedspread. Within five minutes M. de Coantré had put out his light.

No sooner was his nephew out of sight than M. de Coëtquidan had gone to the fireplace, where the fire was dying down. Delicately he had cut two hairs from his beard with a pair of scissors and put them in the shovel, which he now held over the embers. Soon the hairs began to sizzle, and an expression of amusement, of childish glee, appeared on the old man's bearded face, a sort of gargoyle's grin which lasted until the crackling noise of the hairs had ceased. Ah! there was no thought now of starving, or even of being night-watchman in his brother's bank! Life was good, so long as one could play these little games. The old man remained for a few moments staring at the fire. It was ten o'clock. The cook, who went home at night, normally left at about nine. M. de Coëtquidan took up his lamp and advanced cautiously on to the landing. The house was silent; all that could be heard was the sound of a piece of coal falling inside the stove. Trying not to make a noise (although the banisters shook as before), M. de Coëtquidan went down to the kitchen. He took three lumps of sugar from the sugar-bowl and three nuts from a fruit-dish, and pocketed them. A bottle of wine had already been broached; he put it to his lips and drank about a glassful, wiping his mouth with his coat-sleeve. He dipped a spoon in the jam-pot and helped himself. He was washing the spoon—still in absolute silence—when, from behind the door, a tremulous voice cried:

'Who's there?'

'Hrrr. . . .'

M. de Coantré appeared, his face drawn. M. de Coëtquidan pushed the sticky spoon into a corner.

'Oh, it's you, Uncle! Well, you did give me a fright. You know, all this talk about money must have gone to my head. I was woken up by a noise and thought it was like that other time . . .' (an allusion to a burglary scare which we shall hear about later on).

'The window was banging and I came to shut it,' said the old man, averting his eyes like a delinquent child caught redhanded. 'She always forgets.'

And with a sly expression, glad to be able to humiliate the person who had discovered him *in flagrante delicto,* he added:

'Mustn't be so panicky, my boy!'

The two men, each with his lamp, left the kitchen.

'You go up first,' said M. de Coëtquidan. When his nephew had gone up a few stairs, he followed him. He had had his first revenge, with that wounding remark. Now he had a second. On the way up, his eyes lowered and without making the slightest noise, he turned the stove up a little higher.

2

IN MAY 1869, the smart people of Paris were invited to attend the weddings of the Coëtquidan girls, Angèle and Emilie—'the love-birds' as they were called, for they were twins. They were married the same day, Angèle to a young de Coantré whose ambition was to be a gentleman of leisure, Emilie to a naval officer, M. de Piagnes, who was a paragon of virtue. M. de Coantré was marrying his 'love-bird' because he had had his share of wenching and now wanted someone absolutely respectable. 'I should prefer her to be stupid,' he had specified when his aunts asked him what sort of girl he wanted them to look for, and when they mentioned the Coët-quidan girl his first question had been: 'Is she nice and stupid?' They had reassured him. As for M. de Piagnes, he was attracted only by girls who did not open their mouths at dances. Not only did he regard this as a proof of their virtue; he was also sorry for them, because the young men left them high and dry: he was the St Vincent de Paul of the ballroom. Emilie danced three *cotillons* with M. de Piagnes, in the course of which she never uttered. He was so overwhelmed that he proposed there and then.

The 'love-birds' were reputed to lack intelligence. This reputa-tion was unjustified. Society people are apt to believe that a girl who puts on an act, or who is a 'character', or who is taking her *baccalauréat,* or who flirts, or who, quite simply, is badly brought up, is an intelligent girl; and heaven knows how it is in reality! Having given too much credit to some, society withholds too much from others: the more homely girls are wantonly condemned. And yet, given a choice between stupidity plain and stupidity adorned, how could one but prefer the former? At least it is harmless and does not contribute to that vast confusion of values which is one of the most devastating and most neglected social evils of our time. The 'love-birds' had little wit, but they were pious, upright, retiring, docile, ready for any sacrifice, fundamentally charitable—in other words they had all those Christian virtues which are always an object of derision in a Catholic society. Besides, were they so devoid of wit? Often they would utter remarks full of shrewdness or common sense, of which none of their brilliant friends would have been capable. But since these remarks came from them they either passed unnoticed, or were laughed at. However, one of the twins, Angèle, was reputed to be more intelligent than her sister. But she drew no advantage from this reputation, because only their nearest relations and a few intimate friends could tell the 'love-birds' apart. Anyone who ran into either of them was tempted to ask her, 'Let's see now, are you the intelligent one?'

The 'love-birds' had two brothers. The elder, Octave, was at the time of their marriage a young man of twenty, who had just become an employee of Latty's Bank, of Paris, because he was a close friend of the chairman's son. The younger, Elie, was the most promising of all the Coëtquidans. He was studying political science, for which he was quite unsuited, since he disliked society and was always buried in his books and papers.

His daughters married, the old Baron de Coëtquidan went back to his château at Trenel, near Saint-Pol-de-Léon. He had insisted, at the time of the weddings, that the Coantrés, in return for an allowance, should keep Elie with them until he got married, since he was so engrossed in his books and so well known as 'a bit of an eccentric' that he was considered incapable of looking after himself. M. de Coantré pulled a face, but was obliged to acquiesce. M. de Coëtquidan had chosen Angèle for this wedding present because she was to remain in Paris, where Elie had to stay because of his studies, whereas the Piagnes were going to live at Lorient.

M. de Coëtquidan, who had married at the age of fifty-five, was now eighty. It was malevolence that kept him alive, for malevolence, like alcohol, is a preservative. After a certain age, every biting word uttered, every anonymous letter posted, every calumny spread abroad wins you another few months from the tomb, because it stimulates your vitality. This can also be seen among animals: a particularly cruel hen, a stubborn horse or a vicious dog will live longer than its fellows. M. de Coëtquidan was extremely pretentious; the way he said 'people like us' was enough to make you want to guillotine him on the spot. At Trenel he sank into the melancholy dotage of those without the prospect of constant promotion in the Legion of Honour to buttress their old age. He was wedded to an old copy of *Tout-Paris* which he covered with mysterious notes concerning all the families he knew. Wherever he opened it this sacred book provided food for profound reflection— just as the believer, wherever he opens the Gospel, is said to find an answer to what he seeks.

M. de Coëtquidan's other activities were more humdrum. It was he who wielded the feather-duster, chopped the wood, lit the fire and did the cooking, for he had made himself so detested that no one would work for him. By increasing their wages, he might perhaps have kept his staff, but that would have meant surrender. Continually creating a desert around him, and persecuting the few who ventured into it, he reached a point where even the tradesmen refused to come up to the château. Nobody now called but the postman, who arrived panting and footsore, for M. de Coëtquidan had taken out a subscription to *Le Temps* with the sole intention of forcing this excellent man to walk sixteen kilometres daily from the post office to the château and back. Abandoned by the tradesmen, who were delighted to forgo his money at the thought of leaving him at death's door, M. de Coëtquidan lived on fruit from his orchard and biscuits and cakes which he had sent to him by the makers, and would have died of this régime had not Mme Angèle discovered it by chance and sent him a manservant, with enormous wages, who left forthwith because M. de Coëtquidan had given him orders and he only accepted requests. M. de Coëtquidan would have had to fall back on the biscuits if his other daughter, succumbing to the lure of martyrdom, had not come to live at Trenel. Food restored M. de Coëtquidan's faculties: he proceeded to paint a set of plates with the arms of all the provinces of France as they were in '89.

Eventually the old rogue had a stroke, and died after three days.

Five years later M. de Piagnes died, as a result of an accident in the arsenal at Lorient. Mme de Piagnes, a childless widow, went to live in Paris with her brother Octave, who had remained a bachelor. Meanwhile the Coantrés, still flanked by M. Elie who had also clung to his celibacy, had acquired a son and a daughter, Léon and Marie.

By 1890, nothing had changed in the Octave-Emilie partnership, but M. Octave was now head of something or other at the bank and was growing pompous. The Coantrés had had another daughter, Madeleine; Marie had died at the age of sixteen. Marriage had brought about one unfortunate transformation in M. de Coantré. His main occupation hitherto had been debauchery. A dutiful husband, he gave this up on marrying. But he had to keep himself occupied; his passionate interest in women had to be diverted into some other channel. So he busied himself by trying to increase his fortune on the stock exchange—in other words, in the time-honoured fashion of his kind, by ruining himself. By 1890, he was well on the way to bankruptcy.

That year, Léon de Coantré went to do his military service at Toulouse. He had been a pampered child, who was made to keep his long curls until the age of seven, and then a brilliant pupil of the Jesuits, brilliant but temperamental and undisciplined. His mother spoiled him madly, from a mixture of love and weakness. His father spoiled him from inclination—the Coantrés were an easy-going race—and on principle. The fact was that M. de Coantré did not find it easy to stomach the presence in his home of such a disagreeable person as Elie de Coëtquidan, more and more unmarriageable; he had rather an aversion for the Coëtquidans. In spoiling his son he was protesting against the harsh theories of his father-in-law; too strict an upbringing, he claimed, automatically produces a reaction when the child grows up. What had become of old Coëtquidan's children? Angèle and Emilie had kept in marriage the same cowed demeanour as under their father's régime, and their social life had suffered from it. Elie simply did what he liked, and moreover (as we shall see) had turned out to be a non-starter.

Having passed his *baccalauréat*, Léon de Coantré started reading law. At his first year's examination, one of the examiners thought he remembered having met some de Coantrés as a young man. Without explaining to Léon the reason for his curiosity, he asked him a few questions about his family. Léon's reaction was worthy of the elder Coëtquidan. 'What's it to do with you?' he asked the august personage. He was promptly ploughed. The two years that followed until his military service, still reading law without either inclination or success, were as characteristically futile as the student years of most average Frenchmen.

He was a gifted youth, in a variety of ways. He excelled at writing Latin verse. He drew and painted agreeably, without ever having been taught. He could draw expressive harmonies from the piano, although his ignorance of music was such that he could scarcely identify a single note on the keyboard. He was interested in physics and mechanics and would shut himself up to carry out experiments. He was astonishingly clever with his hands, and could produce models of houses or boats, executed in such elaborate detail, with such taste, skill and technical ingenuity as to make them little works of art, good enough to be shown in an exhibition.

In the army, where he became a sergeant, he made friends with a fellow-sergeant called Levier, whose father was foreman in an engineering workshop. His horror of social constraints of any kind induced in him a fellow-feeling for the people, made him choose working-class youths as friends, sewing-girls and maidservants as mistresses: with them he did not have to stand on ceremony. Society people were his bugbears: he was physically incapable of conceiving a desire for a well-born woman. Towards the end of his military service, Léon told Levier of a certain apparatus he had in mind for enlarging photographs, something much more advanced than the existing method. Levier was enthusiastic. In a few months they would be civilians. Why not go into partnership? Léon would produce the idea and the capital, Levier undertook to provide the materials.

All the family joined in. They had faith in Léon's genius: did he not compose at the piano without knowing the notes! And moreover, how splendid to see a young nobleman rolling up his sleeves, loving the workers, being progressive! Levier gave all the necessary guarantees and made a good impression. They saw big. It was no longer simply a question of exploiting an enlarger; they would also deal in cameras. One member of the family put twenty thousand francs into the business, another fifteen, another ten. Within two years it was bankrupt. Levier, who was a man of his word, had remained straight as long as Léon remained serious. As soon as Léon, incapable of application or method, and moreover obsessed by women, ceased to turn up and assumed the role of the titled amateur, Levier proceeded to take advantage of the situation—and it is true that Léon's ignorance and naïvety in business matters would have tempted a saint. Then Léon announced that he could no longer work with Levier because his breath smelled, and one may guess how the family, whose financial feathers were falling like snowflakes in this storm, received such an argument. The enlargers cost the Coantrés eighty thousand francs, not counting their initial shareholdings, which Levier promised to pay back gradually. At this very moment M. de Coantré completed their ruin by his stock exchange speculations. As a result, he died. Mme de Coantré was left with sixty thousand francs' worth of debts.

Léon, impulsive as ever, wanted to kill himself. The Coëtquidans, furious with the Coantrés who had brought all this on their sister, naturally maintained that he was shamming. But he was found with his throat cut. His mother was frantic. Léon said to her, 'I think I'm going mad. I must give up everything at once, not think about anything, or I don't know what I mightn't be capable of. Give me five thousand francs and you won't hear of me for two years. I give you my word of honour that I won't ask for a penny for two years.' Mme de Coantré, who imagined him blowing his brains out if they did not yield at once to his every whim, gave him the five thousand francs.

He set off—not for California but for Chatenay (Seine), where he stayed two years. He took a room in a widow's house, and did nothing but potter around, shooting, fishing, doing odd jobs; out all day long; dressed like a tramp; chaste as a gelded cat (we shall see this metamorphosis in slow motion later on); happy as a king.

Like the *kalenderi* of Sufism, his principal aim was to escape from custom and convention, and to avoid worries. Foolish and improvident over important things, he was the soul of wisdom and prudence as regards minor details. Noting down his smallest expense to the nearest sou, not once did he exceed by as much as five francs the monthly sum he could allow himself. Mme de Coantré went to see him once a month. Only twice in the two years did he accept the small sums which she offered him on each visit.

When the two years had elapsed, he returned home. What was to be done with him? Mme de Coantré thought of marrying him off; after all, he had a name. He made no objection. But he refused to move in society. He would only marry a bourgeoise or a working-class girl, not an aristocrat. His tool-box never left him, and one day Mme de Coantré found him with a chisel removing the coronet and crest from all his personal silver. 'Kind hearts can do without coronets,' he said.

In the role of suitor, he anticipated Tristan Bernard's Triplepatte.[1] His poor mother wore herself out trying to arrange interviews, with the help of the family. Everyone would at last be brought together, after enormous pains, and Léon would fail to turn up. That was how he was: smart people made him see red. And then having to *dress*, what torture! and be *on time*, what agony! With all this there were flashes of disinterestedness and pride which leave one hesitating whether to praise or blame. Negotiations have reached an advanced stage with a rich family called Duruel. Léon discovers that these people, who were to be found under D in last year's *Tout-Paris*, are under R in this year's. Hey presto! In vain does Mme de Coantré try to persuade him that 'It's a good thing for families to try to improve themselves'. He intimates that all is over; for him, these people have been judged and found wanting. A big industrialist family, one of those whose names are known the world over, are not averse to the idea of offering him their daughter. Interview. Mademoiselle is wearing lipstick. The hermit of Chatenay launches into a tirade against young women who paint their faces. Imagine this monster in the society of today: a man without a job who is not

[1] A character notorious for his indecision and procrastination.

ambitious, a poor man who does not care for money! Surely he must be devout enough to go into a monastery! Far from it. And what place is there for a man who is in the world but has no ambition and dislikes money? Ambition and greed are the two legs of the worldly man; he who is without them is a legless cripple in the crowd. But we, dear reader, we raise our hat to this cripple.

This matrimonial farce lasted three years. After his two years of solitude and chastity, it would have needed a great deal of tact to reconcile Léon with society. Instead, his family did their utmost to put him off it for ever. Out of stupidity. They showed kindness, even great kindness, considering the memories Léon had left behind him. But there it is, they were stupid people. Whatever you might think of him, Léon was a creature apart. The family treated him as though he were an elegant young charmer. We shall refrain from passing judgment on the methods by which marriages are ordinarily made in France in the social class which concerns us here. Léon saw it all, and found it repulsive. Eventually he announced that he would only marry a woman he liked, in a country church, with no ceremony, no invitations, no presents; he even wanted to do without witnesses. Mme de Coantré threw in her hand.

During these three years, Léon de Coantré lived with his mother. There was no question of his working. Mme de Coantré was afraid he might slit his throat if she breathed a word on the subject. Clearly, he had had a brilliant idea when he had slit his throat or pretended to. This new life under his mother's wing, with all expenses paid, as carefree as a little boy, was much to his taste. He asked for nothing better than to continue with it. He did so for twenty years.

Opinion was hard on him. To have wasted his talents, to have been partly responsible for his mother's destitution, and now, still young and healthy, to be sponging on her, although she found it difficult to make ends meet!

Opinion was too hard on him, for this reason. Mme de Coantré, finding herself a widow and in an extremely devitalized position both materially and morally—and moreover deprived of her daughter who had just married (satisfactorily enough) an engineer called M. de Bauret—had left her mansion in the Rue de Lisbonne and moved into a small house in the Boulevard Arago. There was a garden there, and Léon devoted himself to this garden. Brown corduroys, old worn-out shoes, blue apron, no collar—it was Chatenay all over again! Soon he took on other jobs, such as looking after the stove, fetching the coal from the cellar, painting walls, even polishing floors. It will be said that he did it because he enjoyed doing it. He did. In this life of his, completely devoid of thought, worry, and social responsibility, he was happy. In spite of being a nobleman, a count, the head of the house of Coantré, in spite of having excelled at Latin verses, painted and made music without having learnt, and invented a photographic enlarger, his true vocation was to be a common labourer. But the fact remains that the services he rendered were of a kind that, had he not been there, would have had to be paid for. When Mme de Coantré had made quite sure that it was not another fad of his, that it was going to last, she got rid of her housemaid and kept only the cook and a charwoman.

For twenty years, almost literally, M. de Coantré never left the house in the Boulevard Arago. New Year visits and funerals of close relations (he did not go to weddings) were his only contacts with the outside world. Not once, in twenty years, did he go out after dinner. There were some years when, in the entire twelve months, he did not go through the garden gate more than five times. Notwithstanding his mother's mute supplications, he never went to do his Easter duties; though if you had said a word against religion in front of him he would have scratched your eyes out. To avoid having to comb his hair, he had it practically shorn off; in order to avoid having to shave, he let his beard grow. He wore his shirts (workmen's khaki shirts) for a fortnight. There came a time when he no longer used soap except on Sundays; the rest of the week he simply gave his face a wipe with a wet towel—which at any rate is in a great tradition.

Mme de Coantré let him be. She was worn out. Having fought with her husband, fought with her son, fought with her family, fought with the creditors, she did not want to have to fight again to

31

persuade her son to wash himself. For the moment he was harmless, and he made himself as useful as he could, poor boy. She could still see the scar on Léon's throat . . . A single misplaced word, she told herself, and there might be a recurrence of such dramas; Léon was someone not to be roused.

Occasionally, indeed, he treated her in an almost loathsome way. Léon had the good nature, the cheerfulness, the superficial kindliness of the Coantrés. But when a man has only a grain of malevolence in him, he is liable to store it up for his aged father or mother. Sometimes it was only out of nervous exasperation that Léon fumed at his mother—whenever he heard the faint clicking of her rosary beads, or when her face was more lugubrious than usual. This, in particular, was a matter of course; as soon as he saw her suffer, it was as though, like a hen when it sees another wounded, he flung himself at her, climbed on top of her, trampled her down, pecked at her skull until he drew blood. But most often it was, theoretically, for her own good that he abused her. For example, if she had refused to see the doctor, or if, contrary to the latter's orders, she had not eaten enough at meal-times (concealing in her napkin, with the pathetic childishness of the old, a few pieces of the raw meat prescribed for her).

Needless to say, these tirades did far more damage to Mme de Coantré's health than she herself had done by getting rid of a little of her raw meat. Afterwards Léon, impulsive but tender-hearted, would ask her forgiveness with tears in his eyes; but the damage had been done. The crowning absurdity of Léon's behaviour in doing harm to his mother out of love or so-called love for her, showed itself in a scene that frequently recurred. Mme de Coantré was liable to fall asleep in her armchair in the middle of the day. Léon could not bear to see the old lady's ravaged face, eyes closed, mouth open, either because it brought to mind what she would soon be like in death, or because, in his feeble-minded way, he thought the worst had happened, that she *was* dead, so he would wake her with an anguished cry of 'Mother!' and if she did not wake up at once he would shake her roughly. It so happened that Mme de Coantré was racked night after night by the most appalling insomnia, and these snatches of day-time sleep should have been piously respected. But that would have been too much to expect of Léon, who was incapable of controlling his imagination and his nerves.

And what of M. Elie, that other paragon? Well, M. Elie was still living with his sister and Léon. And we shall see what had become of him.

What is one to think of the kind of hoodoo that seemed to bewitch these two men? Was it the shade of old Coëtquidan that hovered over them? Was it the fact that both lived under Mme de Coantré's wing, cut off from everything human, in conditions that would only be suitable for great thinkers or creators (and for very few of these)? We shall see the uncle's life take the same course as was later to be followed by that of his nephew. Surely there must have been some flaw in the machine that propelled these two lives?

Taken in from the age of twenty by his sister, in accordance with their father's wishes, Elie ceased to take an interest in anything whatsoever except his old papers. The family were dazzled by the extent of his knowledge. They were incapable of making the distinction between intelligence and education and thus realizing that Elie was an imbecile endowed with a good memory. That sort of animal goes far in society, and Elie might have become as important as his brother had not his Coëtquidan extremism, finding no counterbalance in reality, since he lived cut off from reality, rapidly eaten up the little merit he possessed. After the birth of Léon, the Coantrés, in order to have more room, moved house from the Rue de Bellechasse, where they were then living, to the Rue de Lisbonne. One morning, Mme de Coantré noticed that her brother had stayed at home instead of going to his political science class. On being questioned, Elie explained that he could not continue his studies because the Rue Saint-Guillaume was too far from the Parc Monceau. 'I can't spend an hour and a half in a bus every day.' His sister, his brother-in-law, and finally his brother all tried to persuade him of the folly of destroying his future for such a childish reason; but he refused to budge. (There was no question of renting him a room near the Rue Saint-Guillaume, since Mme de Coantré had made a solemn promise to her father to keep him with her until he got married.) Thus Elie's eccentricities foreshadowed, twenty years ahead, those by which Léon was to ruin *his* life, down to the lunatic reasons he gave for his behaviour.

As to that, of course, the pundits who always find high-sounding motives to explain men's actions will tell you this is impossible, that the reason given by Elie was an excuse, that there must have been some ulterior motive. But there was not. M. de Coëtquidan gave up the idea of ever being a man of consequence simply because he did not want to do an hour's bus journey every day.

From that moment, almost overnight, Elie began to do nothing. It was in 1903 that Léon, at Chatenay, settled down to this pursuit. But already, in 1880, Elie had shown him the way. And this is how this paragon organized his empty life.

He woke up at nine, and stayed in bed until half past ten reading, playing with the cats and picking his nose. At eleven he went for a stroll in the neighbourhood, returning home for lunch. After lunch he read for a while, then walked round Paris from three till seven, browsing in second-hand book-shops and going from café to café. He never had a meal in a restaurant, although he often longed to do so, because his board was paid for at home. He never went away even for a week. He never went out in the evening, and was never invited. Out of moroseness and a horror of putting himself out, he had abandoned social life, no longer calling on people except when he knew he would not find them in. As a result, not surprisingly, society abandoned him, and whereas at first he avoided it solely out of caprice, a time came when there was an additional reason—the fear of being snubbed.

His conversation was a tissue of inanities. Nevertheless—and this is the serious part of it—for every four or five inanities there was one strikingly accurate judgment. Almost invariably he took the opposite view to the majority, and since the latter is more than likely to be astray, it was inevitable that from time to time he should accidentally hit on a truth which anyone but an 'eccentric' would have missed. He had a kind of genius for dressing in an outlandish way, but he was aware of this, and persisted in it out of a taste for the sordid. At family weddings and funerals, he stayed near the back of the church, saying that in his get-up nobody would want him even as a door-keeper. The pathetic life of Léon de Coantré —the army, servant girls, enlargers, creditors, the jungle of Chatenay-sous-Bois —was an epic of heroic romance compared to M. de Coëtquidan's, in which nothing ever happened at all. For four years M. de Coëtquidan got up at half past ten, played with the cats, read the newspapers, and probed the mysteries of vermouth in the course of innumerable meditations at Scossa's, Perroncel's or Weber's. His normal disposition was of the kind we feel when we are waiting our turn at the post office and find some young whippersnapper in front of us who has brought a dozen parcels to be registered for his boss; this disposition was rage, and the urge to insult.

For M. Elie, like his father, was vicious. When he saw a notice saying 'Sale by order of the court' he was pleased; when he read in his newspaper an account of some disaster he would say: 'Another few useless bastards out of the way!' The hatred of this idler for people who were taking a holiday! The hatred of this failure for people who were unsuccessful! He would pinch children on the sly in crowded shops, or, sitting on a bench in a square, would let them brush past him as they ran, and then suddenly trip them up. But this unemployed knight-errant put on lordly airs only when he could do so with impunity; he tyrannized over waiters and cats, who cannot answer back; he insulted people in letters, and would have insulted them over the telephone, had he tried this machine, but not once in his life did he do so. His perpetual spleen was attenuated by a congenital Coëtquidan timidity, which old Coëtquidan curbed by dint of malice, and M. Octave by dint of money, but which, far from being curbed by anything at all in M. Elie, was aggravated in his case by two of the most crippling sentiments imaginable: the consciousness of being badly dressed, and the consciousness of being sexually null.

From the latter point of view, all the Coëtquidans were rather cold. M. Elie was not exactly cold—in fact he had a ribald imagination—only he did not take things to their logical conclusion. However, as with Léon, we shall examine later M. Elie's attitude towards the fair sex.

Her husband dead and her daughter married and living in her own home, Mme de Coantré thus found herself living with her brother and her son when the war came. M. de Bauret was killed almost at once, and his wife did not long survive him: a heavy blow for Mme de Coantré. To have provided a home for her brother and her son was enough: she offered to take in her grand-daughter. But Simone de Bauret, who was then seventeen, and gave signs of becoming a real post-war girl (need I say more?) refused point-blank to bury herself alive with 'Gog and Magog' as she called them, and went to live in Brittany with an old but rich cousin who had taken a fancy to her.

M. Elie was too old to be conscripted. Léon, for some obscure reason, was rejected as unfit. His heroism was of the unassuming kind: he offered his services to an auxiliary hospital in Paris. But it would be no exaggeration to say that to drag himself out of his Arago shell cost him more than it cost many combatants to drag themselves out of their trenches, which is why we may talk of heroism. M. de Coantré's feelings about the hospital can be summed up as follows: deep friendship and absolute devotion towards the wounded, because they were men of the people, and hatred for the nurses, the management, the visitors—in short for anyone belonging to the well-to-do classes. The odd thing is that, in spite of all they might have thought of this man in good health and out of the firing line, titled, poor, madly incompetent, looked down on by the rest of the staff, and on the whole rather ridiculous, the soldiers liked him well enough.

Eager, painstaking, and still fairly good with his hands (though a good deal less than of old), Léon carried out menial jobs as an assist-ant medical orderly for three weeks. Then, after committing several blunders, he was condemned to a sort of Chinese torture, which consisted in giving him nothing to do at all, but literally nothing. He wandered from ward to ward, his arms dangling, feeling himself a burden to everyone, trying to make himself as small as possible as though to weigh less, like a man in an overloaded boat, not daring even to raise his eyes, sensing the gibes behind his back, seeing the faces suddenly straighten when he appeared, but nevertheless telling himself that this was his war effort, that it wasn't a hard one, and that he must grin and bear it.

This situation gave rise to a rather splendid scene. One of the patients, a corporal who in more respects than one was far removed from M. de Coantré—he was a school-teacher, of the humblest origin—said to him one day while they were alone on the terrace: 'Monsieur de Coantré, will you allow me to give you a word of advice? Don't stay here. You count for nothing in this hospital. All the bigwigs are against you. One of these days they're going to do you down. So go while the going's good.' Léon thought this over and, the next day, asked the matron if he could be given some work to do, otherwise he would ask for his freedom. 'Certainly we'll give you some work to do,' said Mlle Kahn with her most gracious smile. A few moments later, the youngest nurse (aged seventeen) handed Léon a broom and told him to sweep the ward. He did so, then went to say good-bye to each of the patients, and left for good. But he sold (dirt cheap) a rather fine silver paperweight and had some cigarettes sent round to the hospital with the proceeds.

Mme de Coantré had spent twenty years flapping her wings like a frightened bird over which the hawks are hovering. The hawks were her creditors. She grew pale when the door-bell rang, and put letters away unopened in a drawer for days. 'One must play safe,' the poor woman would sometimes be heard to say, or 'One must strike while the iron's hot.' Such remarks are typical of victims; Mme de Coantré had no more defence against the unbelievable malice of the world than has the surface of the water against a stone that is thrown into it. She had known ill-shaven lawyers who spoke to her with cigarettes dangling from their lips; all that frightful legal gibberish, a disgrace to a civilized nation; solicitors' bills demanding up to forty francs for 'correspondence charges' and fifty francs for 'stationery', whereas the 'findings' and the 'settlements' cost only a franc or two; lawyer-relations who look after you gratis for three years and then in the fourth year, dissatisfied with the imitation Sèvres you have sent them as a token of gratitude, leave you in the lurch with your affairs in a hopeless and inextricable tangle; 'opinions' requested from arch-pettifoggers in the hope that they will support you in the course you have already taken, and when they advise against it you nonetheless continue on this course out of reluctance to start again from scratch; decisions on which your whole livelihood depends that have to be taken in a quarter of an hour, not because there is any real necessity but because counsel cannot be kept waiting, he has other people to think of besides you. All this she had known, as well as the Calvary of being continually on the verge of bankruptcy, the indifference and the appalling frivolity, comparable only to that of the medical profession, of the men to whom one entrusts one's fortune and with it one's health and one's life. The whole thing tore her to pieces.

When the doctors told Léon that his mother's days were numbered, he softened towards her and looked after her perfectly. However, her death was partly eclipsed for him by the struggle he had to wage with the nurse they had engaged. The latter ate continually—a trait peculiar to all those who are paid to look after the dying—asked for more wine, was impatient because Mme de Coantré took such a long time to die. The doctors had decided that Mme de Coantré would not last beyond the 14th, and when the 17th arrived and she was still alive, the nurse made a rather splendid remark, 'Poor Mme de Coantré! What *is* she up to?' (meaning: what does she mean by it? Can't she see that she's keeping us waiting?) The nurse thought she could do what she liked because she was an old friend of the family, and M. de Coantré's hatred for her was aggravated by violent jealousy because in these last hours his mother spoke more often to the nurse than to him. In a word, although one could not go so far as to say that Mme de Coantré's death passed unnoticed in the struggle between Léon and the nurse, at least it lost some of its sting.

After his mother's death, Léon, who for twenty years had not had a care or responsibility in the world, had to take over the running of the house. Somehow he managed, but only by taking pains out of all proportion to this simple task. Within a week his face changed, he grew puffy round the eyes, he had constant nightmares; even a Prime Minister feels less weighed down. Sometimes he was so overcome by it all that he could not bear it any longer and would go and rake the garden or mend his socks. At the same time he had to grapple with his mother's estate. We have seen what it consisted of. When, after having explained the lamentable situation to Léon and his niece, Maître Lebeau's assistant asked them whether they wanted to accept or refuse the estate, Léon was indignant: refuse his mother's estate! Later, he had another aristocratic impulse. Even though he knew already that he would inherit next to nothing, he announced to his niece that he would give her all the furniture left to him by his mother, although strictly he had no right to do so and although this mad gesture might make them liable to estate duty. The furniture was not worth a great deal—the valuation was twenty thousand francs (Mme de Coantré had reduced the insurance policy from fifteen thousand to twelve and finally to ten thousand francs as a measure of economy)—but the money he could have made from selling it would have saved him from destitution. Neither he nor Mlle de Bauret was aware of the almost insane disinterestedness of this gesture, which moreover gave no pleasure to the girl. His sacrifice, like all good sacrifices, was entirely in vain.

While we are on the subject of aristocratic gestures, we must cite one by M. de Coëtquidan: we should never get to the bottom of 'Gog and Magog' if we regarded them as mere puppets. One night, not long before Mme de Coantré's death, Léon heard a noise downstairs. He got up, and sure enough, there was someone moving on the ground floor. He crept, bare-legged, into his mother's room, and found her sitting up in bed, her eyes wide with terror. Whereupon Léon double-locked the door and lay low there in his nightshirt. Let the burglars remove the ancestral portraits, everything in the house if they liked! As for dear Uncle, alone on the first floor, he was left to his sad fate.

Meanwhile the old man, with complete composure, had been putting on his trousers, and, seizing a table knife he had brought up to his room the night before because he wanted to eat a pear before going to bed, he took up a position on the landing and waited; disagreeableness sometimes has its advantages. He too abandoned the ground floor to the burglar. But if the man came upstairs he would have a Coëtquidan to reckon with!

After a moment or two he saw a shadow on the staircase, and then found himself face to face with the intruder. 'What!' he exclaimed, an expression which admirably sums up his feeling: indignation at being treated with disrespect. The intruder must have been a novice; or else the descendant of the Crusaders, who in the day-time was a frightening enough spectacle, must by night, and with a knife in his hand, have looked like the wild man of Borneo. The visitor turned tail and rushed down the stairs. Thus it can be seen that M. Elie, who in the course of this narrative will be seen to be shy, pusillanimous, and on more than one occasion a moral coward, was physically brave. And he added to the merit of his conduct by not mentioning it to Léon. But he thought about it nonetheless, and privately gloated over it, as though it had been a real 'judgment from heaven' proving quite clearly what history had of course proved already but which there was no harm in proving yet again in every-day practice: that compared to the Coëtquidans the Coantrés were nothing but sheep's droppings.

3

BARON OCTAVE DE COËTQUIDAN, after lunching alone (his sister, who lived with him, had lunched out), was sitting in a rocking-chair reading the *Daily Mail*. 'Reading' is a euphemism, since he knew no English—no, let us be fair, he knew a few words. But the baron maintained that one cannot know anything about French politics without reading the British or American press. He had a cup of coffee beside him, but he did not smoke.

He was a tall, clean-shaven man, with white hair cut short, as spruce in his attire as his brother was not. However, if we have noted at the beginning of this book that M. Elie was dressed 'like nobody else', it must be said that the baron also—in *his* case in an aristocratic way—wore an unusual get-up alike for his age, for his position and for the season. In this month of February in Paris, conventionally the season for dark clothes, he was wearing a light grey suit with turn-ups on the trousers and shoulders cut in the American style (which was then a rarity, for the fashion did not catch on until two or three years later). A soft white collar, a white linen bow tie knotted with studied negligence, beautiful brown laced ankle-boots (made to measure, costing three hundred francs, and lovingly *boned* until they had acquired that *genuine*[1] chest-nut glow), white woollen socks like his brother (those delicate Coëtquidan feet!), no ring, no watch-chain, no cuff-links (his shirt was a soft one with mother-of-pearl buttons). On his lapel the rosette of the Legion of Honour, in the smallest available model, which had nonetheless provoked a memorable scene when the baron had bought it after his promotion, protesting against its 'repulsive size' and pretending he wanted one specially made for him that was invisible to the naked eye. For M. Octave had always

[1] In English in the original.

made a point of refusing to be satisfied with 'standard models', and would order, to his own specifications, such things as a shooting jacket in bishop's purple or a beach jacket with gilt buttons, or else a waste-paper basket made of wire-netting but 'of a size that only existed in wicker on the market' or an absolutely sensational trouser-press, of a type abandoned in 1840 though it was the only effective one, or a mysterious looking suitcase designed for luggage-racks which was supposed to have a capacity well above that of the largest suitcase normally allowed in a luggage-rack. All these objects, either because they proved useless or because the baron soon realized that they made him look ridiculous, ended up with the valet or the chauffeur after being used two or three times, and thus allowed their owner to kill two birds with one stone by giving proof, with a mere jacket in bishop's purple, at once of his muni-ficence and the singularity of his soul.

Anyone who saw Baron Octave, member of the board of Latty's Bank and Officer of the Legion of Honour, dressed in this way would have taken him either for a genuine original or for a com-posite personality like an actor playing a part. The second hypo-thesis would have been the right one.

This important man, who by virtue of his wealth and even more his station had a voice in fairly considerable interests, had some-thing of the childishness of his brother, the fruit of a similar up-bringing, totally divorced from life. M. Elie, at different periods of his life, and even at different hours of the day, was wont to think of himself now as an officer, now as a Nimrod, now as a lady's man, and so on. Sometimes, indeed, his ideal was much more modest. One day, for example, an old friend of his passed him in the street and seeing him gradually stop, then start up in the same way, then stop again, at the same time continually turning the handle of his cane, said to him, 'I say, Elie, old man, what *are* you up to?' And M. Elie, still swinging his cane energetically without im-mediately stopping, threw him a 'Do be careful! You might give me time to put the brake on,' as he passed. For the moment, M. Elie believed himself to be a tram. On a somewhat higher level, M. Octave also had his little games. He played at being the 'modern man'—more specifically the 'modern man, American variety'.

The profound eccentricity inherent in the character of the Coëtquidans revealed itself in M. Octave at about the age of twenty-five in this form: I shall be the modern man of the family. In no time the idea had become mixed up with Americanism, and subsequently it had determined all the baron's opinions and attitudes. For example, it had prompted him to love or feign to love the democratic system, to scorn or feign to scorn people's rank, to take an interest or feign to take an interest in the machinery of business and economics, to disparage slightly or feign to disparage slightly the Deity, to the point of affecting a dash of Voltairianism. But quite apart from such lofty matters, this bias also extended to the most trivial things. The desire to be a modern man, American style, explained why the baron's table was systematically vile (a business-man must have an unprejudiced mind, and therefore an unpreju-diced stomach—gastronomy was anyway 'out-of-date'); why he 'did' his shoes himself (an up-to-date man must be able to look after himself—though in fact it was his servant, Papon, who did the polishing and brushing, while M. de Coëtquidan merely gave a final flick with the cloth); why he had a rocking-chair in which he suffered agonies for fear of toppling over backwards but which he had seen described as an American speciality in a picture paper of 1875; why at the slightest excuse he corresponded by express letter or telegram, as if, by such speedy communication, he hoped to make up for being a hundred years behind the times by reason of his birth; and so on. All this, apart from the pleasure the baron enjoyed in being different, had the added attraction of annoying his family and thus gratifying the rebellious spirit which is one of the character-istics of the Breton nobility. M. Elie for his part deliberately exag-gerated the shabbiness of his clothes, with the sole aim of annoying his brother and his sisters.

M. Octave de Coëtquidan had risen to the position he now occupied thanks to his close friendship ever since their college days with M. Héquelin du Page, who was now chairman of Latty's Bank. His business capabilities were more than questionable. In spite of his position, he shared his brother's and his nephew's ignorance of the realities of life, and their inability to adapt themselves to it. He lived almost entirely according to his own idea of himself. The rule is for a man to put on blinkers around his twentieth year and then, for the rest of his life, carry straight on like a carthorse. M. Octave had not failed to keep this rule. One remembers Michelet's cruel remark about Molière: 'Molière knew nothing of the people. But what *did* he know?' One might have said the same of the baron, as well as his brother: 'What *did* they know?' Their prejudices and their mannerisms covered them as though with a varnish preventing all contact between them and the outside world. Marie-Antoinette's famous 'If they have no bread, let them eat cake' has always been considered an odious remark. But perhaps it was simply that Marie-Antoinette believed that cake was no more expensive than bread. M. Octave thought Papon was robbing him when, after an afternoon's shopping all over Paris, he claimed to have spent four francs on trams. Four francs on trams—impossible! On top of all this, having achieved an important position through influence, the baron felt justified in regarding himself as a *self-made man*.[1] He pompously declared that he had 'risen from nothing'. The human mind is endlessly ingenious in self-flattery.

In everything he did M. de Coëtquidan was ruled by principles. In fact he would often get marvellously tangled up in them. For example, when he did something which bored him, he thought he was doing his duty. He would even say: 'If I didn't do what bores me, I would do nothing at all.' One could use up a whole ink-well of deep thoughts on this.

M. de Coëtquidan, then, was sitting 'reading' the *Daily Mail* when Papon announced M. de Coantré. M. de Coantré came in, shook hands with his uncle, and bowed a few inches too low, like a steward.

It was quite a different M. de Coantré from the one we saw in rags at the beginning of this narrative. He was wearing a dark grey suit, of good material and extremely clean. This suit dated from 1905

[1] In English in the original.

and, because of its cut, made an old-fashioned effect which was not, however, out of place on a man of his age. What was indeed extraordinary, if not ridiculous, was the height of his stiff collar, of a shape that had also gone out of fashion twenty years earlier, and below this collar a black silk stock with a stag's-tooth pin. His starched cuffs, cracked with use like an old face with wrinkles, were detachable. But it was perhaps his boots which cried out most eloquently their date of birth—1900 to 1905. They were buttoned boots, square-toed, and immensely long, curling upwards like certain kinds of medieval footwear. Like the suit, they were of excellent quality and almost as good as new despite their twenty years, since M. de Coantré wore them only two or three times a year and looked after them with the greatest care.

M. de Coantré had left in the hall a short velvet-collared overcoat (of a type known as a 'bum-freezer') and a silver-handled cane which was also very 1900. But, in accordance with the conventions of his youth, he had kept his bowler hat in his hand, as well as a pair of gloves which, now that he was seated, he had carefully placed in the hollow rim of his hat, for this pair of gloves was composed of two identical ones, and M. de Coantré assumed that this was not noticeable when he held them in his hand. They were mourning gloves, for M. de Coantré, during the past twenty years, had had no occasion to wear gloves except at family funerals. And they had that pitiful flatness, that lifeless appearance of gloves that have never been worn.

No sooner was M. de Coantré seated than the baron, with the purposeful air he always showed in conference, as though to say 'Gentlemen, let us stick to the point' (a quite artificial purposeful-ness by which he concealed his natural timidity), switched the con-versation in the direction he wanted. Pointing to the *Daily Mail,* he said in a stilted voice:

'Have you read Herriot's splendid speech?'

M. de Coantré knew perfectly well what his uncle was up to. He, too, tried to switch.

'I'm afraid not. With all the worries I've got at the moment I've hardly the time.'

'You should buy *Le Temps* on your way home. It's well worth reading. Absolutely first-rate.'

'What a dream world he lives in,' thought M. de Coantré, 'the dream world of people who have money.' (Yes, but those who have no money live in a world that is worse than a dream—an obsession. It is impossible to discuss anything with them in a disinterested way; everything comes back to their bread and butter.) But he felt full of courage, and plunged straight in:

'To be quite frank, Uncle Octave, I have no feeling for politics. I saw Lebeau two days ago. We worked out together what I would be left with, and found that after I've paid their fees I shall have six thousand francs. Six thousand francs *all told*, and that's assuming there won't be another bombshell.'

'Lebeau is pessimistic on principle, you know,' said the baron.

M. de Coantré recognized his uncle's genius for refusing to face unpleasant facts.

'But Uncle Octave, it isn't a question of optimism or pessimism. Those are the figures, and you can't get round figures.'

M. Octave gave a little laugh.

'You can do what you like with figures. Believe me, I'm an old banker! I remember in 1919 . . .'

He described how he had falsified a balance-sheet. And his face, naturally shrewd, took on a quite remarkable expression, transfigured and as it were spiritualized by the thought of having cheated a fellow-creature. It is easily verified among animals—for example in kennels—that the most intelligent are always the most vicious.

But all this had no connection with the financial situation— all too simple, alas!—of M. de Coantré. 'Will you allow me to summarize the whole thing?' said the count, feeling his courage waning. 'I have a piece of paper here . . .' And he produced the paper he had placed on M. Elie's table two days earlier.

'Go ahead,' said M. Octave with the forced joviality of a man who has already made up his mind. 'But let me give you a word of advice: you ought to get used to doing without notes. That's the way to lose your memory. I simply decided one fine day, "No more notes". That was in '96, the year Aunt Hortense died. Since then (he tapped his forehead) it's all in here. What about an experiment—try and explain your problem without referring to your paper?'

M. de Coantré's features had contracted slightly. 'Tomorrow I shall be on the street,' he thought, 'and all he can do is suggest experiments!'

'You know perfectly well, Uncle Octave, that I've been suffering from amnesia for twenty years. I have doctor's certificates . . .'

'Come now! You have an excellent memory . . . I regard you as an extremely healthy man,' he added, accentuating each syllable forcefully. For he knew all about the Coué system from the newspapers, and was just the kind of man who is impressed by that sort of science.

M. de Coantré suppressed the inevitable grimace of the man who is told he is not ill. He apologized with some vigour for not being able to do the experiment, and after his uncle had said 'I won't insist', he gave him the same account he had given to M. Elie, sprinkling it again with technical words he had picked up here and there.

When he had finished, 'And now I must work,' he added 'That is partly why I came to bother you, Uncle Octave.'

'Have you begun to look for anything?' asked M. Octave.

'Yes, I've written all over the place,' said M. de Coantré, who had done nothing of the sort. For the past two days, so great was his joy at the prospect of leaving the Boulevard Arago, he had concentrated exclusively, eight months in advance, on plans for moving out of it, and deliberately refrained from thinking about his future. It was at once a 'bachelor' trait and a 'Coëtquidan' trait to avoid, for as long as possible, if not for ever, doing anything disagreeable.

'I shall speak to Héquelin du Page about it,' said M. Octave. 'He sees a lot of people. I don't. I lead a very quiet life.'

In this way he was preparing the ground, giving advance reasons for the failure of his feeble efforts. For he had no intention of losing prestige by warmly recommending this dim and ineffectual relative. At the same time he was extremely worried, for he was convinced, as his brother had been, that M. de Coantré would find nothing by himself.

'Yes,' said M. de Coantré,' I should be very, very grateful if you could mention my name to a few people. Do it in memory of mother,' he added, convinced that M. de Coëtquidan would not do it for him, and not averse from making him feel that he knew it.

The object of his visit was to obtain from his uncle a kind of promise that he would not abandon him—a promise which, after all (though the comparison did not strike him), would be no different from the one he himself had made to M. Elie the other day with so much warmth and spontaneity: 'Whatever happens, I shall never desert you.' But since the baron seemed not in the least disposed to make such a promise, he felt less and less emboldened to ask him, and knew that he would leave without having pronounced the only words that had any chance of setting his mind at rest.

'And how is Mélanie, as dependable as ever?' asked M. Octave, trying to switch the subject again.

'More or less. But of course, as soon as she realizes there's no more money in the house . . . The rats always leave a sinking ship . . .'

A vain attempt by M. de Coantré to switch it back in his direction. M. Octave, having found his new track, was sticking to it.

'These Picards are on the whole excellent people. When I had to find a replacement for Borel—one of our heads of department—I said . . .'

And M. Octave explained how he had supported one of the candidates for Borel's job simply because he was from Arras. M. Octave, as the reader may have noticed, had a tendency to regard everything that was said, thought or done in the light of what he himself said or had said, thought or had thought, did or had done. His brother might say 'I'[1] with a more impressive intonation, but the impulse in both cases was the same. For bachelors, the world is a ball attached to an elastic band: however far they throw it, back it always comes.

M. Octave was in the middle of his commentary when the bell rang. M. de Coantré, more and more miserable at the thought that he would never dare to ask for a firm promise from his uncle, leapt

[1] *Moi*, which M. Elie pronounced *moa* with a lordly drawl.—Tr.

at this excuse and got up. He had always worshipped the ineluctable, which exempted him from making any effort of the will.

Presently Papon opened the door, and M. Elie appeared. It was not entirely by chance that the whole of 'Arago' met that afternoon at M. Octave's. He had told the two of them that they could be sure of finding him there on Thursdays; any other day there might be nobody at home. He was not anxious for possible callers to meet 'Gog and Magog'.

M. Elie held out his hand to the baron, who, knowing how damp and sticky it would be, merely touched the tips of the fingers. Then M. Elie turned towards his nephew and flung at him 'Oh, so *you're* here!' in a surly tone of voice that would have been the height of rudeness had it not been habitual with the old man and therefore of no significance. Almost before he had time to sit down, M. Octave pointed to the *Daily Mail* and, adopting his affected tone, said to him:

'Have you read Herriot's speech?'

'Do you think I read that filth?'

'What?' said M. Octave, raising his eyebrows.

'Herriot! A traitor! If I were in charge I'd have him shot!'

'You don't know what you're saying,' said the baron contemptuously. However, if, when he had spoken of Herriot to his nephew, it was in order to switch the conversation, this time he had done it simply to exasperate his brother.

Seeing M. de Coantré make for the door on his way out, M. Octave picked up the *Daily Mail* and gave it to his nephew.

'Here. There's no point in your spending money on a newspaper when I can give you one. *I've read it.*' (The Coetquidans, as we have seen, were always remarkably generous with the newspapers they had read.) 'Be sure to read the bit where he says that what makes France a power in the world is the moral strength she draws from democracy. That's what people in our world don't understand. Come, *farewell.*[1] Keep me informed about your affairs, won't you? And don't forget what I told you about notes. It's a very bad habit you're getting into. *Very bad!*'[1]

[1] In English in the original.

49

Although it was part of M. Octave's stock-in-trade to spatter his conversation with English words, this time he had done it mainly for his brother's sake. And these English words did indeed infuriate M. Elie, firstly because he knew no English, secondly because 'it was a modern habit', and thirdly because, for him, in spite of 1914, Wellington was still the enemy.

M. de Coantré found himself on the landing feeling somewhat crestfallen. He had come to obtain the promise which would set his mind at rest, and had obtained nothing but the *Daily Mail* and some good advice on how to develop his memory. Nevertheless he told himself that Uncle Octave was now forewarned. 'He looks a bit like a dummy, but I know he's a good-hearted man. He'll chew it over. The first step has been taken. Besides, he told me to keep in touch. If he wasn't interested in my future he wouldn't have said that. No, it isn't going too badly.'

Meanwhile the baron had returned to his study and was apostrophizing his brother:

'So it appears you're leaving Arago?'

'Yes, feet first. *Ça*! Nothing for it but to starve to death.'

'What do you mean, starve?'

'How will I be able to live on five hundred francs a month?'

'You're sure you can't afford more?'

'How do I know!'

'What do you mean, how do you know? Surely you know how much you can put down?'

'No, I don't know.'

'But surely you keep accounts?'

'Accounts! For the few francs I've got!'

'But after all, Elie, when you run out of cash, what do you do? What happens at Lebeau's?'

'At the end of each month I go to Lebeau. He gives me the five-hundred francs for the shack. I ask him for one hundred and fifty or two hundred for myself.'

'All right. You see that gives you an income of seven hundred francs a month already. And what if your expenses come to more than two hundred francs?'

'What expenses? I spend nothing. I'm penniless.'

'All the same, your clothes . . .'

'My clothes? These rags!'

'But you had to buy them at some stage.'

'Well, I say to Lebeau, "I must get a new rig. Give me six hundred francs extra".'

'And he gives them to you?'

'Yes.'

'And he makes no comment?'

'He says, "I shall have to sell a share." So I say, "Sell it."'

'Ah! Ah! That's not so funny. Have you sold a lot of shares like that?'

'Don't know.'

'You don't know! Doesn't Lebeau send you an account?'

'Yes, he sends me odd bits of paper from time to time. I don't even look at them. Wipe my a . . . with them. He puts down anything he likes: I don't understand a thing. They're all robbers!'

'My dear chap, the first thing you must do is to go to Lebeau and say to him: "How much capital have I got? What is my income? I must have details." When you know exactly how much you can spend per year without touching your capital, we'll see what sort of life we can afford to organize for you. Go and see Lebeau tomorrow. He will probably want three or four days to work it out. Come back and see me as soon as you get his answer. And get it in writing, otherwise what you tell me will be worthless. . . .'

M. Elie did not reply, and they began to talk of one thing and another. From time to time M. Octave glanced at his watch, which was lying on his desk; these relations of his took up an unconscionable amount of his time! At last Elie got up. But instead of going towards the door as his brother expected, he went across to the window, took in the room at a glance, and said:

'Pretty big, eh! How many rooms have you got altogether?'

'Well, there's . . . let's see . . . eight rooms,' replied the baron, innocently.

'Eight rooms for you and Emilie! Well, well, splendid, you've got some breathing space! Hrrr . . .'

The baron understood. That meant: 'Couldn't you put me up?' He shuddered at the thought of sharing a house with his brother. That, never! He felt like a healthy man who is visiting a consumptive and, ashamed of his paunch, finds himself on the point of saying to the dying man: 'You're lucky! At least they take you seriously. Now, my catarrh, if you only knew what hell it is!' The baron said hastily:

'Big, I grant you. But what a place! Ceilings crumbling, no central heating, badly situated, never any sun!'

Now M. Elie, with the eye of an expert valuer, was inspecting the contents of the room. Everything bespoke the solid affluence of a man who has no desire to impress but does not count the cost when it comes to buying something he likes. M. Octave found this inspection acutely embarrassing. He could read his brother's thoughts. He imagined the shabby bed-sitting room where Elie would have to live in six months' time. Once more he looked at his watch. The glance did not escape M. Elie.

'I see, you're throwing me out.'

'Not at all. Only I have to prepare my report for tomorrow . . .'

M. Elie had already left the study and was now in the hall. But there, instead of going to the front door, he went into the drawing-room, the door of which was open. Suppressing the urge to say 'What do you want to nose around in there for?' the baron clenched his teeth and followed him in. The drawing-room was vast, and much more luxurious than the study. Whenever anything happened to annoy him, the baron stifled his displeasure by buying some *objet d'art* he had been coveting. There is an art in avoiding suffering, and the baron was a past master at it. Meanwhile his brother looked round the room and sniggered.

'I say, Octave, you couldn't fix me a job as assistant caretaker at your bank?'

'Assistant caretaker?' the baron muttered in a toneless voice.

'Yes, me. Do you think I'll be able to live on five hundred francs a month! I'll just starve to death.'

'One doesn't starve to death when one has a brother.'

No sooner had he heard these words than M. Elie went back into the hall and made for the front door, as though he genuinely regarded this promise as the price for his departure. Like his nephew, he also had come to seek a pledge of support. He now had it. He could clear out.

On the threshold M. Octave did not give his brother a vague 'Keep in touch'. He said:

'If you go to Lebeau tomorrow, you'll probably have his answer by Monday. Come back here on Tuesday at two o'clock; I'll be alone. And we'll see what needs to be done . . . Would you like the car to take you back?' he added.

Three years earlier M. Octave had bought a car, which he found extremely agreeable. It enabled him to traverse swiftly and without having any contact with it, a world which he dimly felt he neither knew nor understood and which only a sort of miracle—the friendship of M. Héquelin du Page—had saved him from. At first he had placed the car at his brother's disposal whenever the occasion arose, and M. Elie had made use of it a few times. But ever since M. Octave had said to him one day, 'You ought to give Georges (the chauffeur) a tip, you know . . . It's the thing to do,' Elie would have walked from one end of Paris to the other rather than use his brother's car; and he no longer even acknowledged Georges' salute now that he felt obliged to him. So that the baron, having seen through his brother, now took pleasure in offering him the car at the slightest opportunity, delighted to have discovered this means of being brotherly on the cheap. This time, as usual, M. Elie said no, muttering 'You want to have me killed. Doesn't know how to drive, your chauffeur. And anyhow I'd dirty your cushions.' Having thus succeeded in combining, in a few short phrases, rudeness, calumny, and acerbity, the old man withdrew.

The two brothers had been together for three-quarters of an hour. Not once had M. de Coantré's name been mentioned.

4

M. DE COANTRÉ had not taken the slightest trouble to find himself
a job after hearing from Lebeau about his new financial situation.
Nor did he do so after his visit to his uncle. He plunged once more
into his preparations for the move, which gave a tangible meaning
to the break with 'Arago' and the advent of a 'new life', and in
which he could make use of his abilities, dusting, packing, hammer-
ing, pasting, tying and painting. Invariably bewildered by any
intellectual task, he was all afire at the prospect of tidying up the
Augean stable of this Arago house in which everything was systematically kept so that nothing would ever have to be bought. Anyone
who wants to appreciate the lyrical frenzy that comes from moving
house has only to watch M. de Coantré.

Moreover, the idea had occurred to him that he might fall ill
before having completed his preparations. He imagined the fatal
day, October 15th, arriving with the house still in disorder, an
extension being refused, and his belongings being thrown out into
the street. Thus did his dire imagination work. By sorting everything out now—'I want everything settled as if we were leaving in
a fortnight'—he was setting his mind at rest.

He threw out everything that was not worth keeping, all that
was briefly listed in the inventory as not being worth detailed description. The rest was brushed or cleaned and packed in trunks or
packing-cases on which he had painted large numbers. Then the
description of each object was noted on a sheet of paper with its
appropriate trunk or packing-case number, so that Mlle de Bauret
would have no difficulty in finding anything she wanted. (It will be
remembered that he was giving her everything.) He assumed that
his niece, having no other home but her old cousin's château, would
put it all in store until she got married. As soon as the decision to

leave Arago had been made, he had written to inform her that everything in the house—except what was in his own room and Uncle Elie's—would be got ready for moving wherever she wanted it moved by a given date. Mlle de Bauret had not replied to this letter, but M. de Coantré was not surprised because he knew she was an up-to-date girl.

A week after his visit to M. Octave, M. de Coantré was nailing down a packing-case when, glancing absent-mindedly through the window, he was struck by an extraordinary sight. A small boy of six or seven in a black school smock was roaming about the garden. A young living creature, in this backwater where none but the old were ever to be seen! M. de Coantré felt ill at ease. Not only because there was a stranger 'making himself at home' there, but chiefly because this stranger was a child. Léon was naturally friendly and easy-going. But children made him feel awkward; he never knew what to say to them, and his embarrassment sometimes amounted to acute physical discomfort.

A few seconds later he discovered a new source of anxiety. The garden tap had been left on and the water was overflowing the tank. M. de Coantré, who would have sacrificed a million, as he was sacrificing his twenty thousand francs' worth of furniture, with a smiling detachment tinged with unawareness, worried himself to death over a few sous. Besides, even if this wasting of water did not mean an extra bill (of three or four centimes), it wounded his sense of order (itself, however, extremely ill-ordered).

He went downstairs with the intention of turning the tap off, but stopped first in the kitchen to ask Mélanie who the little boy was. She said he was the daily woman's son, and he had asked her permission to play in the garden.

So M. de Coantré went out into the garden. But, once there, instead of going to the tap he stayed near the kitchen and began pulling up weeds. To reach the tap meant passing the little boy. The little boy might speak to him, he might have to make conversation, and that terrified him.

His apprehension was reinforced by a new circumstance: he had just noticed M. de Coëtquidan at the bottom of the garden—

M. de Coëtquidan standing motionless as a statue, his stick dangling from a waistcoat pocket. Normally at this hour, whenever he was at home, M. Elie would be prowling around outside the kitchen waiting to tease the cats when they came in for lunch. It was clear that M. de Coëtquidan was 'blockaded' at the end of the garden by the presence of the small boy. He must have been loitering there, waiting until it was time for the cats, or else urinating against a certain tree, a sort of sacred tree against which it was a solemn ritual for the two gentlemen to relieve themselves, when the small boy arrived, and now he dared not go in for precisely the same reasons that prevented M. de Coantré from turning off the tap.

(It was an old story. Often, in summer, Mme de Coantré would be sitting in the garden when a caller arrived, whom the old lady would receive under the shade of the trees. If either of the two gentlemen happened to be there, as soon as the bell rang he would disappear into a tool-shed by the garden wall and stay there, sometimes for as much as an hour, crouching in the dark among the rats and the cobwebs, unable to get back to the house without passing the visitor. Better a whole day imprisoned with the rats than to have to put themselves out for a few minutes with a guest.)

Meanwhile M. de Coantré had decided that he must at all costs turn off the tap; this water overflowing was like blood flowing from his veins. As he went forward, he saw the little boy raise his head, smile and come towards him. His courage failed him, and on an impulse of irresistible panic he turned tail and retreated towards the kitchen.

But alas! the little boy was of a naturally friendly disposition. He followed M. de Coantré, and the latter, thinking it better on the whole for an encounter in which he would cut a poor figure to take place without witnesses rather than in front of the cook, wheeled round and bravely stood his ground.

'Don't you pick ticklers?' asked the little boy.

'I'm afraid not . . .'

'Why? Won't your mummy let you?'

M. de Coantré, who was a sentimental soul, found the question charming, and smiled. But he was so embarrassed that he could think of nothing to say. Then the small boy held out a handful of those hard little fruits of the wild rose which undignified people call 'ticklers' and which are the delight of children and birds in their mysterious picnics.

'Here you are, would you like some?'

'Eh? What would I do with them?'

No sooner had he spoken than he realized, both from his gruff tone and the look of surprise that had superseded the cheerful expression on the child's face, that he had replied churlishly to this friendly offer. He felt he ought to say something, take the hips and put them in his pocket—but he had for so long been cut off from human intercourse that he could not bring himself to do so.

At that moment he saw a shadowy figure pass hurriedly behind the little boy and sneak into the house. It was M. de Coëtquidan, who, taking advantage of the fact that the child's attention was distracted, had put on speed from the bottom of the garden and made port. Emboldened by the pleasure of having spotted his uncle and having rendered him this high strategic service, M. de Coantré summoned up the strength to say to the little boy 'Well, now, enjoy yourself . . .' and then to lunge forward, as though leading a cavalry charge, turn off the tap and return triumphantly to the house without being further troubled by the child.

They sat down to lunch and were in the middle of discussing the social implications of this encounter ('A charming youngster! And so clean! . . .'—'In my day working-class children *looked* like working-class children. Now they're all like little gents.'—'There aren't any classes left.') when the bell rang and Mélanie said: 'It's the postman.'

For twenty years, whenever the postman rang, M. de Coantré had seen a wave of anxiety cross his mother's face. Yet, like everyone else, she sometimes received quite pleasant letters, and nine out of ten were at worst indifferent. But no: for her, the arrival of a letter could only mean trouble. Since his mother's death, M. de Coantré reacted to the postman's visit in exactly the same way: his face became suffused with anxiety. But when the envelope was in

his hands and he saw the crest *Maître Lebeau, Solicitor,* he ripped it
open feverishly, tearing the edge of the letter. And he read:

Sir,

A new matter has arisen in connection with the estate of
Mme la Comtesse de Coantré, and I should be obliged if you
would be so good as to call at this office on Friday the 22nd
inst, around 3 o'clock.

Yours, etc.

That was the letter he had always been expecting, and now it had
come. Trouble, for sure: the sad thing about worriers is that they
always have reason to be worried. M. de Coantré read the note
to his uncle and then tried to eat, but his throat was constricted.
Meanwhile, he could see M. Elie casting surreptitious glances at the
letter, which he had put down beside his plate. At last he understood.

'Here you are, Uncle, if you want the stamp . . .'

'Why, yes! Thanks . . .'

And M. de Coëtquidan proceeded to spit on the stamp. Suddenly
M. de Coantré stood up.

'I'm going there today. The appointment is for tomorrow, but I
must know now. I can't bear to wait.'

In vain does a hunted man, who is terrified of a knock at the door,
decide to lie low and wait for it to stop; after the second knock
he can stand it no longer. He must know, he cannot bear this
presence, this mystery behind the door; rather death, if that is what
it is, than the agony of the unknown. . . . He opens the door.

'But you've got plenty of time,' said M. Elie. 'It's only twenty to
one!'

'I must shave, and change my clothes. And I don't want to rush.
I must keep calm, very calm.' (He clenched his teeth.)

He went upstairs and shaved. His hand shook and he cut himself.
'I know what it is, by Jove! It's a new creditor. Anyhow, whatever
it is, it can only mean trouble.'

So little did he trust his own memory and presence of mind
that, whenever he went to Lebeau's, he took with him a large

bundle of papers more or less connected with the estate, imagining always that at some stage of the interview an essential point would slip his memory, and also, theoretically, in order to be able to check what the lawyer said to him. He had great confidence in this man, Bourdillon—but after all, one never knows! Like all incompetent people, he was suspicious. All these papers, many of which should have been in the waste-paper basket long ago, were meticulously classified and numbered and covered with caballistic signs scrawled in coloured crayon. And yet he was rarely able to find the one he wanted: partly because any bit of paper, however unimportant, that looked as if it might be connected with 'business' was for him something mysterious, sacred and awe-inspiring, and he kept everything down to shoemakers' bills going as far back as 1898, and partly because, whenever he felt he was being watched, or whenever he had to act quickly, his brain clouded over, his hands trembled and he lost control of his faculties.

An hour later, having, in spite of his oppression of mind, carefully brushed his clothes, cleaned his stiff collar with a piece of bread he had brought upstairs, and arranged his handkerchief in his breast-pocket in such a way that the little of it that showed was not soiled, M. de Coantré left the house.

During the ten years between his return from Chatenay and the war, M. de Coantré, as we have seen, had scarcely been out of the house. When he had joined an auxiliary hospital in 1914 he had chosen one quite close to the Boulevard Arago; to reach it he had only one street to cross. Afterwards, for another ten years, he no longer went out. Thus, when his mother died and he had to go through all the formalities death brings in its wake, he was completely crushed, the more so because his mother's long illness and death-throes had already worn him down.

Outside in the street, everything seemed blurred in front of his eyes, and his ears were shattered by the din of buses and trams. He was a terrifying sight as he crossed the road, jumping like a frog whenever a car appeared; he should have been run over a dozen times. When he came to the main avenues and wider squares, he would not cross them without the help of a passer-by. He had steeled himself against taking taxis, not only because of the expense but because he was just as frightened when he was in a car. So he wandered through the streets, continually on the look-out for 'means of transport' whose details he had studied for an hour before leaving in out-of-date time-tables, so that the antics of these vehicles were never the same in reality as they were on paper, unless it was he who lost his way in them. Sweat poured down his face, with the same prickly effect as the hairs which the barber leaves under one's collar. Why was it only he who tripped over his own feet? Why was it only he who could never find the number of a house? Now he would imagine that people were making fun of him, were deliberately getting in his way. And anger would well up inside him, the anger of a man who knows that he has reached the very depths of human weakness; he would thrust his way through, jostling people to left and right, and anyone who challenged him would have been treated in a very lordly way. But whenever possible he would move away, go and sit on a bench and try to recover. And he was utterly exhausted by the time he returned, in the evening, to the silence of his room, where no one wished him ill and where gradually a modicum of equanimity and self-respect would be restored to him. Afterwards, he would need several days of relaxation at home to recover the flat calm of mind and soul which alone kept suffering at bay.

But gradually he had grown used to these journeys, and in particular the route to the Boulevard Haussmann, where Uncle Octave and the solicitor lived, had become familiar. Nevertheless, since he was always afraid of arriving late and hence annoying the person he had come to see, and since, moreover, he had extravagant notions as to the distances which caused him such agonies, he continued to exaggerate to a ridiculous degree the time needed for his journeys. If he had an appointment at three, he would arrive at 2.15 (a notable improvement, this; six months earlier it would have been 1.30). In fact his early arrival had become part of the programme. There was a certain bench in front of Lebeau's office, and a certain café not far from his uncle's house, where he would sit, always at the same end of the bench or at the same café table. And he would wait until it was five minutes to three before getting up, feeling a childish pride if he managed to reach M. Octave's house or Bourdillon's office on the stroke of three and one or other of them welcomed him with some such phrase as: 'Well done! What punctuality!' Such a compliment would suffice to give him the self-confidence he so sorely needed when he met these gentlemen.

At half past two M. de Coantré went into Lebeau's office—and however low he had fallen socially, one could tell he was a real gentleman from the fact that he polished his boots on the edge of the luxurious stair-carpet on the way up.

He was received by an office boy who immediately said: 'But it wasn't today!' This pleased him; obviously he counted for something in the firm, since everyone knew about him and remembered the date of his appointment. He was on the point of confessing that he couldn't bear to wait when he pulled himself up in time to say 'Yes, but I happened to be passing.' He asked if he could see Bourdillon just for a moment; he was quite prepared to come back next day to talk at leisure. Bourdillon sent back a message asking him to wait.

M. de Coantré felt happy. Bourdillon and Uncle Octave were his two guardian angels—the saviours, the magicians whom he expected to clear up all his problems. He found Bourdillon rather awe-inspiring, because he had a big black beard (like Cacus, whom Hercules strangled, and who, we feel positive, must have had a fabulous beard).

A longish time went by. M. de Coantré sat in the hall, which was used as a waiting-room—this famous hall where all the Coëtquidans had sat in turn, M. Elie always keeping his hat on, even if the heat was stifling, for fear somebody might think he was being polite if he took it off. There was a hum of low voices which was punctuated by the high-pitched clatter of a typewriter and which suddenly increased in volume when the typing stopped. M. de Coantré threw surreptitious glances at one of the typists, a most agreeable young woman with a splendid moustache, for she was the daughter of a retired major from Périgord. Suddenly Bourdillon came out of his office, and the count leapt to his feet, thinking it was for him. But Bourdillon went past him, saying: 'One moment, please . . .'

'Just one word, Maître Bourdillon,' said Léon with an imploring look. 'Is it anything serious?'

'Of course not! It will all sort itself out. So don't worry,' said Bourdillon in his deep, oily voice as he vanished into another room. M. de Coantré called him 'Maître' out of toadyism, knowing he had no right to the title. Even a de Coantré is not above such wiles.

M. de Coantré sat down again, somewhat relieved. 'It will all sort itself out' obviously meant some difficulty. But he had complete faith in old Bourdillon, that excellent man. The firm of Lebeau had been running the affairs of the Coëtquidans for half a century; it represented security, was almost part of the family. Of course, the firm's spokesman might bring him bad news, but they would never let him down.

Suddenly a furious old gentleman rushed out of Bourdillon's room. His sky-blue eyes, his hairy nose and his florid complexion all stamped him as a military man. He swooped on M. de Coantré with his eyes popping out of his head and shouted:

'Are you the plaintiff?'

'I don't think so . . .' said M. de Coantré, getting up, as though he were addressing his superior officer, and turning his eyes towards the mustachioed young lady to ask her opinion on the matter. But the cavalry officer (for it was indeed one) veered away without waiting for a reply, and disappeared in the direction of the offices, leaving the count gaping.

Once more he waited, and at last Bourdillon called him into his office, an absolutely traditional office with bogus medieval windows, faded photographs of whiskered gentlemen—the founders of the firm—and a clock with a black marble base and a bronze figure on top, a weeping Niobe, lamenting her lost dividends.

'Well, M'sieu de Coantré,' said Bourdillon with his common accent which endeared him to Léon because he sensed the man of the people, 'We'll never see the end of this business!'

But he said it with such a genial air that it was almost on a jocular note (as who should say: 'It's such a hopeless muddle that it's really rather a joke'), so that Léon asked: 'Well, what's the trouble now?' and added: 'I shudder at the thought. You terrify me!' Knowing how inept he was in such matters, he had taken to joking about it to Bourdillon—'I'm a child in all this. It's double Dutch to me. They can do what they like with me'—with the object of suggesting that he was not such a child as all that since he laughed about it. He believed that the reaction to someone who says 'You know, I'm an awful fool,' or words to that effect, must be to think: 'Aha, my man! I know what you're up to.' M. de Coantré would have given a great deal (if such an expression can be applied to him) to know that it was suggested behind his back that he feigned ignorance to achieve his ends. But it is extremely doubtful that anyone ever expressed such an opinion.

Bourdillon leafed through the file of Mme de Coantré's estate, which literally swarmed with counts and countesses, barons and viscounts, mostly with the words 'Profession: none' written opposite their names. '*Provision: none* would be more like it,' M. de Coantré, who liked his little joke, had said one day. There were pages covered with figures, with geometric doodles pencilled in the margins. There were eleven yellow folios in which Mme de Coantré eleven times acknowledged that she owed eleven separate sums to M. Antoni; there were papers on which, beside receipt-stamps that were exactly the colour of lice, M. de Coantré renounced one thing after another, and it was splendid to see his lordly signature (a 'real grandee' nonchalantly 'scratching the parchment') at the foot of these documents in which invariably he was dispossessing himself, as though he were in fact signing a peace treaty which was to bring him the duchies of Lorraine and Brabant.

Bourdillon took a letter out of the file. M. de Coantré pulled down his shirt-cuffs, which were two centimetres too short.

'Do you know someone called Defraisse?'

'Yes,' said the count, his face falling. 'But the Defraisse business was over long ago.'

'Well, he doesn't seem to think so. He's claiming five thousand francs.'

'And . . . he's justified in doing so?'

'Everything suggests that he is.'

M. de Coantré swallowed his saliva. Along the upper surface of his thighs something began to quiver.

'But it's diabolical! Life's hardly worth living under the constant threat of these bombshells. Five thousand francs!'

What could have been clearer in his head than the sum which would soon be his all? Had he not repeated it often enough? And yet, now, try as he might, he could not remember it. He searched among his papers, but failed to find the one on which the operative figures were recorded.

'Looking for something?'

'Yes, I want to know how much I had left before the Defraisse claim. You must have the figure, since it was you who gave it to me.'

Bourdillon consulted the file again.

'Here we are, this must be it. "Remainder: eleven thousand". Yes, that's it. You had eleven thousand francs left. I remember now, that was the figure we arrived at the other day.'

'How much will the fees come to? Two thousand?'

'Oh, no!' the big man heartily exclaimed. 'We're not going to fleece you. I should think a thousand will see you through. More or less.'

M. de Coantré brightened a little. Sometimes, after all, there was good news! Some people, at least, were honest! The lawyers would take a thousand francs, but it might have been two thousand or two thousand five hundred; he would have had to pay up. Instead of which, here was a thousand francs 'recovered' in an instant!

'Well,' said Bourdillon, 'what would you like me to do? Of course, I'll have this Defraisse round first of all to check his claim. But afterwards, we can either keep him waiting or settle at once . . .'

At this point the office boy half-opened the door and called Bourdillon, who went out.

As soon as he had gone, M. de Coantré rummaged through the papers he had brought. And since he was alone, and nobody was looking at him, and he had no need to hurry, and therefore did not lose his head, or only half lost it, he immediately found the note with his accounts on it. And he read the following, which was underlined: *Once Lebeau has been paid off, I shall have six thousand francs left.*

'When Bourdillon comes back we'll be examining this question of paying Defraisse, and if I hadn't found this note, everything would have turned on my having eleven thousand when in fact it's six! As if it was the same thing to pay out five thousand francs when you have eleven as when you have six! And to think that I put my trust in this man!'

M. de Coantré was a pathetic creature, but one who was prone to fits of violence because he was incapable of controlling his nerves. When Bourdillon came back, it was in a highly intemperate tone that he addressed him:

'Well, M. Bourdillon! It isn't eleven thousand, it's six thousand francs I've got left. I found the paper. Eleven thousand and six thousand may be all the same to you, but not to me. . . .'

And he threw the paper on the table.

What did Bourdillon think about it? Did he think: the slave turns into the master? His face betrayed nothing. He read the note and said after a moment:

'Yes, it's six thousand. Actually I'd been thinking eleven thousand was rather a lot. Now the question is, what are we going to do about Defraisse?'

How calmly Bourdillon went on with the discussion! He seemed to find it perfectly natural to have made a mistake, and on an essential point! The effrontery with which he claimed to have thought eleven thousand francs 'rather a lot', when in fact he had said quite confidently: 'I remember, that was the figure we arrived at the other day!' For M. de Coantré everything was collapsing at once; he was being robbed once again, and he could no longer put his faith in his guardian angel. He took a deep breath, as if the air he inhaled might calm his nerves, which he could feel pulsating inside him. At this moment, a man of about thirty, elegant but dissipated-looking, came into the office without knocking and began chatting to the chief clerk. After a minute or two Bourdillon said to the newcomer:

'But . . . you don't know M. de Coantré? M. de Coantré. Maître Lebeau.'

Lebeau! This limp young man, round-shouldered, cadaverous, with his long undergraduate's hair falling down over his temples, and his look of sloppy depravity! M. de Coantré had never seen him before, since he dealt personally only with his smarter clients. The first time Léon had seen Bourdillon, he had addressed him as Maître Lebeau: the majestic beard could only mean the boss. And this time he had mistaken Lebeau for a new kind of clerk! He remembered having heard at Arago that 'the young Lebeau' had succeeded his father, but to have guessed that this lounge lizard was the grand panjandrum . . . To think that his fate was in such hands! Lebeau, a rake, and Bourdillon, whom he had just caught red-handed making a blatantly frivolous mistake.

Lebeau greeted him and said:

'Well now, what's happening about this estate?'

M. de Coantré, furious with Bourdillon and full of antipathy for Lebeau, answered crossly:

'What's happening is that M. Bourdillon tells me five minutes ago that I've got eleven thousand francs left when in fact it's six thousand. And now the question is how to pay Defraisse.'

Having said his say, he pulled down his cuffs. After this revelation, he thought Bourdillon would 'get a rap over the knuckles'. But Lebeau merely turned towards the chief clerk with an inquiring look which clearly meant 'What's all this! He's a queer fish, this client of yours. . . .'

Needless to say, Lebeau knew nothing, or next to nothing, about the Coantré estate. In fact he knew very little about any of his firm's affairs. His role in the office was that of all incompetent bosses: it consisted in complicating matters by poking his nose into everything in order to show he was the boss.

Bourdillon outlined the situation for him. Lebeau appeared to be listening attentively, with his head bowed, but in fact his eyes were fixed most of the time on the documents which the office boy had just given him, and which he read while the chief clerk was speaking to him. The trick did not escape M. de Coantré. But his temper had subsided, and as always happened with him, the result was a feeling of helplessness. It was all too much for him—the ill-concealed indifference of Lebeau and Bourdillon, the sudden blow which reduced his entire fortune to two thousand francs. And still these cuffs refused to show themselves! He would have felt much more self-confident if his cuffs had been visible.

'Well, then,' said Lebeau when he realized that Bourdillon had stopped talking. 'What does it come down to? It comes down to the fact that all the assets are going to be eaten up. You would have done better to renounce the estate.'

'I'm not the sort of man who renounces his mother's estate. And my niece Mlle de Bauret, to her credit, was in complete agreement with me.'

'Still, there are times when . . .'

Lebeau and Bourdillon exchanged a knowing smile.

The toneless voice of a typist could be heard reading out a document for someone to check, and sometimes, when a door was opened, a piping voice with sharp consonants (the voice of a Catholic lecturer) dictating: '. . . that the termination is an estab-lished fact . . .'

'Well, do you want to sell or do you want me to argue?' asked Bourdillon. 'I mean you and Mlle de Bauret. You'll need her consent.'

'My niece has given me power of attorney,' M. de Coantré said loftily. 'She said to me: "Anything you like, so long as I don't have to bother."'

Bourdillon could not repress a smile.

'What a splendid family!' he thought. 'We need more like them.'

'What do you advise?' asked M. de Coantré.

'Oh, I don't want to give you advice,' said Bourdillon, indicating for the first time that he had taken in what had happened earlier. 'But I must know the advantages and disadvantages of the two alternatives.'

'If you pay up now you'll be rid of it. If I try to come to terms it will take some time, but we'll probably get a reduction, as with Mme de Saint-Huberty.'

'It seems quite clear to me that we ought to try and scrape up something.'

'But you must provide me with the means to do so. *I* have in my file the list you know about, which your mother gave me, with the entry: Defraisse, four thousand. With the interest, it will make five thousand. But *you* can contest it. It depends whether you have any documents, any letters from Defraisse . . .'

'But there are stacks of papers at home! I found the attic full of them. If I have to go through them all . . .'

Bourdillon shrugged his shoulders gloomily.

'In that case, it would be better to pay up straightaway, and get it over and done with.'

'Yes,' said M. de Coantré with an expression of resigned fatigue, 'I think it's better to pay up. It will put my mind at rest.'

'All the consequences of an authenticated act . . .' the piping voice continued in the other room as someone opened the door.

The desire to pay one's debts can arise either from honesty or from a pathological state. The latter was the case with our count. He could never be at peace with himself unless he felt that he was under no obligation to anyone. Moreover, he was afraid of reprisals from his creditors, as he was afraid of everything in such matters. When, some weeks after his mother's death, he had found two one-thousand franc notes in her desk, he was so terrified of being accused of having hidden them that he immediately informed Bourdillon by express letter.

'All the same,' said Lebeau, who was sitting on the edge of the table like a smart young bounder perched on a stool in an American Bar and poisoning the atmosphere with the fumes of his strong cigarette, 'All the same, it's silly not to contest a doubtful claim.'

'Well, if that's your opinion, let's try and make terms,' said M. de Coantré, pulling at his cuffs. It was a quick volte-face, but he was beginning to feel hypnotized by the bounder because, after all, this bounder was the boss.

'Oh, please don't do it for my sake,' said Lebeau. 'I simply said it would be silly . . .'

'You must understand,' Bourdillon put in, 'that what M. de Coantré wants first and foremost is peace of mind. And he's ready to pay the price for it. If we settle with Defraisse without further argument, he won't have to worry any more.'

'Obviously!' Lebeau said facetiously.

'In spite of this procedure . . .' said the voice of the Catholic lecturer.

'Do *you* think Defraisse would compromise?' the count asked in the tone of voice in which one might ask a doctor 'Do you think I'll get over it?' which is to say that it was an idiotic question.

'My dear M. de Coantré, how do I know? You're the one who's got the papers, if there are any.'

There was a long pause. One might have assumed that M. de Coantré was carefully weighing the pros and cons. In fact he was thinking of nothing—literally nothing. His eyelids were beginning to droop, as though what he really wanted to do was to drop off to sleep.

'Look here,' said Lebeau, 'we're all wasting our time.' (Complacently he flicked the ash from his cigarette.) 'If M. de Coantré values his peace of mind above everything else, he had better pay up. Otherwise, we should probably have to ask him to see Defraisse . . .'

The cruel politeness of 'We're all wasting our time' made M. de Coantré writhe. Could there possibly be a more courteous way of saying, 'You're wasting *my* time?'

'All right, let's pay him, and get it over with,' he said.

'Very well,' said the chief clerk heartily. 'But don't say I forced your hand. I'm still quite prepared to see Defraisse and argue with him, provided you help me, of course . . .'

'No, no,' said M. de Coantré. 'Sell as many of the shares as you need to, and let's hear no more about it.'

They chatted a bit longer and then, 'having said all there was to be said,' M. de Coantré got up to go. It was only then that he realized that Lebeau had left the room—without saying good-bye to him.

69

Scarcely had M. de Coantré gone before Bourdillon was running after him with a half-mocking, half-pitying smile and handing him his bundle of papers, which he had forgotten. Every time he left the lawyer's office he forgot something.

Once outside, he began to walk aimlessly. He felt so disgruntled that he stopped at the first tobacconist's to buy a packet of cigarettes. Six months before, when he realized his new financial position, he had given up smoking to save money. But now his willpower was crumbling. On the most favourable assumption, if no more creditors turned up, he would have two thousand francs left! 'But after all,' he thought, 'there's still time to tell him to contest it. I'll have a look through my papers. In any case, even if I have to pay, there's always Uncle Octave.' He noticed that involuntarily—as a horse whose rider has fallen asleep automatically takes the accustomed route—his steps had led him to the Boulevard Haussmann. He went upstairs without taking the lift, for he was afraid of such machines (similarly, without either of them having mentioned it, M. Elie never took the lift).

M. Octave was out. Léon pretended to look for a visiting card in his wallet (for twenty years he had had none) and exclaimed 'I've *just* given the last one away!' having forgotten, as Papon, who eyed him in silence, had not, that he had already been through this little act twice before in Uncle Octave's hall. Then, on a slip of paper which he afterwards put in an envelope, he wrote 'My dear uncle, a new creditor has turned up at Lebeau's: five thousand francs. Once this is paid (and a thousand francs saved elsewhere), I shall have two thousand left. No comment. I shall, if I may, call on you tomorrow at five. Your affectionate Léon.' When he saw himself signing 'Léon' on a note to M. Octave, he had the impression that he was on a footing of great intimacy with his uncle, and that his uncle wished him well. He put 'your affectionate' because it was a formula used by the Duc d'Orléans.

He did not get back to the Boulevard Arago until eight o'clock, having a genius for taking three or four hours, so fantastic were the means of transport he adopted, on a journey which a messenger boy (not by nature in a hurry) would have done in one. M. Elie had started dinner without him. He went straight upstairs to change, partly to spare his 'best' clothes but also because he always felt slightly uncomfortable in them. And when he saw these clothes laid out on the bed, he remembered all the trouble he had had earlier in the day, brushing them, finding a clean shirt, cleaning his boots, shaving, etc, and the pill he had just swallowed seemed even more bitter. When one 'dresses up', he thought, one ought at least to be rewarded by the success of whatever it was that made it necessary.

In the dining-room, taking advantage of Mélanie's momentary absence, he said to M. Elie:

'Uncle, I have some bad news for you . . .'

M. Elie looked up sharply and stared at him, showing his big, pale pupils.

'What's that?'

'There's a new debt on the estate, and when it's paid I'll have only two thousand francs left.'

M. de Coëtquidan breathed again. An odd way to express oneself, typical of the de Coantrés of this world, to speak of 'bad news' to a third party when the news is only bad for *oneself*.

'Actually,' M. de Coantré went on, 'it isn't certain that we'll have to pay. I must go through my papers. If I happened to find . . .'

'Ha! there's Minine,' said M. Elie. 'He wants to come in.'

He had heard a miaow behind the front door. He got up, let the cat in, and gave it a few scraps of meat which he tore off roughly with his fingers like an Arab.

'Yes,' M. de Coantré continued, 'it may be that my having found the letter from M. d'Aumagne, which if it had been couched in terms . . .'

'Ah, Minine! You want to go out?'

The cat had gone back to the door and was indeed now miaowing to be let out. The cats of the Arago household had this in common with humans: they always wanted to be somewhere else. So M. de Coëtquidan, a devoted slave to their every wish, was always opening a door somewhere or other, and the phrase 'He wants to come in' or 'He wants to go out' had become a private joke between

Mme de Coantré, Léon and Mélanie. It should be noted, in passing, that M. de Coëtquidan addressed cats in the second person plural, which sounds rather grand, instead of saying '*tu*' in the normal way. Did they say '*vous*' to cats at the court of Louis XIV? Perhaps they did until the latter part of his reign, when it was felt that the time had come to 'brighten things up a bit'.

M. de Coëtquidan came back. But by now Léon had understood, and said no more about his affairs.

Soon after dinner he went up to his room and wrote three letters. Impulsive as he was, he would have suffered if something had prevented him from writing these letters at once, even though they could not be posted until the next day. One was addressed to the son of the old lady in whose house he had lodged at Chatenay; another to a decayed nobleman, a sort of jack-of-all-trades who dabbled in marriage-making and had done so for him; the third to one of the doctors at his auxiliary hospital. He had had no dealings with these people for twenty, fifteen and ten years respectively, but they were the only names he could think of when, during dinner, he had made this resolution: 'There's no time to lose. It's time I found myself a job.' In these three letters M. de Coantré explained his situation in a few words and asked if he could 'do something'. He emphasized his talents as a male nurse.

When he had written them, he felt he had taken action. Three letters! Proudly he weighed them in his hand. And, no doubt, writing a letter *is* an action. This impression of having 'taken a step forward' somewhat assuaged his bitter feelings.

(It is amusing to observe that M. de Coantré's handwriting, firm, upright, well-formed, the signature strongly underlined, would have credited him, in the eyes of a graphologist, with all the characteristics—concision, energy, pride, vitality—in which he was most conspicuously lacking.)

That night, he woke up at two o'clock, a thing which never happened to him, and did not go to sleep again.

Next morning he went up to the attic, where there was a packing-case full of letters addressed to his mother, which for the past six months he had not found time to sort because the idea of it was too irksome. There, perhaps, some document lay buried which would enable him to avoid paying the five thousand francs. He took out three packets of letters, and immediately was overwhelmed by the magnitude of the task; it is always astonishing to see, in a dead person's room, how many letters someone of no social importance has managed to receive.

Before going to Lebeau's, Léon had made up his mind to spend the next morning at a job he adored, a job he wallowed in, a job that had almost become a vice with him—and vice is the word, for it gave him an almost sensual pleasure: mowing the lawn. And he needed this pleasure all the more today because he had to compensate himself for the ordeal of having to go back to Lebeau's. After debating with himself for a few moments, he decided to indulge himself and forget the five thousand francs. He closed the packing-case and went down from the attic to play with the mowing-machine. When an unpleasant thought occurred to him, he simply told himself: 'Anyway, I made a thousand francs yesterday' (on the lawyer's fees).

That afternoon he wrote to Bourdillon: 'In spite of my searches, I have found absolutely nothing which might enable me to contest the Defraisse claim. Will you therefore take the necessary steps to see that this man is paid.' (*This man!* When one pays someone what one owes him, one naturally acquires the right to insult him a little.)

He wrote the address on the envelope with scrupulous care. Ever since he had noticed the envelopes of letters he had addressed to Bourdillon carefully pinned on his file, he sensed that the contents of these envelopes might be enough to hang him. And he sent Mélanie to post the letter, although M. Elie might have done so on his way out. But he was afraid that M. Elie, unable to resist the temptation to unstick the stamp, might spend his afternoon walk delivering the letter himself; and *what on earth* would they think of the rectangle of glue on the envelope?

Once the cook had gone, M. de Coantré experienced a kind of euphoria comparable to that of a martyr going to the stake or, better still, a man who has slit open a vein and whose life is ebbing away: the languorous pleasure of utter impotence. There was something beatific about the ease with which M. de Coantré shed his possessions. And this is clearly what the masses feel when they interpret the famous passage, referring to a certain category of beings, to mean that theirs is the kingdom of heaven.

5

To BE the 'plutocrat of the family' is not a state one would wish on anybody. It would take a long time to work out the total sum that his relations, one after the other, had extracted from M. Octave. He had painstakingly supported Mme de Coantré when she was assailed by the money troubles brought down on her by her husband and her son. He had taken in Mme de Piagnes when she became a widow, and, incredible as it may seem, the rent she paid him in 1924—four francs a day—had not altered since 1906. He had showered presents on his great-niece Simone de Bauret and 'taken her around', until the old cousin took a fancy to her. And this is to mention only the family. In fact no stranger ever approached him in vain.

M. Octave had acquired the habit of dispensing largesse—or rather had it instilled into him—to such an extent that he was now obsessed with the idea that, whatever happened to him, he was most unlikely to get through it without having to put his hand in his pocket. This was highly distasteful to him, not so much the giving away of his money, for he was not by nature ungenerous, as the fact that he did not know how to give it. We have said that all the Coëtquidans were shy. The 'love-birds' made no attempt to over-come their shyness: it bound them hand and foot. Old Coëtquidan and M. Elie conquered it by being gratuitously rude and cantanker-ous; they would quite suddenly adopt a totally outlandish manner, which was their way of defending themselves by anticipation. M. Octave conquered it with money, which enabled him to withdraw from embarrassing situations by giving some of it away—though this in itself put a cruel strain on his shyness and on the peculiar awkwardness he suffered from, typical of those who have never penetrated below the surface of life.

The pain M. Octave suffered from continually being 'touched' was aggravated by the fact that, like the pain of a husband whose wife is deceiving him, it had to be concealed. And needless to say, every act of generosity brought its trail of worries.

Just as, at the age of seventy, he had still not found the right tone in which to speak to his subordinates, whether his own servants or employees at the bank, alternating curtness, which came naturally to him, with a forced bonhomie, which made him sweat blood, and changing his policy in this respect every twenty-four hours, M. Octave had never mastered the art of knowing when, how, how much or even whether he ought to give. In this connection, an incident in his youth had put him off for life. At the end of a short stay in the country during which friends had taken him for several drives, he decided, after long deliberations with himself which practically ruined the last few days of his visit, to slip the coachman fifty francs. Politely but firmly, and in front of everyone, the tip was refused, and he was left squirming with embarrassment. (After this, appalled at the thought of having hurt the man's feelings, he had tied himself up in knots in an effort to make amends, blurting out some nonsense that gave every appearance of an apology, and did not consider himself absolved until six years later by a First Communion present he gave the man's son.)

Ever since then, giving frightened him. It infected even the simplest things, especially any kind of service that was done for him. Should he give? Had he given enough? Had he given too much? He asked everyone's advice, and then, having given, how anxiously he would scrutinize the recipient's face to find out his reaction! When, one day, he was heard to say 'I don't like people to do me favours', it was regarded as an example of revolting pride. In fact the baron had plenty of egoism, a fair amount of vanity (as much as is hygienically necessary), but no pride. He disliked receiving favours because he felt obliged to return them, and this presented problems which tortured him. Every time the baron came to someone's aid monetarily, the person concerned had to come to the baron's aid physically. This man had been seen, even when well into his fifties, blushing like a girl when he told someone that they could count on him if they were in difficulties. And simply to say this had cost him dear; he had called round twice before with this end in view, but each time, with the words on the tip of his tongue, he could not bring himself to utter them, feeling precisely the same embarrassment and shame as if he were asking for money instead of offering it. 'His generosity will kill him' was the unfriendly verdict of Léon's father (who pecked at the Coëtquidans as much as they pecked at the Coantrés), but this, it is true, was before he had had to submit to this generosity, which paid off part of his debts and was both big in cash and infinite in delicacy.

This general attitude of the baron's as regards charity was not quite the same when it came to his nephew. He could not, of course, leave his sister's son in want. At the same time, he knew that Léon had powerfully contributed to his mother's ruin, and although Mme de Coantré concealed from him her son's tantrums, he had had little difficulty in smelling them out. The enlarger business had not left him unscathed. He despised Léon for reasons that are easily guessed—and contempt, we are told, is 'the most pitiless of emotions' (André Suarès). Finally, however anxious he was, as a reaction against his father and because he believed that the Americans award merit only to the individual, to free himself from 'family' prejudices, he could not help feeling some antipathy towards the Coantrés—a family who had had a disastrous influence on his sister's life, who were shallower, less punctilious and less noble than the Coëtquidans, and who, moreover, had an easy-going cheerfulness, a suggestion of debonair ease which the Coëtquidans lacked and which therefore weighed on the same side as their failings in the Coëtquidan scales.

When M. Octave returned home to find Léon's scribbled note, he gave an exasperated 'Ah!' and then, at the thought of the handful of money which his nephew would be left with, realized that he would have to make an effort to find him a job if he was not to be saddled with him. He spoke to his sister about it over dinner.

Mme Emilie had a pale face which she made even paler by covering it with rice powder, forehead included; a flaming red wig; and teeth that were as yellow as those of a horse; the general effect, though it gave her a face in the Papal colours (which was praiseworthy) was not exactly pretty-pretty. Added to which she was thin, stooping, flat-breasted, with sparse eyebrows blackened with mascara and the Coëtquidan hands, which were her chief pride, so small at the end of her arms—scarcely wider than her wrists—that they were somehow grotesque, like atrophied limbs or the feet of a tadpole. Léon, living on his mother and naturally idle, did not conceal the amount of spare time he had. Mme Emilie, living on her brother and having nothing to do and no responsibilities, never had a minute—an example of feminine genius. A childish, querulous soul, utterly stupid, yet with some features that compelled respect, the flashes of wit and common sense she had shown in her youth had been absorbed, as it were, into the vague, pallid mush which was her substitute for the inner life—like one of those children who impress one with their enormous eyes, but when we meet them again later on, their eyes seem to have shrunk simply through not having grown in the same proportion as the rest of the face.

Mme Emilie's reactions, whatever the subject which provoked them, were always choice.

'Poor Léon! Only two thousand francs left! How dreadful!' she wailed when her brother told her the news.

M. Octave had been sufficiently stirred by his nephew's situation to decide to do something, and to speak to his sister about it, but no sooner had he heard the word 'dreadful' on Mme Emilie's lips than he decided that the situation was not so dreadful as all that. This was not only because it was by contradicting that every Coëtquidan managed to shape a personality for himself (ever since the Coët-quidans of the fourteenth century, who owed their existence to their systematic contradiction of the king), but because he regarded his sister as of no importance and because she was dependent on him. As a rule he did not reply when she spoke to him, but continued to read his newspaper, and she would be left staring at him in silent reproach.

'Dreadful?' he said. 'What do you mean? He won't be the first to have to earn his living. He ought to be able to work, he's done nothing for twenty years. As for the two thousand francs, I shall remain sceptical until Lebeau confirms it. You know what Léon de Coantré is like: he's *highly strung*. And Lebeau is pessimistic on principle.'

There is always something remarkable about the baron's statements. This one is worth looking into. It is remarkable, for instance, that M. de Coëtquidan should have inferred, from the fact that Léon had not worked for twenty years, that he would find it that much easier to do so now, as though these twenty years of inaction had somehow stored up inside him a potential of unused energy—whereas in fact an aptitude or an organ are weakened by prolonged inaction. Then the assertions that Léon was 'highly strung' and that Lebeau had a tendency to look on the black side were calculated to dispense M. Octave from worrying unduly about his nephew. We must, incidentally, salute this cliché about Lebeau's pessimism—an old acquaintance, which we shall be meeting again: it was one of those indestructible family words, secretly worshipped because they are a substitute both for thought and for observation. And finally we must note that M Octave said 'Léon de Coantré' and not simply 'Léon', thus indicating that in spite of everything his nephew was something of a stranger to him.

'Work!' said Mme Emilie. 'But what can he do?'

'I'll talk to him about it, but he is obviously more or less good for nothing,' M. Octave replied, for he wanted on the one hand to try to avoid helping Léon by affirming that he was perfectly capable of working, and on the other to belittle Léon by saying that he was incapable of it. These two propositions were mutually contradictory, but M. Octave was reluctant to dispense with either. So he alternated them.

There was a silence, during which he foresaw how it would all end, and then he sighed:

'After all, I gave quite enough to poor Angèle.'

True enough. But Léon was not his mother, and would hardly be able to buy bread with the money M. Octave had given to Mme Angèle, who had given it to her creditors.

When, at five o'clock that evening, Léon climbed the stairs in the Boulevard Haussmann, he had that faint feeling of apprehension he always had when he went to call on his uncle or on Bourdillon, the fear that something might have happened since their last meeting to alter for the worse their attitude towards him, the fear of seeing a new expression on their faces, and worst of all the fear of never being able to find out why. Thus did he treat his life, innocent though it was, as if it was full of guilt. But M. Octave, at this moment, was just as embarrassed as he was, having not the slightest idea what he was going to say to him.

The baron, who believed in preparing everything in advance, regarding spontaneity as bad form, had prepared a digression which would enable him to gain time (his usual running away from reality). It consisted of a comparison between the premature mildness of the weather and the occasional warm spells at the beginning of November during his childhood at Saint-Pol-de-Léon. But this plan was upset by M. de Coantré, who was not without his little wiles, and had brought his uncle a small blue vase, worth next to nothing, in which his mother used to put flowers. He offered it to him as a souvenir, telling him that it was in this vase, a few days before her death, that his mother's feeble old hands had arranged their last bunch of flowers. This was a pure invention, which could nevertheless be called 'pious', although its sole object was to soften up the old man. So the conversation started off on a sentimental note, which opened the door to reminiscences into which M. Octave plunged with a vengeance.

Léon was supremely indifferent to M. Octave's reminiscences, but he listened with a great show of attention, put in a word from time to time, and thought, 'He'll be pleased with me for listening to him, and glad of the chance to talk about himself'—for he flattered himself that he 'understood' his uncle. But secretly his attention was concentrated on the problem of how to explain his plight and make himself interesting, and he watched for the first pause so that he could rush in.

When all this gossip had been wrapped around the object of their meeting, like the straw which Léon wrapped with such artistry round the crockery in his packing-cases, M. Octave, indulging his talent for never broaching a question openly, adopted an oblique approach and instead of referring to the new factor, which was the new debt, said:

'Well, have you done anything about finding a job?'

'Yes,' said M. de Coantré, 'I've written six letters.' (He had written three.) 'But I haven't yet had a reply.'

M. Octave then realized how rash his question had been. Remembering that Léon had asked him to make some inquiries on his behalf, he said:

'I haven't forgotten about you. I mentioned your name to Héquelin du Page. But he immediately asked me: "What exactly can he do?"'

'Thank you, Uncle Octave!' M de Coantré fervently exclaimed. Once his uncle and M. Héquelin du Page together were looking after him, he was saved! And like an electric bulb when the light is switched on, a gleam of emotion and gratitude suddenly shone in his eyes. This look was painful to M. Octave, who had not spoken to his friend or taken any steps at all on Léon's behalf. But since he hated to suffer, he thought: 'I didn't do it yesterday, but I'll do it tomorrow. So it's as if I *had* done it.'

To the question of what exactly he could do M. de Coantré answered by detailing his capacities. M. Octave picked up a pencil and from time to time made notes on a piece of paper: 'gardening . . . knowledge of cuttings . . . auxiliary hospital . . .' to show how seriously he was taking it all. But *in petto* he was thinking: 'Him a male nurse! He needs somebody to nurse him!'

When Léon said that he would not jib at manual labour, M. Octave proceeded to sing its praises:

'Peter the Great was a good carpenter, Louis XVI mended locks. I polish my own boots, I clean my own clothes, and I would mend the curtain runners myself when they break if I didn't feel dizzy on a step-ladder. There are things which the people who look after us, even if they are specialists, don't know how to do, and which one must do oneself. For example, a barber will never give you as close a shave as you will yourself. When the girl at the bootmaker's ties your laces, you invariably have to undo them again and tie them yourself. And when a policeman is trying to look up a street for you, you invariably have to take the directory away from him and look it up yourself, because he *can't* find it the way he's looking. Elie is being hopelessly old-fashioned when he talks about the Coëtquidan hands. When one of the chaps in my section in '70, a worker, said to me: "What white hands you've got! Honest, considering what you do with them!" I went and rubbed my hands on some old scrap iron. Besides, the Americans. . . .'

It was astonishing to hear the baron reciting this eulogy of manual labour—or rather not so astonishing, since the *sacred* character of manual labour is a specifically bourgeois invention. M. Octave's speech was interrupted by Léon who, always passionately devoted to his uncle and longing to do him a favour, both in order to oblige him and in order not to be continually at the receiving end, pounced on the detail about cleaning clothes and gave his uncle the name of a stain-remover far superior to anything else of the kind, a name which M. Octave made a note of, out of politeness, even checking the spelling, although he had made up his mind never to buy this product, which was doubly suspect because it was not he, M. de Coëtquidan, who had discovered it, and because it was Léon who recommended it.

In this connection, Léon gave free rein to his 'bachelor' spirit with a string of domestic anecdotes in which the name Mélanie cropped up at every turn, as a normal man has an itch to bring the name of his mistress into everything he says, however dangerous it may be. According to whether the conversation revolved round him or a subject that had nothing to do with him, the baron's face alternately lit up or clouded over, as the sun alternately appears and disappears in a sky that is clear but dotted with small clouds. Léon, on the other hand, even when he was not talking about himself, kept his eyes lit up by an effort of the will, feigning a violent interest in every-thing connected with his uncle.

'And what if I haven't found a job by October 15th?' he asked at length, sensing that the atmosphere was propitious.

'I think between the two of us we'll manage somehow,' said the baron, looking down at his fingers and making an odd face. Léon, jumping for joy as well as anxious to compromise his uncle, rose in his seat and, leaning forward, grasped the old man's hands.

'Ah! Uncle Octave, I knew you wouldn't desert me. Think how happy you're making Mama! You really haven't changed a bit!'

M. Octave, his hands still in Léon's, had drawn back a little, squirming with embarrassment. As soon as he could do so without being rude, he extricated his hands and on the spur of the moment treated his nephew to a splendid, traditional panegyric of poverty, with the object of convincing him that he ought not to read more into what his uncle had said than his uncle had meant, and that in fact he would always be poor. He finished up with these words: 'You, my boy, ought to be able to put up with poverty more than most. You're lucky to have simple tastes and few needs. And then socially . . . how shall I put it . . . you, at least, if you're short of money, nobody notices. Whereas if I were obliged to lower my standard of living, it would be obvious to everyone.'

M. de Coantré was glad to learn that he was, after all, in a privileged position. They parted on a note of optimism.

On his return home, Léon wrote in the notebook in which he was wont to record succinctly the day's events and sometimes a short reflection: 'Sentimental session with old Oct. We shall see! . . .' This may shock some lady readers, who would prefer 'poor Léon' to be unreservedly lovable. But it is not for us to create lovable characters, but to show them as they were. And it is certainly true that Léon's remark in his diary revealed him as a man who, for all his naïvety and his often touching sentiments, was not entirely innocent.

When his nephew had gone, M. Octave wondered whom he could approach on Léon's behalf with any chance of success. He ruled out automatically all his colleagues at the bank. He had no desire for these people to know that he had a nephew who was prepared to work with his hands, and, moreover, it was a strict rule of his never to mix family affairs with those of 'the house' (as, characteristically, he called the bank, having transferred to his profession, in his 'American' way, the respect which people of his class usually reserve for their family). He also ruled out M. Héquelin du Page, because, having always obtained whatever he wanted from his *alter ego* without having to do anything in exchange, he made it a point of honour never to ask him for anything. And he ruled out others simply because he did not want to use up his credit with them, doubtless to no purpose. When we ask people in high places to help this or that person and they say they can do nothing, we are incredulous, we question their goodwill. But the process of elimination, which worked for M. Octave, works for us all, and if we ourselves look round among our acquaintances for people who would really be useful in any given circumstance, we find that their number, when it comes to the point, is always remarkably small.

The baron eventually hit on the idea of tackling one of his friends, an ex-solicitor called Maître Beauprêtre. He was about to telephone him, but was overcome by diffidence, which he translated as scruples; even on the telephone, which is a godsend for shy souls, asking favours embarrassed him, and he decided to write instead. But suddenly, with his pen already poised, the letter seemed difficult. He addressed and stamped the envelope, and placed it in front of him against a replica of the Statue of Liberty, as though the envelope was more than half the battle and might give out a sort of aura of encouragement and inspiration—but the letter would not *come*. And, unfortunately, letters do not usually count until they are written and posted.

A card of introduction serves no purpose at all. A letter of introduction seldom serves any purpose. Only a visit carries weight, a personal approach in the most warm and pressing terms, and moreover one must return to the charge. All else is vanity. Yet people refuse to recognize this, and go on asking for scribbled notes which one gives for the sake of peace and quiet. The baron's letter, without his realizing it, was the prototype of all such letters, which are in the last degree futile since they exude the unmistakable impression that the writer is not interested in what he is asking for and does not believe he will get it. And indeed M. de Coëtquidan hated asking. He had never done it for himself, having been given everything, and he found it galling, if not unjust, to have to do it for others, and especially for someone as *uninteresting* as his nephew. Nevertheless, he wrote four pages to M. Beauprêtre.

Then he wrote another—or rather, more or less the same—four-page letter to a first cousin who was reputed to be kind-hearted and went in for good works. 'If you can't find anything that looks at all suitable,' he told her, 'don't bother to answer.'

That evening he was dining with a stockbroker, an ostentatious vulgarian. While he was dressing, he thought of approaching him about Léon. In the smoking-room, in the drawing-room, all through the evening it worried him. But it seemed somehow improper to mix these sordid matters with a social occasion, and to ask a favour of someone who had just plied him with extremely expensive fodder. So that, though the words were always on the tip of his tongue, he continued to keep them to himself.

M. Octave gauged what he did for other people not so much by its efficacy as by the trouble he took doing it. Having written two letters, each four pages long, he considered that he had done enough for the time being, and that there was nothing more to be done but 'wait and see'.

Léon, for his part, having written three letters, each four pages long, and received a promise, or an ostensible promise, from his uncle, also considered that he had done enough for the time being and that there was nothing more to be done but 'wait and see'.

However, the days went by and mail after mail brought him nothing, either from the people he had written to or from his uncle, to whom he dared not write again for fear of irritating him. When the postman rang, instead of going at once to the kitchen he waited for ten minutes in order to conceal his impatience from Mélanie. Then his face would light up at the sight of an imposing packet of letters on the kitchen table. But, on closer inspection, what a disappointment! Prospectuses from motor-car dealers, wine merchants, jewellers—everything that is likely to be sent to a count whose name appears in *Tout-Paris* and the *Bottin Mondain* with H.P. (*hôtel particulier* — town house) beside it—together with begging letters from charities, which reminded him of a remark of his mother's in the bitterness of her last years: 'The only thing you get through knowing the best people is trade cards.'

It also happened that for two days running the postman did not come at all. (Previously he had been obliged to come every day, because M. de Coantré subscribed to *L'Action Française*; but he had not renewed his subscription the previous month, both as a measure of economy and because any intellectual exercise, even reading a newspaper, had become more and more of an effort.) 'No mail?' he could not help asking Mélanie, thinking that she might have forgotten to give it to him.

'No, monsieur. How quiet things are!'

'No question about it, we're certainly being left in peace,' said Léon with a forced laugh. His whole life had been spent in such a way as to guarantee his being left in peace. But now this peace frightened him. It is a time-honoured process: those who are anti-social at thirty live to regret it at fifty.

Léon's plight required not so much, perhaps, a strictly financial effort as someone to examine it *seriously*. Over a dozen people knew about it, but, like a bunch of racing cyclists, nobody wanted to go into the lead. Most sufferers know the cure for their ills, and people around them also know the cure. And yet from all this knowledge nothing comes to bring them relief.

In this way a week went by after Léon's visit to M. Octave. At last, on the eighth day, Léon received a letter from the doctor at his auxiliary hospital. It was full of kind words: they remembered his devotion to 'our dear wounded'; they could offer him nothing for the time being, but promised to bear him in mind, 'although at the moment, in every branch, there are many applications and few vacancies'. The letter ended with 'kindest regards'.

This was not quite what Léon had expected; he expected to be given an interview. But still, the doctor was *au courant* and his letter was 'very friendly' . . .

Léon went to the Boulevard Haussmann, to 'report' to his hierarchical chief.

Unfortunately, since his last visit, M. Octave's movements had been as follows. It will be remembered that he had asked his brother to obtain from Bourdillon a written statement of his present income and to bring it to him on an agreed day. That day, and those which followed it, he waited for Elie, who never came. He turned up the following week and declared quite simply he had not been able to see Bourdillon because 'that damned shop was always closed . . .'

'Always closed?'

'Arrived at quarter to six: not a soul. A bunch of idlers! There's your modern Frenchman!'

The baron, convinced that he would never get the details of his brother's finances unless he himself spoke to Bourdillon, went to the lawyer's office. The chief clerk told him that Elie had an income of nine thousand francs, which in itself was enough to put M. Octave's nose out of joint, since he realized that his brother would never be able to manage without his help, when Bourdillon added parenthetically, after having confirmed Léon's even more disastrous situation: 'M. de Coantré isn't very easy to deal with. He spoke to me the other day in such a way that if it weren't for his family ties with yourself and your brother, I would have answered him back in kind.'

Bourdillon was too clever not to have sensed that he was giving pleasure to M. Octave by speaking ill of his nephew. The baron was outraged: Léon was penniless, and yet presumed to be insolent!

Added to this, M. Octave had received a visit from Beauprêtre, who said to him: 'Let me be perfectly frank: don't send your nephew to see me. I'm a sensitive soul . . . for example, when I see a beggar on the pavement, I cross to the other side, because I know that if I looked him in the face it would be too much for me, I'd give him something. What will happen? I shall feel sorry for your nephew, and ruin myself for him. Well, I don't *want* to do that: I owe it to my family.'

Moreover, it was a fortnight since he had written to his cousin about Léon, and she had not answered. 'For fifty years I've got on extremely well with Marceline—from a distance—and this fool of a nephew has to come along and spoil it! Because after all I can't feel at ease with a relation who doesn't even bother to answer a four-page letter! It's typical of Léon de Coantré. He brings bad luck all round!' True, he had said to Marceline: 'Don't answer if you can't think of anything suitable.' But of course that was simply out of politeness.

When, that evening, Papon announced Léon, M. Octave did not hide his feelings from his servant; in fact, succumbing to his fury, he almost paraded them. He threw up his hands as though he were about to tear his hair, and shouted: 'This time, no, no and no! Tell him I'm out.'

Papon complied. But he did it so well (with a secret spite?), laying it on so thick, saying that Monsieur had 'just this minute' gone out etc, that Léon guessed the truth, and went away filled with a sense of catastrophe. He always expected Bourdillon's letters to bring him bad news, and indeed the news they brought was nearly always bad. He always expected that the moment would come when Uncle Octave would turn on him, and at last that moment had come. We have said it before and we repeat it now: the tragic thing about anxious people is that they always have cause for anxiety.

6

OLIVE-SKINNED, with slender, well-bred wrists, eyes that would set a haystack alight at a range of ten yards (Mlle de Bauret was Provençal), two beauty spots on the front of her neck and one in the crook of her left arm (which was blue, like a patch of sky reflected in water in the hollow of a ditch), Mlle de Bauret, having arrived unexpectedly at one o'clock, was sitting in the dining-room at Arago, the picture of charm and grace. She was holding in her hand one of those literary reviews that a self-respecting man will never read in public without wrapping his newspaper round it, lest he should be taken for a humbug. Her low forehead bespoke her lack of intelligence but added to her facial attraction; her bosom, *miserabile dictu*, was on the whole conspicuous by its absence; the aura of warmth that always emanates from a woman's body was in her case an aura of *fresh* warmth, for she was still nubile although twenty-five years old; and so charming withal that if you looked at her for any length of time you gradually experienced (no joking!) a slight feeling of levitation—a sensation which, however literary, is not so far removed from that expressed by Mélanie when she said, 'How elegant Mlle de Bauret is! When you see her move, you'd think she was walking on air.'

Mlle de Bauret had refused the cup of coffee her uncle had offered her. 'No thanks! I don't want to be poisoned,' she had said to herself, for she had failed to penetrate the secret of the house, which was that although everyone dressed in rags there was no cheese-paring over food or heating, contrary to what happens among the common run of humanity, who invariably cut down on food as soon as they are threatened with a shortage of money. The coffee that was offered to Mlle de Bauret was in fact excellent. Her eyes travelled from the grimy pellet of breadcrumbs, which M. de

Coëtquidan was feverishly rolling between his fingers, to the old man's face, and she produced an exaggerated version of that scowl of contempt at which young ladies always excel. She longed for M. Elie to realize that she despised him; but he was miles away, and, moreover, even if he had noticed, he would have been glad: to be despised by someone we ourselves despise is like nectar to us, for it justifies us in our own eyes. Mlle de Bauret's glance now wandered towards the genealogical tree, painted on parchment, which hung on the wall (the duly authenticated line of descent of the Coëtquidans since the year 1431, with the appropriate coats of arms) and the fine oak sideboard on which were engraved side by side the arms of the Coëtquidans and those of the du Couësnons (Mme de Coantré's maternal family), and seeing these splendours cheek by jowl with the cheap painted 'Breton' plates, fixed to the wall as though they were expensive porcelain, the copper pots worthy of the flea-market, and the carved wooden bear bought in a Swiss emporium and lacking the smallest artistic merit, the girl thought to herself that even if she was paid a 'tidy' sum to live in this house she could not have done so.

What with the war and the premature death of her parents, Mlle de Bauret had had no upbringing at all. But our age is such that nobody noticed, unless, like the old cousin, who could trace her descent in direct line at least as far back as Hildebrand, they found a lack of breeding 'such fun, don't you know'. The stupidity of children is invariably and without exception the result of the stupidity of grown-ups. Mlle de Bauret had a taste for literature and the arts, but her literary knowledge only began with the end of the nineteenth century—in other words it was non-existent. She saw and judged the world through the pet theories of a few fashionable authors: for example, she honestly believed that every man had been in love with his mother as a child, and if someone confessed to her that he had been tempted to push a stranger under a tram, she would say to him: 'You've been reading too much Gide'—at which her companion would stare at her blankly, having never even heard of the author of *Les Nourritures Terrestres*. She proclaimed a cinema clown called Charlie Chaplin a genius. When she lapsed into a reverie, she called it an 'interior monologue'. When M. de Coantré told her that Uncle Octave was reluctant to face reality, she translated it into her jargon thus: 'He is taking refuge in escapism.' And so on. This infantilism of mind gave her, at the age of twenty-five, the same sort of silliness as a sixteen-year-old who enters the class of philosophy and discovers the human mind and soul through the manuals of M. Paulin Malapert. In politics, needless to say, Mlle de Bauret had progressive ideas.

Mlle de Bauret's real failing, which was partly the failing of her age and partly that of the period in which she lived, was that she regarded novelty as synonymous with value. This is a sure sign of barbarism: in any society, it is always the people with the lowest intelligence who long to be 'in the swim'. Incapable of assessing anything by their own taste, culture and discrimination, they automatically judge a problem in accordance with the principle that what is new is true.

Let us, however, concede one good point to Mlle de Bauret: although she was a great intellectual, she did not spell her Christian name 'Symohne'.

Thus equipped, the poor girl was an obvious prey for the charlatans of the pen and the palette. She mixed in that world, and as she was popular there because of her rather credulous nature, she turned it to good account and earned from it what she called, in her frightful jargon, her 'bread and butter'. With the vile tendency towards parasitism peculiar to her generation, both male and female, during those years, she lived six months of the year with the rich cousin in Brittany, and six months in Paris with up-to-date friends, the sort of people M. de Coantré, for all his filth and rags and for all his good nature, would have hesitated to shake hands with. In partnership with a young caricaturist, she launched a new drawing-room doll which was fashionable in 1922. She acted as a go-between in the fake antique business. She decorated studios, and from the beginning of 1924 had started to look for flats for her friends on condition that she herself would decorate them 'if the deal went through'. The whole thing is so vile that one hasn't the stomach to go on with it. Suffice it to say that for the past two years she had made forty thousand francs a year out of these various deals, which after all was something for a girl who had *nothing* to her name. Although heterosexual, she had not married, because she had nothing; and she had even preserved her virginity—though it was hardly worth preserving.

Mlle de Bauret's feelings towards 'Gog and Magog' corresponded to the feelings each of them bore towards her: animosity for M. de Coëtquidan, affection for M. de Coantré. Her relations with Uncle Elie were stiffly polite. With Uncle Léon she had established herself, when still quite small, on a footing of familiarity that was ever so slightly patronizing but which he found agreeable. Though he was terrified of boys, as we have seen, the genius of the race overcame his fears when it came to a little girl. He was fond of his niece, whom he called 'Pinpin'. He had been surprised to find her disinterested in connection with the estate, oblivious of the fact that this girl, who cared nothing about the money she might receive when it came from the family, would have had the lawyers in action over five hundred francs which one of her 'clients' was disputing.

While the two men drank their coffee, M. de Coantré gave his niece the latest news about the estate. In the meantime M. de Coëtquidan kept his nose in his cup, refusing even to look at his great-niece, so much did she stir up his fury and bile. At length M. de Coantré led the girl into the drawing-room, where seven packing-cases or trunks were stacked together, and said triumphantly:

'And there are eleven more upstairs!'

'What!' cried Simone, pulling a long face. 'I'm going to feel the draught all right.'

'What do you mean?'

'The bill from the repository, of course! It's going to cost me three thousand a year.'

M. de Coantré was silent. Such cries from the heart, or rather from the purse, were not at all what he had expected. Mlle de Bauret went on:

'Thank you, dear Uncle. In giving me your share you have made, as the papers say, a splendid gesture. But why the devil didn't you wait until you saw me before packing it all up? I'm sure half the contents of every one of these cases is not worth keeping.'

(Mlle de Bauret's rudeness makes one shudder.)

'But I warned you. I wrote and told you that I was starting to pack.'

'Well, you see, I can't read long letters.'

(On reflection, one wonders whether Mlle de Bauret's rudeness makes anyone shudder; probably nobody notices she is being rude.)

'Naturally,' she went on, 'there's no question of undoing it all. You've gone to enormous trouble. . . .'

She also was going to enormous trouble, to be amiable—for she was under the impression that she was extremely amiable. The effort she was making completely altered her appearance.

She hoped Léon would say: 'But of course I can take everything out. It's no trouble.'

What he actually said was:

'I've made lists of all the main items in each case, with the number of the case opposite each item. So if you want anything you can find it at once.'

'Oh, but I have everything I need at Cousin Martha's.'

(Well, now, yes or no, *does* Mlle de Bauret's rudeness make one shudder?)

She looked at the cases, and was burning to say: 'I don't want to give you all that work. I shall bring along an odd-job man and we'll sort it all out.' But she could not; the thought of the poor man seeing all his handiwork turned upside down, when he had taken so much trouble, and was giving it all to her so generously . . . no, it was out of the question, she would sooner pay the three thousand francs. As for M. de Coantré, he sensed his niece's secret wish. But he felt that his complaisance had gone far enough. She could have the cases opened if she could bring herself to do so; *he* would have nothing more to do with them.

Eventually, with the speed of decision she showed in all 'practical' matters, she decided to put all the cases not in a repository but in a garage which she would hire for a month. She would go there with someone, sort the stuff out, and send three-quarters of this bric-a-brac to the saleroom. But what a lot of bother, which could so easily have been avoided if this old idiot had had a ha'p'orth of common sense!

They were standing in the hall, at the foot of the staircase, and she was getting ready to leave, when there descended from the first floor, raucous and violent, as though amplified by a megaphone, one of those noises men make with their mouths after a heavy meal. (The extreme fastidiousness of the post-war Frenchman prevents us from giving this noise its proper name.) Mlle de Bauret drew herself up and, in an undertone, flung at Uncle Elie by way of retaliation the name of a domestic animal, a name that is usually taken in bad part.

'It was for *you* that he did that, take my word for it,' said M. de Coantré. 'He has even worse habits, but not that particular one. Obviously he wanted to prove to you that in spite of your youth and elegance and money he is not in the least impressed and has no intention of putting himself out for you. Don't pay any attention; he's a pathetic creature. Come into the garden a minute, I have something to tell you. And if we stay here he'll start again. It will be a bombardment.'

When they were outside, seated on the iron chairs which were so rusty they might have spent a thousand years at the bottom of the sea, M. de Coantré said:

'My little Pinpin, I can't remember whether I told you that although I'm supposed to be keeping the furniture in my room for myself, I intended to give you my piano.'

'I don't know whether you told me, but pianos, you know, for me . . .'

'Good, I'm glad, because I'm afraid I must tell you I haven't any money left. I have two hundred francs to take me to the end of the month, when your Uncle Elie pays his rent. So I thought I might sell the piano. I'm sure I can get at least two hundred and fifty francs for it. Only, as I intended to give it to you, I wanted to ask your permission first, because if you would like to have the piano, I don't want to deprive you of it.'

'Do you think I play those contraptions? No, but really, can you imagine me doing my scales? As a matter of fact, if I were dictator my first edict would be: "Anyone found in possession of a piano, grand or upright, will be shot". So keep your contraption, and get as much money as you can out of it.'

'Ah! Pinpin, you're a good girl. Do you realize that you've just made me a present of two hundred and fifty francs? Because, after all, you could have told me you played the piano, and accepted it simply in order to sell it . . .'

'Two hundred and fifty francs . . . that means two hundred and forty-nine raspberry ices,' Mlle de Bauret said dreamily, and added after a pause, 'and one vanilla.'

'I realize you're making a big sacrifice,' her uncle said, half joking, half serious. He took her hand and squeezed it hard in the way people do when they want to show that this is a handshake full of meaning, having nothing in common with ordinary handshakes. He was astonished at the almost preternatural softness of this girlish hand, and wondered whether it would be proper to prolong this pleasure. But she withdrew her hand.

'Are you really as hard up as that?' she asked. 'How is it possible?'

He gave her a short summary of his financial situation.

'If you ever need anything . . . You know I'm earning a bit of money now . . .'

M. de Coantré's eyes moistened.

'I would never have believed that I could reach the point of borrowing money from my niece,' he said. 'Anyhow, yes, I promise that if ever I find myself absolutely at the end of my tether—but only then—I shall turn to you . . .'

Concentric wrinkles formed round his mouth, and for a second or two his lips shrank inwards slightly, as happens with very very old people.

'It's hard, you know . .' he murmured.

She turned her head away, then got up, and they went towards the garden gate. He muttered to her:

'Take a look at your Uncle Elie's window without letting on . . .'

She looked, and saw the old man watching them from behind the half-closed blind. When she raised her eyes, he withdrew into the room.

'I should be delighted to escort you some of the way,' said the count, 'but dressed as I am,' he pointed to his clothes, which were shabby and full of holes, 'I would disgrace you.'

'What difference does it make!' she said with complete sincerity. And she picked a thread from his jacket. Ah, women!

'No, no . . .'

'But anyway, why are you in rags? You must admit you like it.'

'It's true,' he said, passing from emotion to cheerfulness like a child, 'it's true I feel more at ease in these old togs. When I'm wearing clean clothes I don't feel myself . . .'

'It would be a pity if you weren't yourself,' she said with veiled insolence, but laughingly and without malice.

'Do write to me, then,' her uncle said. 'Of course I don't ask you to write to an old fool like me for fun. But you might at least answer. Whatever I write to you about, even an important piece of information I need for Lebeau, you never answer.'

'I can't write letters. I happen to be made that way,' she replied with the same serious air she had shown earlier when she said: 'I can't read long letters.'

He watched her walk away with long strides down the wide avenue enveloped in the June sunlight, through which the buses sailed like liners on a torpid sea. She hailed a taxi, and as she stood there in the middle of the road with her hand raised and her feet together like a banderillero 'sighting' a bull from a distance, the vehicle came like a languid wave to expire at her feet. Returning to the house, M. de Coantré felt a weight in the right-hand pocket of his jacket. He put his hand inside and found it full of pebbles. While they were sitting in the garden talking, Mlle de Bauret had amused herself by quietly dropping gravel into his pocket. This girlish pleasantry delighted M. de Coantré, and the barometer was set fair when he went up to his room to devote himself to the important business of sleeping until five o'clock.

We must apologize for having spoken of Mlle de Bauret with a sort of shudder which is quite out of place in this narrative. But we were unable to suppress it.

For three months M. de Coantré had been marking time. M.

Octave had recommended him to the organizer of one of those 'social' clubs where, under some pretext or other, a number of respectably dressed people who want to get on in the world are brought together and where, in return for one hundred francs a year, they are supposed to be able to 'make contacts'—the avowed aim of all the riff-raff of Paris. Gentlemen and crooks, adventurers and respectable, even prominent people, rub shoulders there in a promiscuousness which none of them find distasteful. The club in question was an 'aero-social' club, although nine-tenths of its members had never set foot in an aeroplane in their lives. It was run by an 'aero-social' gentleman who could not utter a word without mentioning 'my friend Foch' or 'my friend Painlevé' or 'the Aero-Club, where I'm a big shot'. This man thought M. de Coantré's title might impress some cretins, and made him the following proposition: that the noble count should have a fixed retainer of one hundred francs a month and twenty-five per cent of the subscriptions of the cretins he would bring into the club. M. de Coantré could not get away from him fast enough.

He put an advertisement in *l'Action Française,* and M. Octave paid for another in *Le Temps*: 'Bachelor, 50, well-educated, well-connected, responsible, seeks suitable employment. Moderate requirements.' The advertisement was sent in under Mélanie's surname. It is not surprising that Léon failed to realize the absurdity of this wording. But M. Octave! How are we to answer those sour people who tell us that half the people in responsible positions in any given society are not only imbeciles in the general sense of the word, but that they do not even know anything about their own line of business and have got there by the grace of God?

The advertisement in *Le Temps* brought him a letter offering him a job at twelve thousand francs a year on condition that he brought in one hundred and twenty thousand. Another letter, marked 'urgent' on the envelope, read more or less as follows: 'Why look for a job when for a tiny sum you can be a house-owner?' and was accompanied by a circular advertising a cheap housing scheme. Then there was a letter from a school on the outskirts of Paris where they wanted ushers for the beginning of term; board, lodging, and laundry and two hundred francs a month (three or four times less than a footman, for men into whose care the youth of France are entrusted). M. de Coantré, who would have been delighted to accept a job wrapping up parcels, trembled with shame at the thought of being an usher.

M. de Coantré could quite easily have found a job as a packer, or something of the sort. But it would have meant that the people he applied to took his wishes and tastes seriously instead of trying to find him something in the sphere in which they themselves would have looked if they were in his place. It would have meant that he himself knew which door to knock at. There is a book by Duhamel called *Les Hommes Abandonnés*. He means the veterans of the war. But eight people out of ten—whatever their social position—are abandoned, lost, in peace-time—lost in big things as well as in small. Is there an air-line for such and such a town? What time do the planes leave? How to find a husband. What to do if one's neighbour has a fainting fit. Which monastery to retire to. How to protect the young against venereal disease. What we are looking for is always there, waiting for us. But always the same ignorance: where to look? And human beings! Somewhere our sighs are always echoed by another's. But we do not know where, and our thirst remains unquenched, and life goes by. Oh no! It is not only in war-time that men are 'abandoned'. It may seem a trite thing to say, but it must be said: the lack of connections is one of the great misfortunes of society.

The last letter M. de Coantré received claimed to have the very thing he wanted, and gave him an address and an appointment. But when the time came, he was so bored at the idea of shaving and dressing up and, never having been able to apply himself methodically to anything, he was already so tired of having to repeat what he called 'the same old patter', that he remained at Arago. It was Coantré Triplepatte again, the man who had skipped all those match-making interviews.

He wrote to an old cook who had worked for the family and was now living on her son's farm in Vendée. He offered to pay her one hundred and fifty francs a month (where would he get it? From the baron's pocket, no doubt) and help in the fields, in return for board and lodging. 'It will give you an extra pair of hands,' he naïvely explained. Her reply was a polite refusal.

In the meantime he had written to the director of his hospital, ostensibly to inquire about something but in fact to remind him of his existence. The answer he received began 'Sir . . .' He was so taken aback that he looked up the doctor's previous letter. It began 'Dear Sir . . .' What had he done in these three months to alienate the sympathy of this man? Gloomily he expunged the doctor's name from his address book.

It was exactly as in the war: attempts to break through without success. So now he gave up, convinced of the futility of his efforts and, moreover, persuaded that he had done what he could, that his conscience was clear, that such prodigious efforts had earned him the right to relax. The baron, for his part, had made up his mind to give up searching on his behalf. For he had been mortified, not only in his own eyes but in those of Léon, to find that he had failed; it might cast doubts on his power. However, since, every time they met, Léon told his uncle that he was 'constantly preoccupied' with his future and M. Octave told his nephew that he was 'mentioning it to everyone', neither of them was excessively worried, the one thinking 'Old Octave won't leave me in the lurch', and the other 'He'll end up by getting hold of something. Better leave him to his own devices. He's a crank. He'll only be satisfied with what he finds himself.'

Of Léon's preoccupations and daily routine during the summer of 1924 one can get some idea by glancing at his diary, in which, in his splendid, magisterial handwriting, he would note, for example:

June 13. No Eugénie today [this was the charwoman].

Or:
June 17. Paid laundry-woman: 88 francs. Still owing to her: 0 fr. 60. Wished Mélanie many happy returns.

Or:
June 21. Saw old Octave. He said, 'You're bursting with rude health. I've never seen you looking so well.' I'll say!

Or:

June 26. Mélanie tells me Eugénie has been stealing our 'sparrows',[1] which she took away in a little bag slung between her legs.

He made frequent calls at the offices of the gas company, the inspector of taxes, the town hall, etc. For, since there were mistakes to his detriment in every bill he received from these organizations, and since these errors were accompanied by threats of frightful penalties if he failed to pay up within three days, he saw his gas being cut off or the bailiffs arriving, and could not rest until he had had it out direct with clerks who ridiculed him for having taken these official ultimatums literally. He could have telephoned, but he had never used a telephone in his life, and in any case did not know that one can telephone from any café.

At other times he consoled himself with his beloved gardening—the simplest gardening, a sort of horticultural pottering about, which consisted of weeding, trimming shrubs, mowing the lawn, clipping hedges. Always destroying, as with his own life; though it is true that whenever one comes upon professional gardeners at work they too are always cutting something down.

But M. de Coantré's favourite pastime nowadays was sleep. He had always loved to stretch himself out on his bed in the daytime. Sometimes he used to take up pencil and paper and pretend to be thinking up and noting down ideas concerning the amelioration of his financial situation—what he called 'making plans'. Sometimes he would lie there inert, thinking, 'At this hour people are going about their business, having to stick to a time-table,' and he would keep his mouth half-open as though better to demonstrate his own relaxation. But now, when he lay stretched out like this, he fell asleep, and it had become his ambition to sleep as long as possible during the afternoon. He even went so far as to order from Mélanie heavy dishes for preference, stews and thick soups, so that digestion would encourage sleep. He would wake at around four o'clock, yawning as though sleep had made him sleepy, his eyes watery, the

[1] Lumps of anthracite known as *têtes de moineau* (*sparrows' heads*).

creases of the pillow engraved on his cheek, and would say to himself: 'Well, another one gone!' (Ever since the decision had been taken to leave Arago, ticking off the days had become his chief pleasure. As each day passed he crossed it out in his pocket calendar, so eager was he to reach the date of departure. Sometimes his impatience was such that around noon he would delete the current day, as though it had already come to an end.) And then, at about six o'clock, he was overcome by a new wave of contentment, because the end of the day was at hand. By nine o'clock he was in bed.

A few days after the scene with Mlle de Bauret, M. de Coantré sold his piano for four hundred and twenty-five francs to a music shop in the neighbourhood. He was dazzled by these four bank-notes, but the baron told him that he could have sold the instrument for one thousand or one thousand two hundred francs: a Pleyel! At the time Léon also wanted to sell a collection of oddments: odd pieces of china, old flower-pots, fire-dogs, various scraps of iron-mongery. Annoyed, he raised his price ludicrously high, asking two hundred francs from the second-hand dealer whom he had invited round. The woman burst out laughing but, sizing up her man, said in order to flatter him, 'You drive a hard bargain, M. de Coantré!' At which he preened himself but stuck to his guns. She offered him forty francs. Then his eyes flashed and he told her without more ado to be off.

'All right, fifty, as it's you.'

'Go away, I tell you!'

She went down the stairs insulting him: 'Count, eh? Count Flatpurse!' M. Elie, who had heard everything from his room, grunted with joy—'Hrr . . . hrr . . .'—like an ant-eater in its cage when someone brings its feed. Such were Léon's outbursts of pride, as surprising and unexpected in the midst of his apathy as geysers in a calm sea. The following day he went to another second-hand dealer; but having arrived at the shop he was afraid to go in, and walked past. Then he came back, stopped, and looked in the win-dow, but once again could not bring himself to go in. Returning to the house, he dropped these objects which he had been unable to sell one by one from his window into the garden, and with the aid of a shovel and a rake, smashed them to smithereens.

It was at about this time that he received a letter from Bourdillon:

> Dear Sir,
>
> Would you kindly call at the office one of these days? Meanwhile I hasten to inform you that the melancholy business which has preoccupied you for so long is well on the way to being settled.
>
> Yours, etc.

On reading this, his face clouded over and he had a fit of anxiety—'I foresee the worst'—like a peasant who, when you show him a clear sky, says, 'It bodes no good for tomorrow', or a nervous young woman on a liner that is in spanking form and apparently gliding along faster than usual, who says, 'We must be trying to get away from a storm.'

Since the scene which we described between M. de Coantré, Bourdillon and Lebeau, M. de Coantré's comings and going to and from the lawyer's office had not ceased. Some title deeds had to be sold—an operation which took a long time because of the red tape that accompanied it, and which was a splendid source of agitation for our count—not to mention a number of other transactions of this sort, which it would be too boring to recount, and in any case unnecessary, since the reader has seen enough of M. de Coantré face to face with money problems.

On this July afternoon, then, Bourdillon informed M. de Coantré that they had only to wait for a few more paper formalities, and the presence of Mlle de Bauret, before proceeding to wind up the estate, and that he could therefore relax, since it was unlikely that any new hitch would arise.

On leaving the office, M. de Coantré called on the baron to tell him the good news. After chatting for twenty minutes, M. de Coëtquidan excused himself and left the room, saying he had something to tell Papon. When he came back, they had hardly exchanged a word when he suddenly pulled an envelope out of his pocket and handed it to Léon.

'I haven't forgotten it's your birthday on the 13th. Here's a little something to buy yourself a present with . . .'

His face had gone purple, and he immediately added, to cut short his nephew's effusions:

'Have you seen the new café they've just opened next door? Those coloured parasols look extremely attractive. How inventive people are these days. . . .' etc etc.

When he reached the landing, M. de Coantré opened the envelope and found, together with a card on which the baron had simply inscribed the date of his nephew's birth, a five hundred franc note. He was wafted on to the pavement on wings of joy.

O men and women of Paris, those lives of yours, bitter, wearisome, frantic with struggle! But on this July 11th it was Paris in slow motion: people would be going away in three weeks, and showed that they had already left in spirit by taking things easy, like the clerk who puts down his pen and stops work at five to eleven because he is due to leave the office at 11.30. With this unexpected banknote in his pocket, and the blissful knowledge that the Lebeau affair was over, Léon experienced a sensation that was quite new to him: a decided reluctance to go straight home to Arago. Instead of going to catch the bus at the Gare St Lazare as he usually did, he strolled towards the boulevards, enjoying everything he saw as though it were for the first time.

People whose faces had been puckered up with concentration until six o'clock, because *time is money*,[1] were now idling away the time they had gained by means of taxis, secretaries and shorthand. There were Frenchmen there, not exactly handsome (but let that pass), and Frenchwomen, of indifferent looks (because 'unfeminine') but well-dressed and often pleasing (one would think that, with us, it was man who was created from the rib of a woman: women have all the advantages). And amongst these French people flowed the dregs of every nation, by whom the French were in no way incommoded, and whom they did not even recognize as dregs. From café to café, just as the crater of a volcano releases the fire within, the loudspeakers served as outlets for all the false sentiment,

[1] In English in the original.

the false pathos and the false glamour in the heart of this crowd. In fact everything that was offered to them along these boulevards, of whatever category, was false—although in our age at least, authenticity is the *only* luxury. Shops displayed hollow 'bronzes' and 'pearl' necklaces for one hundred francs; street traders hawked 'watches' for ten francs, 'scent' that was really coloured water, 'fountain pens' that would not write; cafés served orangeade in which there was no orange, barley water in which there was no barley; gramophones played tunes which bore little relation to the tune created by the composer; banks advertised fictitious rates of exchange; newspapers presented made-up news, fake photographs, sporting results that had been decided in advance; cinemas showed films in which there was no difference in talent, or rather lack of talent, between the millionaire star and the smallest bit-player. And was all this peculiar to Paris? Indeed no, but here it was following a great tradition. The works being played or sung in this neighbourhood, and the way they had been played or sung for centuries past, testified to the fact that with us nothing is beautiful except what is false, only the false is agreeable. When, in a play put on in Paris in the nineteenth century, a shepherd said to a shepherdess, 'The grass is wet. Sit on my jacket,' this remark, simply because it expressed a true and natural and amiable sentiment, was enough to kill the play: it was considered naïve, and your ordinary, asinine Frenchman cannot bear naïvety.

M. de Coantré walked boldly through the crowd. His outings during the past year had toughened him; he no longer felt dizzy. And then the two pleasant surprises he had just received gave him additional confidence. He was as happy and pleased with himself as a dog trotting along with a fir-cone in between its teeth.

Around the bleating ballad-singers, typists stood enraptured and sergeant-majors cried their eyes out, forgetting the iron rules of their rank. There were two sorts of street-vendors: those who wanted to sell, and those who did not. Those who wanted to sell performed incantations that were calculated to stun their audiences, to induce in them a mystical condition whereby they would pay forty francs for a comb they could buy for twenty in any shop.

The incantation consisted of a string of words between which there must never be the slightest pause to allow the listener to recover his wits and take flight; so the man had phrases ready made to be slipped into the slightest gap—'I know the ropes all right', or '*I don't care, I nicked 'em . . .*' And at the thought that perhaps the man really had stolen them, the whole audience brightened up and warmed towards him. M. de Coantré paid little attention to the hawkers. He picked out the younger women among the groups of listeners and, edging in beside them, he brushed against them and sniffed the smell of their hair, a smell which is generally good among the women of Paris, even ill-dressed women of the people. This must seem an extraordinary thing for M. de Coantré to do, and so we must retrace our steps.

As a young man, M. de Coantré had had mistresses—laundry-women, sempstresses, servant-girls, street-walkers—with a marked preference for dairymaids. What excited him more than anything else in the world was a worn-out woman's shoe or an ill-fitting stocking, and a woman he saw entering a cheap restaurant was sure to win his heart: because with her he would not have to stand on ceremony. A lot of fun, a lot of pleasure, no love. It lasted like this for ten years. When he was working on the enlargers, he met an eighteen-year-old girl whose widowed mother sold sweets, lemon-ade, waffles, etc in a kiosk on the Cours de Vincennes, and without much difficulty became her lover. She was skinny, and sexually unsophisticated; the pleasure he got from her at first was only moderate; but he liked her gentleness. Soon this gentleness acquired a kind of radiance. Her caressing ways, her constant need to snuggle up to him, the way she always closed her eyes when she held out her face to be kissed—but rarely kissed herself, being always rather passive. Unintelligent, slow-witted, knitting her brows in order to grasp the simplest thing, she was nevertheless sweet and trusting and loyal and disinterested. And so graceful, with her slightly Japanese looks (she resembled the actress Marie Leconte), so well-mannered, so withdrawn, like a little Spanish infanta. M. de Coantré began to love her tenderly. After ten years of pure sensuality, he had dis-covered a new category of experience, that of sensuality mixed with tenderness. However splendid pure sensuality may be, this other category is to it what paradise is to limbo. They have no common denominator.

One day, Mariette and her mother left Paris for Lyons, where they were to spend the summer holidays. She wrote to him once from Lyons, and then no longer answered his letters, which he addressed to her poste restante. He went there and looked for her, alone and through friends. The two women had left their hotel without leaving an address. On returning to Paris, he found the kiosk reopened with a new tenant. He could get no news of Mariette.

After a few weeks he returned to Lyons. In vain. He was handicapped in his search by the fact that this sweet little thing, like nine out of ten girls or boys of her age, was a monster of falsehood, duplicity and guile towards her mother, who knew nothing of what had been going on. He was afraid of compromising Mariette.

He remained obsessed by the memory of this child. This memory poisoned everything else for him; it was a cloud overshadowing his whole life. '*Un seul être vous manque et tout est dépeuplé*'—how well he knew it! Now he felt nothing but disgust and nausea, yes, nausea for human beings and their bodies—even the most delectable— because he no longer had what he loved. Three or four times he wrote to Lyons, more letters flung into the void; he returned to the Cours de Vincennes and wandered there, sick at heart, devouring the dried-up avenues with his eyes, as though the concentrated strength of his desire would squeeze that beloved form from the atmosphere and force it into being.

For four months he remained like this, in an abyss of melancholy, his whole emotional and sexual life steeped as it were in this memory, without the energy either to exhaust the possibilities of finding Mariette (putting a private detective on her track, or even the police), or to turn resolutely elsewhere and try unknown women until he found the right one. He remembered that it had taken ten years and about sixty women to find one who could arouse in him that marvellous tenderness which now he felt he could no longer do without. At this rate, how many barren and exhausting experiments, how many false starts, would he be faced with before meeting with a similar success, how many melancholy caricatures of the lost paradise!

He was in this paralysed condition when the collapse of the enlarging business occurred. In his misery, he flung himself into the streets and picked up some creature who in the darkness of the night had made some impression on him but who, seen in the light, turned him to ice. A whole night through, this woman who was either insatiable or else had found in Léon something that excited her, clasped him in her arms, wrestled like an obscene monkey with his inert body, offering him wide open her mouth with its decaying teeth, which he incessantly refused, covering his face with kisses which he did not return, sliming him all over with her sweat, embracing him as he lay there unresponsive, still as a stone, paralysed with loathing and disgust. Shortly afterwards he left for Chatenay.

In a desert such as Chatenay restraint was obligatory. He could have made excursions to Paris, but two considerations held him back: an experience such as he had had with Mariette seemed to him more and more like a miracle which could not be counted on to occur again, and that last, truly infernal night of 'love' reminded him forcefully of the risks involved in trying to renew the miracle. Add to this the fact that he had no money left—though this is incidental: a man can always find enough money to make love. More important was the fact that, at Chatenay, M. de Coantré had begun to dress like a tramp and had given up washing. Soon, the idea of possessing a woman began to arouse in him powerful objections: having to dress up, to wash, to spend money, to cut a dash. Far too much bother! True, he would not have been averse to a little bit of fun. But the price to be paid for it in trouble and inconvenience was too high. The game was not worth the candle.

This continence lasted for twenty years. Impossible! it will be said. Young people imagine that monastery walls conceal unspeakable debauches. It is our belief that monastery walls generally conceal a great composure of the flesh. The more one makes love, the more one wants to. Conversely, if one abstains completely (provided one has got beyond the first flush of youthful ardour and has had one's fill) the desire for it disappears: the sexual organs fall asleep and atrophy.

If he had known many other women, and even if he had loved one as he had loved Mariette, he would still have remained faithful to her. Fidelity resides not in actions but in the heart. We think we can tear the scab off a little sore with impunity; we do so, and hours after the wound occurred it starts to bleed again. For twenty years M. de Coantré bled whenever he thought of Mariette: her memory was always fresh inside him. Time made no difference. For the first ten years after their liaison (and even during it) he had never dreamt about her, but thereafter, once a year, with mysterious regularity, she appeared to him in his sleep. In his waking hours it was rare for a couple of days to pass without his thinking of her and his life relapsing into a hushed recollection and regret. She lay deep inside him, her face as always held out towards him with the eyelids closed. The smallest thing would bring it to the surface of his consciousness.

7

THAT night, on the boulevards, M. de Coantré felt himself quivering, as it were, in the breeze from the open sea. His packing over, and now the estate. . . . The second mooring rope cast off. One by one the rest would fall; he would leave the shore and sail away towards the unknown, which in his ignorance he envisaged in the brightest colours. When he brushed against a woman, he had no intention of having an adventure, first of all because his linen was dirty and secondly because he did not feel inclined. What he wanted (and even then rather vaguely) was to talk to a friendly woman, to find out where he could meet her again (perhaps) one of these days, to get to know something of her life. Later on, it was conceivable that . . . After all, he had five hundred francs in his pocket, unexpectedly. A sum that arrives out of the blue can be spent without its affecting your financial position. . . .

M. de Coantré strolled back along the boulevards, holding his gloves in one hand, like Diocletian his staff of office. (These gloves were no longer the famous mourning gloves; they were old, threadbare kid gloves, but in his pocket was a pair of new cotton gloves which he had brought to put on at M. Octave's and had taken off when his visit was over so as not to wear them out unnecessarily.) With his other hand he was clasping against his chest a portfolio full of documents concerning his mother's estate; Bourdillon had given him back all the papers he no longer needed. Outside the office of *Le Matin* a group of men and boys, almost foaming at the mouth with excitement, were examining a notice-board on which the results of the latest stage of the Tour de France were advertised, and jotting down names in greasy note-books. A press campaign lasting three weeks would have been enough to make them accept some political deal with disastrous effects for France: but this evening their eyes were popping out of their heads because a Frenchman had taken the lead in the race. M. de Coantré, soaked in perspiration, sat down on a bench. How could he help but sweat? Apart from his 'bum-freezer' (and he had not shed even that until a month after everyone else), he was dressed exactly as in winter, flannel vest included. He must have seen aertex vests in the windows of drapers' shops. But as he had always kept his flannel vests on in summer, he continued to do so. And he believed he was sweating because the weather was hot, when in fact he was sweating because he was dressed for winter.

The same, in fact, applied to most of his fellow Parisians. Here on this bench they were wearing their winter suits, including waist-coats, and starched collars, starched cuffs, hats, ties, tie-pins, rings, trinkets, ankle-boots, even gloves. They fanned themselves and gasped: 'How hot it is!' It was twenty-two degrees Centigrade.[1] Perhaps, under their trappings, they really were hot, but every one of them would rather die of heat than risk being taken for anything but a good bourgeois, for whom these trappings were a uniform. Perhaps the words 'How hot it is!' were simply a polite formula for the benefit of their neighbours, as devoid of meaning and consequence as the mysterious 'eeny meeny miny mo' of little girls.

When a newsvendor offered him the evening papers, M. de Coantré bought one. It was three months since he had read a news-paper, but that evening he wanted to renew contact with life. The news bored him; but when his eyes fell on a page of advertisements they lit up at once. People *wanted* one another—even if it was only to cook or polish floors! There was give and take. How easy every-thing seemed!

On the terrace of a nearby café a woman was sitting alone at a table. Nothing special, but young. He sat down at the table next to hers.

People were drinking yellow, green and orange liquids, which looked extremely good. M. de Coantré had never been a drinker, and moreover for twenty years had tasted nothing but table wine.

[1] 72° Fahrenheit.

He did not even know the names of these prettily-coloured drinks. Caught off his guard, he ordered a *café au lait*.

When he looked at the woman, she held his gaze. When she looked at him, he turned his head away. He had no doubt that she had taken the cue, and frowned a little in order to give himself a more virile look.

However, when, after a time, she got up to go, he remained seated. Hadn't he the whole evening in front of him! He thought she looked disappointed, and felt flattered.

Faces passed by, matt female faces, shining male faces. The men had fountain-pens in their breast pockets, and sometimes propelling pencils. Only in Paris do you see this: the French are all intellectuals. Saint-Cyrians in their plumed helmets passed by, followed, like priests, by a wash of malevolence, and women whose youth and gay clothes gave them the appearance of living cakes, and pale adolescents with slender calves, blond girlish hair, and sickly, acquiescent faces. There was a neatly dressed old man (bearing a certain resemblance to M. de Coantré) carrying a basketful of blessed medals and pictures of Sister Thérèse which he was ostensibly selling, and perhaps *was* selling, to the café customers. All these people, silhouetted against the pale gold light from the setting sun, presented a not unpleasing spectacle. A large number of them gave the impression of being alert, almost intelligent. Most of these faces had a certain character: these people had their own ideas about the world, their own individuality. Only one expression was common to them all: an absence of pride.

In the mind of M. de Coantré, now far from being his usual self, a sensational plan was forming, which was to dine in a restaurant and then to go to Montmartre—Montmartre, whose basilica, seen through the side-streets, seemed strangely close, almost within hand's reach. Oh! no more than a stroll! He would go no further than the Boulevard Rochechouart, and would be home by ten o'clock. He got up, and at the first post office sent an express letter to M. Elie, saying that he had met an old Catholic College friend, Max de Bastaud, who was a 'grass widower' for the month of July and had asked him to dinner in a restaurant. M. de Coëtquidan should not wait up for him. (White lies always came easily to Léon de Coantré.)

Then he took a bus in the direction of Montmartre, got off after two or three stops, and walked northwards through sombre streets. In Paris everything is black, but it is not a deliberate black, the true black of Spain, but the grey black of dirt: grey houses, grey clothes, grey faces, grey blood. It was half past seven. Now that the sun had gone down, waiters pushed back the awnings in front of the cafés. People enjoying the cool of the evening stood framed in their open windows against the dark background of their rooms, like figures against the dark background of old paintings. The evening meal sent up above each roof a little wisp of smoke which fluttered in a sky as colourless as these faces.

M. de Coantré found himself in the Place d'Anvers. The people sitting there were glued to one another like flies on a sore. Faced with this swarming crowd, he hesitated; then he went in and sat down on a bench in front of a name scrawled on the gravel with the point of a walking-stick: Gaston. O Gaston, bring luck to our noble count! On the neighbouring bench a young woman was sitting, a charming female field-mouse. She was reading a book that was either indecent or silly, and probably both, for from time to time she laughed to herself—and at these times she could have been easily aroused. Beside her on the bench was an old Jew in a bowler hat and slippers. M. de Coantré thought that when the man had gone he would go and sit beside her.

On the other benches, sempstresses sat and sewed, showing off the kiss-marks on the inside of their arms (but they had made them themselves—for fun, of course) and continually raising their heads from their handiwork, convinced that people were watching them. The mothers, too, raised their heads from their knitting to see where their children had got to. M. de Coantré's next-door neighbour was a handsome little girl, knitting away with hands pink and shiny as prawns. She was eating a croissant, and he could smell the aroma of munched bread. From time to time she crossed her legs or heaved a sigh. And other little girls revolved round her, shrieking and swooping like September swallows. The air was quite still, but the leaves of the plane-trees, more sensitive, stirred continuously, like spectators seen from a distance moving on the tiers of an arena. And there was a smell of children, in other words a kitten smell.

M. de Coantré would have liked to speak to the little girl—with the most honourable intentions—ask her what stitch she was using, how old she was, whether her father had been killed in the war. But he did not dare. He had to admit that he no longer enjoyed that famous 'Coantré ease of manner' which, in his youth, had so annoyed the Coëtquidans. 'I'm like a racing cyclist,' he said to himself. 'Once I'm started it's all right. But I need someone to give me a shove-off.' Earlier, on the boulevards, he had had the feeling that dusk would bring him the self-confidence he lacked in the sun. Now that dusk had fallen, his excuse was all these people cluttering up the square; in half an hour, with the light nearly gone and the square cleared, he would recover his faculties.

The sparrows wriggled, twittering, in the dust, as though experiencing the same pleasure as human beings in water. They were capitalist sparrows, so fat that their chests, on which a watch-chain would not have been out of place, nearly touched the ground. An apprentice with grimy hands was taking his little brother round the square for the tenth time so that he would sleep tonight like a log and not wake Mum and Dad at two in the morning to ask them to buy him a scooter. And still, around the benches, the poor children were a constant prey to the live wires they had the misfortune to have as mothers. 'Don't touch!'—'Why?'—'Mustn't touch anything.' The child (wearing trousers so short for him that his 'little dickie' was peeping out from one leg) would try something else. 'Will you stop running!'—'Why?'—'Because.' The child would try something else again. 'Play, stupid! You didn't come here to stand around like an idiot!' The child would try something else. 'What sort of a game is that? Come on, you can find something better to do.' The child would try again. 'René, do you hear what I say! Play at once, or else! . . .'

Suddenly the old Jew who was sitting beside the field-mouse got up and left. 'I must wait a moment,' M. de Coantré said to himself. 'To change benches like that, suddenly, would look odd . . .' After a

while he thought, 'Come on, otherwise someone will take the seat.'
But it seemed to him as though the eyes of all the people on the other
benches were focussed on him, and this change of benches would
look suspect and ridiculous. So he decided to walk half-way round
the square, and if the seat was free when he came back, that would be
a sign of destiny. (In other words, he wanted to provide himself
with the possibility of not having to act.)

He walked half-way round the square, during which time the
seat remained free. Returning, on his little legs, to within ten yards
of the bench, he swooped. Too late. A workman with a haggard face
had just sat down beside the field-mouse.

M. de Coantré sat down in a chair a few feet away from them.
He had to acknowledge that he was not at his best. In twenty years
the machine had grown rusty, his tongue paralysed by long silence,
his will deadened by disuse.

The light, its task completed, had retreated to the sky, and now
touched only the roof-tops. And the statue of Victory, at the top of
its tall column in the middle of the square, retained the sun only on
its nobler features, its forehead, its helmet and its wings. The square
was emptying. Big rats, encouraged by the solitude, trotted from
one flower-bed to the next. On the bench where M. de Coantré had
been sitting earlier, only the little girl remained, playing alone like a
cat playing with its tail (no doubt she could not return home
because her mother was out with the key; it was her mother she
was waiting for). An old woman was nibbling at a small loaf of
bread, breaking off the pieces inside her bag so that no one could
see she was eating, for this was her entire dinner. Beside the young
woman, the workman smoked and smoked, as a man smokes when
he has nothing to eat, or a consumptive pauper who smokes 'to
prevent himself from coughing'. Any normal man would have
longed to stab this body that had interposed itself between him and
the coveted one, and see it collapse like a bundle of rags, but M. de
Coantré never dreamed of doing so, he merely thought, 'What a
brute!' At last the young woman got up and went off. M. de
Coantré followed her at a distance, having buttoned his jacket to
make himself look slimmer and more elegant. How terribly fast she

walked! M. de Coantré had no idea what he would say if he caught up with her, or even whether he wanted to catch up with her. It looked rather as if he did not want to. When he had persuaded himself that there was no hope, that she was walking too fast for him, he went into top gear, certain of being spared his ordeal by circumstances beyond his control. As the distance between them continued to increase in spite of his efforts, he finally gave up. 'Is it my fault? After all, I haven't got wings.'

Then, having unbuttoned his coat, he told himself with a feeling of gratification that it was time for dinner. All this had made him ravenous.

But no sooner had he entered a ten-franc restaurant than he was captivated by a charming waitress. Without bothering to examine her in detail, he booked his table and went to wash his hands, which he had had no intention of doing on arrival. What natural grace! Blonde, with a slightly turned-up nose, a touch of powder, scarcely any lipstick, and serving all these frightful dwarfs with the same happy look as if she had been dancing a ballet, smiling at the slightest word, half opening her mouth each time she bent down towards a customer, as though it was the act of leaning forward that opened her mouth by inflating her a little. But perhaps the real secret of her charm lay in the tradition it represented, for it was a face from eighteenth-century France; through it one could see, with a thrill of emotion, the continuity of the race; she could not be called anything else but Manon. And with it all, with that exquisite face and body, these hands which she stretched towards you as she served you! Hands? No, paws, red, swollen, chapped, with black nails, hands that were used for scouring dishes, fingering sordid scraps, unravelling strings of intestines, terrifying hands. M. de Coantré never took his eyes off her. But, charming as she was to everyone, she was no more so to him than to anyone else. M. de Coantré left the restaurant without even having tried to enter into conversation with her. Sure of being able to find her whenever he wanted to, since he knew where she worked, he could surrender with a clear conscience to the luxury of abstinence.

He had even cut short his dinner, because the restaurant was so full that people stood waiting for tables. M. Elie would deliberately have ordered an extra course. M. de Coantré, partly out of good nature, partly out of annoyance, went without his coffee.

If M. de Coantré, instead of a light dinner, had eaten a more lavish meal than usual—we can dismiss even the hypothesis of his having drunk more than usual—it is possible that everything that happened after dinner would have been different. Everyone knows that our life can be altered by an act committed in a state of intoxication. But few people realize that a man who is accustomed, say, to eat in six-franc restaurants is drunk after a twenty-franc meal.

How reluctantly the day was dying! It was after nine o'clock and night had not yet fallen; for three hours it had been dragging on. Shop-windows and street lamps were lit up in the dusk, touching lights which seemed to be telling the night to hurry, that everywhere there were dainty feet nervously tapping the floor or the ground, the feet of women waiting for the night to bring them happiness. Soon M. de Coantré emerged into the Boulevard Rochechouart, and at once found it just as he had left it nineteen years before; the little, brackish pool of Parisian 'pleasure' was still stagnating there.

A leprous crust of dirt covered the houses, the absurd, out-of-date façades of the 'cabarets', the stunted trees, the flabby, anaemic faces, the lifeless, wizened hands, dry as dead leaves, which must have smelt of obscurity and toil, the mouths with their discoloured teeth, 'blind mouths' assuredly. It was as if everything had been steeped in filth, or in the soot that fell from these skies. Radio this, that or the other poured out a sort of musical vomit, as though the diners in all the restaurants had started to throw up in 'concert', a sort of anonymous blancmange, sexless and ageless, the music of limbo, fit for a ghostly dance in slow motion in the fields beyond the grave. There was not a single vital impulse either towards good or evil in this crowd in which not even youth was young, nothing vigorous or instinctive or even natural in this crowd with girls' faces, where the malest of the males themselves wielded women's weapons against each other. This bloodless mass was like a nest of swarming maggots. Seeing the spectacle, any healthy man could have had only one reaction: either asceticism or wild indulgence, but not this! Balzac called Paris 'a great ulcer'. The impression here was rather of a great pustule. And the red neon lights reflected on the pavements might have been the blood of these people that had flowed from their bodies, leaving them pale as death. Crossing the Avenue Rachel, one was struck by a breath of tree-borne air from the cemetery of Montmartre, as though the only life among these living beings came to them from the dead.

And it was because of the ugliness and unhealthiness of these beings that pleasure and love itself here assumed the aspect of vice —if it can be said that vice resides not in any act in itself but in a desire of which we are ashamed because we think the object of it is unworthy—and this is the only acceptable definition of the word 'vice'.

M. de Coantré walked along the central promenade, still holding his gloves in one hand and clasping the files of his mother's estate in the other. He was intrigued by the barmen with their livid, ghostly faces, the giant commissionaires in their gleaming Ruritanian uniforms, the athletic-looking Germans in dinner jackets, and the Algerians with their umbrellas on the look-out for God knows what left-overs, like sharks around a ship. Street-walkers passed by, but M. de Coantré ruled out as hopeless all those who were too well dressed, with the proletarian phrase: 'Too grand for me.' He followed one who stopped at a shooting gallery. She took aim, and bang! bang! scored a bull with each shot. M. de Coantré retreated disconsolately. He followed another, who stopped in front of a strong man act. As he drew near her, he heard only one word she said to her companion, and this word was 'money'. M. de Coantré withdrew. In this he was wrong, for the group around the strong man was as good as the show itself. Instead of looking at the performer, half the men there were looking round to left and right and over their shoulders; for various reasons they were interested only in their neighbours.

Faced with these women, M. de Coantré thought: 'This is all very fine, but after five minutes I wouldn't know what to do with them.' He was conscious of his grotesque, misshapen body, at once heavy

117

and weak; he had a physical perception of the weight of his belly, his puny legs, his skimpy shoulders, his bent back, his lack-lustre eyes, his enormous head, made even bigger by his thick felt hat. A whore overtaking him put some coins in a sleeping beggar's cap. He was so touched by this that he followed her, crossing the road behind her as she went up a side-street. Just then he noticed that one of his boot-laces was undone, and, stopping beside a vast inscription chalked right across the pavement, which read: *Jesus Christ is your only friend* (he had scruples about treading on it), he slowly re-tied it. When he raised his head, the woman had vanished—which was what he had wanted.

He was now so tired that every time he stepped on to a pavement he gave a sort of gasp, heaving himself up and then gathering himself together like a wheezy old horse taking a fence (one almost expected to hear the saddle creak). He sat down on a bench and removed his hat, but immediately a sparrow dropped some dung on his head. He did not wait to be told twice, but moved on. Since under-vitality induces thirst as much as over-vitality, he went into a bar opposite the Pigalle Métro station, and asked for a lemonade— which shows that he was becoming more resourceful, for he had not thought of lemonade in the café on the boulevards. He could easily have revived himself a little by buying an ice or some candy floss at one of the booths in the fun-fair. But his twenty years of retirement had turned him into the opposite of a child; he wanted nothing. Moreover, to order an ice would have caused him something of the same apprehension as he had at the thought of entering a night-club.

Inside the bar he saw a young woman alone at a table, and instantly felt that something new was happening inside him. Why had he given up the others so easily? Now he knew: it was because he hadn't been sufficiently moved by them. This one moved him deeply, with her beautiful black eyes, her slightly olive skin, like Simone de Bauret's, and a vein beating interminably in her temple: a Southern girl, for sure. He sat down at the only free table, two away from hers. Now he knew that something was really happening.

After a while, in order to keep himself in countenance, he opened his portfolio and pretended to read.

If only he could *mean* something to her! If only she could realize that he wished her well!

Now he understood how so many men and women could find sustenance in this deceptive neighbourhood: it was because they received from it what they brought to it, and every one of them had something in his heart. Through all these people, so much happiness could be obtained. These ill-favoured faces each had as much power to give pleasure as the face of a god. The Parisian shadows were ringed with soft light.

Behind the damsel, the leaves of the trees, lit up, were silhouetted in very pale green against the nocturnal sky, as blue and limpid as the skies of the East. This sky was striped with glowing lines—the electric wires of the tramway, reddened by the reflection from the neon signs. In the dark houses, a few windows were still lit up like honeycombs. Above a sordid tenement block a star appeared on the face of the night. Even in Montmartre there were stars!

He turned and looked at her again, and thought how worthy she was of love. (But in his case, this did not mean much.)

She spoke to the waiter, and the way she moved her shoulders when she said 'no' reminded him of Simone de Bauret.

One of the pleasures of the truly rich is to pretend that they are poor. Those silly little things who make eyes at you in a restaurant because you are wearing an expensive shirt—if they only knew! . . . But M. de Coantré, at this moment, was suffering because of his poverty. He did not feel it through a process of reasoning which could have told him that he had no money. He felt it through a number of little details which were not in fact proofs of poverty: his ill-kept fingernails, the smell of his grubby flannel vest which came to him via his collar, the sickly, acrid smell which his fingers retained from the towel in the restaurant wash-room (the smell of towels that have been wet for too long), the dried stain on his lapel, and the long hair covering the nape of his neck (though at least it concealed the rolls of middle-aged fat).

The crowd in the street was growing. He saw from the clock that it was midnight. Without the slightest hesitation he decided to stay. What would he say at Arago tomorrow? Bah! he would think of something.

It struck him that if the table between them became free, he would never dare to move to it. The same defeat as in the Place d'Anvers. His only hope was for her to leave. Outside, he could approach her quite happily.

Young men who were probable if not obvious catamites came and drank at the bar, their faces swollen from alcohol and only the nape of the neck betraying their youth. They ordered sandwiches which they ate with two hands, tearing at them like young dogs. M. de Coantré did his best to make the revulsion he felt for them clear to everyone; he flourished it proudly like a banner. If one of them had stepped on to a tram in front of the noble count, he would have waited for the next tram.

Two little pimps with rodent's eyes and avid, tubercular mouths began to exchange insults at the bar. Or rather, one of them insulted the other, who said nothing, pretending to take it all as a joke. M. de Coantré was glad when they went. This man who in the past few hours had shown *ad nauseam* that 'he was not a man' (in Mediterranean and Arab parlance—and the phrase is rather a splendid one) could summon up enough pride to suffer at the sight of a human being, even of this stamp, allowing himself to be insulted with impunity.

The slow, silent processions of police squads on bicycles could be interpreted in two different ways: they might be taken as a threat, recalling, perhaps, the nocturnal processions of aircraft over Paris, or they might be taken to show, by their tutelary presence, that all is well with a world in which people are peddling drugs, trips to Buenos Aires are being arranged, little girls are selling themselves, everyone carries a prohibited weapon in his pocket, and so on.

A woman of the lowest type came in. Her hideous, rasping voice seemed to come from the most degraded part of her being, and so did what she said, which was without exception vile. One could see that the men who spoke to her despised her, but that she did not disgust them. One could lust after this creature, and yet remain a 'normal' man—a normal, respectable man, a paterfamilias who sits on a jury and whom everybody shakes hands with.

After having wandered round the bar for some time, the creature spotted M. de Coantré, gave him a long stare, then came up to his table and leaned her forearms on it. He saw her black fingernails, and her lips, dual-coloured like a water-ice (natural pink towards the inside, lipstick-red on the outside), and smelt on her breath a whiff of fried potatoes (all she had had for dinner?).

'Won't you buy me a drink, dearie?'

'No,' said M. de Coantré, shaking his head, scowling, and keeping his eyes lowered on one of the papers from his file.

'Why?' she asked, not without a certain artlessness.

'Because I have work to do,' he said, pointing to his papers. He had taken out his pencil and, to strengthen his point, began scribbling away in the margin. His eyes, as they alighted on the document, must have been struck by the word 'renunciation', for this word kept on recurring in what he wrote: 'Renunciation . . . renunciation . . .' We know how much renunciation went on in the affairs of Mme de Coantré (the worst of it being that every time she renounced something she had to pay for the right to do so).

'Working, eh?' she said with an air of profundity. 'What are you working at?'

'I'm a journalist, and I have to submit my article tonight,' he said in a loud voice, by no means loath to let the bar-owner have this explanation of his prolonged presence. 'Come now, leave me alone.'

'Naughty!' she said, tapping him on the arm after the fashion of school-girls, provincial maidens, or girl-cousins.

She went out, and M. de Coantré turned towards the girl. Then—but which of the two began it?—they smiled at one another.

It was half past one. M. de Coantré, having become a journalist, had some writing-paper brought to him and began copying out page after page at random from his dossier. The couple at the next table, who had been separating him from the girl, left the bar. Of course he did not move. But he wondered if the girl understood that he was waiting for her to go outside, and despaired of ever making her understand. . . .

The harridan returned. Whenever she looked at M. de Coantré she began to hum, as though it was from him that she drew this thread of music. He sensed that she was about to accost him again, and he went on copying, copying (he had now got to the under-taker's invoice).

'To the burial of the body of the late Madame la Comtesse de Coantré, opening the family vault, cleaning the interior, waiting for and receiving the body, sup . . .'

He was aware of her standing in front of his table. Lowering his head and screwing up his eyes, he wrote feverishly, waiting for the blow to fall:

. . . 'plying, measuring, transporting, placing, sealing, etc of a slab of Chassignelles stone, thickness 005 at 2 cuttings . . .'

'Haven't you finished writing that b . . . ?'

He did not answer, but clenched his teeth. Suddenly she picked one of the sheets of paper and read with an air of Etruscan stupidity:
'Estate . . .'

He got up and tore the paper away from her.

'Estate! So you're not a journalist, you're a bailiff! You're the man who screws money out of people!'

We know M. de Coantré's 'geysers'. Not since the day before, at six o'clock in the evening, had he been 'a man'. Suddenly he was a man once more. Perhaps this woman had her ponce somewhere nearby, who would come and attack him. The thought crossed his mind, but he paid no attention to it. People are sometimes surprised to find respectable middle-aged gentlemen, as timid as can be, lying on the threshold of some low dive with their throat slit. The explanation is that, at a certain moment, like M. de Coantré, they threw caution to the wind; they clung to their wrath like metal to a magnet. Rising to his feet, M. de Coantré called to the bar-owner.

'I say, look here, can't I be left in peace? I've got work to do, I've got to earn my living.'

(As soon as M. de Coantré began to lie, all his self-confidence returned.)

'Come along, Coquinette,' said the barman, 'leave the customers in peace. Do you want me to throw you out?'

M. de Coantré sat down again. He turned towards the Southern damsel and their eyes met, and once more they smiled at one another, and he said to her with his eyes, 'Look what I'm putting up with for you! Do go outside, you little fool, and I'll follow close on your heels!' Then he bent down over his papers again and continued copying:

'To closing and resealing of vault. . . . 380 frs.'

He went on copying for a long time, glued to this table, telling himself that he would hold out to the end, that this girl would eventually want to go home to bed. Moreover, he was neither tired nor sleepy—galvanized by his desire. Only a few customers came in now, standing at the bar and shaking dice. Outside, the policemen-cyclists still glided slowly round on their silent patrols. Had he had an ounce of wit, M. de Coantré would have gone out and said to them: 'Officers of the watch, bring out this little Provençale, because *I* haven't the courage to accost her in this café, whereas outside I can take care of her.' But that was another thing he did not think of doing.

The harridan was back again. She was now haggling in a corner with two night workers, one of whom said, 'Ten francs for the two of us . . .' to which she replied, 'No, no, fifteen francs . . .' Then came the sound of noisy tart's kisses (much ado about nothing), and the men drank in the seven deadly sins from the distended, rubbery mouth. M. de Coantré went on copying. At half past two the proprietor and the waiter sat down to supper. It was done in a casual way, the boss serving the waiter, evoking sentimental thoughts about the people in M. de Coantré's mind. At this moment a man came in, went straight to the girl's table and sat down. He was a night-club attendant, or perhaps a musician, wearing black trousers and waistcoat, starched shirt-front, black bow tie and a mauve jacket out at the elbows. They spoke to each other in low voices. M. de Coantré subsided in his seat, all hunched up and now quite small, like a fly that shrivels when it dies.

Ten minutes later, the man and the woman went out together,

without her giving M. de Coantré so much as a glance. And he heard welling up inside him that poignant music which men hear when a strange woman who has moved them goes out of their sight and out of their life forever.

He put away his papers and went off, walking aimlessly. Yes, he hadn't thought of that—that she might be waiting for someone. How simple it was, and yet he hadn't thought of it. Just as he hadn't known what drink to order in the café on the boulevard. It was ten to three—the tail-end of the night, when people become at once bolder and less demanding, because something is drawing to a close without their having found what they desired. On the broad-walks in the Place Pigalle men were prowling up and down, having waited, watched and pursued all night long. The tramps sleeping on the benches conjured up images of dead soldiers or a sort of French native proletariat. Adolescents with puckered brows were leaning against the entrance to the Métro like the Spirit of Sleep reclining against a tomb. Street-walkers were still at large, drifting like wrecks in the night. They were no plainer than those who had found takers, but perhaps this was their third outing tonight, like picadors' horses which have been twice wounded but are brought out for a third time. All these women who had escaped him, like water flowing through his fingers! And he had lost them through his own fault. Nevertheless, he did not feel he had suffered a great loss. The troubles he would have had! And anyway, it was the finger of fate. He hailed a taxi, and set off for Arago.

But once he was inside the taxi, and felt that every turn of the wheels was taking him further away from these happy hunting grounds, it was as though a piece of his flesh was being gradually stretched until at last it was torn away. The pools of scarlet light on the pavements had given way to pools of pallid light: death succeeding life. How ghastly it was to be going back to this death-ridden den with empty hands and heart (and no prospect even of finding a letter). When he got out of the taxi in the dark, deserted avenue, he felt a pang of obscure regret. A strong smell of fresh leaves assailed him; but for the moment this country-lover was interested not in trees but in human beings. The taxi had gone. On his way to the garden gate, he saw the pink sky over the centre of Paris, making the stars almost invisible, mysteriously warmed by human lights, or the memory of those lights, and glowing in the great black body of the night like the palms of a negro's hands. He felt then that he could not go in like that, that he must try a little longer, exhaust all the possibilities of the night, and that only when he came back in full daylight would the night have finally said no. And this timid man, rising above himself once more, set off through the precincts of the guillotine, along the sinister wall of the prison, into the heart of the night.

In the Avenue d'Orléans the little jolting carts of the rag-and-bone men, with their lighted lanterns and their minute, scraggy ponies, had an air of oriental misery. The street sweepers swung their brooms in regular semi-circles along the pavement, like mechanical toys. At the Porte d'Orléans only one café was open. He sat down on the empty terrace, vaguely hoping for something that in his heart of hearts he did not expect to come.

There was no real sadness in him. Just as, after having written three letters in order to find himself a job, he had stopped at that, under the impression that he had done all there was to do, so, now, he felt that he had gone through a necessary ordeal, that fate had shown him that he ought not to move out of his shell. What he feared most of all now was that a pretty girl might appear in this café. Once more he would either have to suffer through not daring or if he dared and succeeded, plunge himself into the most frightful complications. 'Renunciation . . . renunciation . . . renunciation.'

He dozed off, still holding his portfolio, on which his sweating hands had left a sticky stain.

When he awoke, figures were looming up continually through the night, which had now grown paler, dark figures of workers coming from the suburbs with their little bags, their boots covered with the dried-up mud of three months ago, and their first two gestures of the day, before catching the Métro, were to go and have a drink and to buy a newspaper. The whole of the south-east region, towards Arceuil, was completely in the shadows, without a single light. This was the 'zone', populated by Italians, Arabs and Jews.

But at this hour, plunged in darkness, it seemed somehow mysterious and rather frightening, like no-man's-land seen from the front-line trenches, the desert seen from the last *bordj*, or the ocean seen from the shelter of a harbour. From the dark depths of this ocean there emerged from time to time, lit up like a liner, an empty bus travelling at high speed on the way from its depot.

Dawn broke through; the sky was the colour of Pernod. M. de Coantré went on sitting there, ordering coffee after coffee, croissants, sandwiches, cigarettes, and smoking like a chimney. Ah! these things, at least, were real! When he sat down, or rather collapsed, at this table, he had been overwhelmed with a nameless weariness, the sort of weariness that fills you with nausea and makes you want to vomit. Now, all these compensatory pleasures—coffee, tobacco, having slept a little, having somewhere to sit—had cheered him up. This hour of dawn, in cities, holds all the mystery and promise of the coming day. Dawn and dusk: the urban hours that beckon to adventure. But M. de Coantré expected nothing, and was content to be like that.

At a quarter past six there was a great cascade of men surging into the Métro. This world of dawn and early morning was very much a male world; at this hour the whole town belonged to the men, like an oriental town. This did not worry M. de Coantré. On the contrary, the feeling that had kept him going throughout the night was being purified. He wondered whether it hadn't all been a misunderstanding, whether what he had really been after hadn't been some contact with the people, and whether he hadn't simply been obeying some old bourgeois atavism in seeking the people through their women. When, at seven o'clock, he saw the first puffs of smoke rising from the factory chimneys, he was moved by it: already men were toiling, when so many others were not yet awake. He remembered the workshop he and Levier had had at the Barrière du Trône, and the embarrassment he used to feel when, returning at five o'clock in the morning in an open carriage from some all-night spree in top hat and tails with a camellia in his buttonhole, he met the first workers, with picks on their shoulders—pleasure and toil passing one another with the same white faces . . . As for the women he had met that night, he was content to be able to tell himself that he had desired. To have proved to himself that one had only to stoop and pick up what one wanted seemed to him enough Already this night was becoming transfigured in his mind; he now had the impression that if he had let these women escape him it was because he wanted to.

At seven o'clock the dustmen passed by, talking in such a strong accent that they might almost have been putting it on. The waiter in the café was cleaning the dominoes. Around 8.15, advancing from the suburbs towards the Métro, came a great wave of women—for the opening of the offices at nine o'clock. Then the flow ceased. One aspect of Paris died away, and its customary aspect reappeared: the bourgeois day began. M. de Coantré considered his 'ordeal' at an end. He took out his wallet to settle his bill at the café, saw the five hundred franc note still intact, and regretted the happiness it might have procured him. His bill was six francs; he put down ten and told the waiter to keep the change. A humble and pathetic gesture: after a whole night spent trying to insinuate himself into the life of the people, he ended up with this age-old bourgeois gesture of giving money. And, as it happened, the waiter misunderstood what he said and brought back the change. So M. de Coantré, seeing that even this gesture had misfired, did not insist but left a fifty centime tip.

As he left, he noticed the name of the neighbouring bar: *Tout va Bien*. 'Yes,' he thought, with a sort of smile, 'all is well.' He imagined how bitter he would have felt if he had spent an hour and a half dressing up the previous evening with a view to an amorous adventure, and all to no purpose. He shuddered at the thought. He hailed a taxi and gave the driver the Boulevard Arago address.

If we have not described more strongly M. de Coantré's feelings during the course of that night, it is because his feelings *were* no stronger.

127

8

Soon after the war M. Octave de Coëtquidan had illegally increased the rent of a new tenant in a modest block of flats which he owned in Passy. There came a time when the tenant, advised and egged on by a newly-acquired son-in-law, a wily lawyer, threatened to sue M. de Coëtquidan. On a technical point operating to the detriment of the tenant, the outcome of the case was uncertain. But, if he lost it and the worst came to the worst, the baron might have to pay over a hundred thousand francs.

In this month of July 1924 the affair had come to a head—and M. de Coëtquidan decided to make a gift of ten thousand francs to a charitable organization.

Here is the connection between these two facts.

M. Octave, with all his social prestige, saw himself being out-manœuvred by these people of no standing. With the help of this display of money he would restore his high opinion of himself. Having appeared in the eyes of his agent and his lawyers as a blood-sucker, and a ridiculous one to boot, for having taken advantage of his tenant and then been punished for it, he could take a hair of the dog that bit him by being lordly with his ten thousand francs.

He had no particular charity in mind, convinced as he was that, no matter which he chose, less than half of the ten thousand francs would be used on behalf of the unfortunate beneficiaries, the rest being diverted to various other uses, and partly into the pockets of the directors. In any case, he was indifferent to the poor.

There was a list of charities in the house. The baron opened it at random and came across the *Oeuvre des Berceaux Abandonnés*. He sent off a cheque for eight thousand francs—having meanwhile decided that ten thousand was too much—and at once began to hate this charity. But the greater his aversion for abandoned infants, for the poor, etc, the more intense became the bitter pleasure he felt at having sacrificed such a sum to an organization whose activities he derided.

At the same time, since he was an honourable man, he was ashamed of having made this gesture in such a frame of mind—especially when he thought of Léon—so much so that, a few moments after having dropped the cheque in the letter-box, he searched his waistcoat pocket for something to give to a beggar he saw on the pavement. He hesitated between fifty centimes and a franc, took a franc between his fingers, and then changed it for a fifty centime piece when he saw that the beggar's hands were clean, which seemed to him to indicate that the man had money. A moment later, having given his fifty centimes, he turned round and saw another person giving the beggar a coin, then another, and he thought, 'He makes a fortune! I've been had again.'

These various impulses having been finally assimilated, he greatly admired himself for his gesture, and in this admiration, as he had hoped and foreseen, his self-dissatisfaction was swallowed up.

Still cherishing the hope that he might not have to give anything, or only very little, to his brother and his nephew, and fearful lest the accidental discovery of his liberality might be a powerful weapon in their hands, he had asked the charity not to divulge his name.

For the next few days, bathed in self-approbation, he waited impatiently for an acknowledgment from the charity, and smacked his lips in anticipation of its terms. He waited more than a week—which he thought outrageous—and the reply when it came, though friendly, was less so than he had expected. The fact was that the members of the board of the charity, whenever they received a new and unexpected donation, immediately thought, 'This is a man who wants to get in on the charity, What's his motive? etc . . .' And instinctively they closed their ranks to keep this interloper at bay, for their only interest in the work was to hasten their advancement in the Legion of Honour. Hence the coolness they had allowed to filter through the polite phrases of their reply to M. de Coëtquidan, in order to warn him that they had seen through his game.

In the meantime, M. de Coëtquidan received a visit from his brother.

Here we must turn back once more, as we did with M. de Coantré, and examine the subject of M. Elie and women.

M. Elie had come of age still cherishing the belief that women were equipped in front with the same attributes as men, and that it was modesty that prevented these marvels from being shown on statues and in paintings. This proves at least that guilty conversations are not all that prevalent in the colleges of the Company of Jesus. The army had no chance of teaching him the facts of life, for he was excused military service on account of rickets. What kept him away from women was religious scruple, the belief that his body was a repulsive object (as indeed it was, but women are not so particular), and above all that congenital diffidence which he shared with his brother, quite unlike the diffidence shown by M. de Coantré during his night of madness, which was that of a man of fifty-four who for twenty years has avoided contact with the world and with women.

Up to the age of thirty-five M. Elie had never known a woman. It was then that one of his fellow café-crawlers, M. de Corson de Beauxhostes, an insurance agent at Bois-Colombes whom he met every evening at Scossa's, introduced him to his mistress, Mlle Léa Meyer. A month later this moustachioed businessman flung his lady-friend into M. Elie's arms out of a mischievous desire to observe his agitation and embarrassment in front of women. Finding himself with Léa Meyer perched on his knee, M. Elie fondled her a little, but felt no inclination to go any further. For all that M. de Corson had told him that Léa was 'not like other Jews', he assumed that she was grasping, and that 'the act' would be a great source of complications and ties, quite apart from the eternal damnation he could expect at the end of the affair, which is a big price to pay for something one has no desire for. So he excused himself on religious grounds. A Frenchwoman would have made fun of him, but Léa said there was nothing she admired more than people who take their religion seriously. Whereupon M. Elie, who would have taken his stand firmly on religion if Léa had teased him, with characteristic contrariness told her that he had lied, that he was deeply in love with someone and wanted to remain faithful. Already he found it necessary to make believe in front of her, thereby showing himself aware of the emptiness of his life.

For twenty-five years, and long after the death of M. de Corson, Léa remained with 'Nunkie'—as she called M. Elie—on a footing of platonic intimacy. He went to see her every Saturday in her little flat in the Rue de La Rochefoucauld, bringing her each time a few francs' worth of *charcuterie* or cakes, mixed up with the shreds of tobacco and other unspeakable oddments in his pockets. He would fondle her a little, without ever undressing. Once a year he took her to a matinée at the theatre, to a play that he himself wanted to see—*La Fille de Mme Angot, Monsieur de Pourceaugnac* (because of the enemas), or a revival of *La Belle Hélène*. And once a year he 'stood' her something, the cost of which was not to exceed about sixty francs (1924 rate).

Léa Meyer was no more mercenary than the rest of us; in other words, she was mercenary within the limits allowed by French convention. But as she was Jewish, she had only to remark that such and such a thing seemed rather dear for people to exclaim: 'She's a real Jewess!' Faced with such a reputation, against which there is no defence, the temptation is to let oneself become what one is represented as being, since mending one's ways will change nothing. If the aristocracy only knew how little credit they are given for the trouble they take not to appear 'stuck-up', they would save themselves this trouble and remain natural. Léa had the decency to continue, in spite of her reputation, to display a merely Aryan sharpness in money matters. She did think it possible that M. Elie might come and live with her if the Arago household broke up, or that he might give her some tangible proof of his affection in his will, the only sort of tangible proof she knew him to be capable of. But her behaviour towards the old man was little affected by such thoughts, which indeed she often lost sight of altogether.

M. Octave and Mme de Coantré were aware of this situation, because M. Elie had been unable to restrain himself from boasting about having a woman in his life. Mme de Coantré believed that Léa had been his mistress when he was a young man, but that this was no longer so. M. Octave, more experienced, was sceptical. Both were so convinced that there was no danger from this quarter that it had never occurred to Mme de Coantré on her death-bed to make her brother swear not to go and live with Léa; he would have sworn, and kept his word, being a man of principle. But in fact M. Elie had always been determined neither to live with Léa nor to leave her anything of importance after his death. So that when it was decided to move from Arago, he was careful not to tell her, for fear that she might pester him into moving into her flat, but waited to present her with a *fait accompli* when the solution he hoped for and confidently expected had been put into effect, in other words, when his brother gave him enough to live in a respectable boarding-house.

On the morning of the day he went to visit the baron, M. Elie made a scene at Arago. Since his slightest wish was anticipated there, he was normally fairly quiet and reserved his spleen for the outside world—for example, if he received a letter addressed to '27, Boule-vard Arago' instead of '27a'. Then, seeing him rave, one would have thought that the 'a' was a sort of nobiliary particle peculiar to addresses. On this occasion, the charwoman had thrown away the piece of soap on his wash-hand-stand. She claimed that there was practically none of it left, that one could almost see through it; he maintained that it would have lasted another week. He stormed and raged, though not without a secret fear; low enough to ensure that no one heard, he muttered that she had stolen the soap. This scene would have been more easily understood had it been known that M. Elie, determined to have it out with his brother that after-noon, was artificially working himself up into the necessary state of fury.

The baron, when his brother was announced, seized one of his jackets and a bottle of stain-remover. M. Elie came in to find him cleaning his jacket with a lugubrious air. M. Octave at once began to prophesy the certain loss of his case, and to complain, in addition, that he had just had a set-back on the Stock Exchange. This ex-plained why he was already beginning to economize—for instance by doing his own jacket instead of sending it to the cleaner.

All this was meant to explain, by way of anticipation and prevention, that he could not be counted on to make financial sacrifices. He did not take so much trouble with Léon. However, after a few exchanges, M. Elie complimented him on his youthful appearance, adding maliciously, 'Honestly! And with all your worries! . . .' which proved to M. Octave that he had wasted his time. (M. Octave pulls a wry face when his brother tells him he looks young, just as Léon pulls a wry face when his uncle tells him he looks well. What an extraordinary creature is man, always tempting Providence!)

M. Elie, who was in excellent form, did not beat about the bush.

'Well, what do I do on October 15th?'

'My dear chap, it is for me to ask you.'

'*Nan,* it's for me to ask you,' M. Elie rapped out with so prompt a fury that it was obvious that it had been prepared in advance. 'You told me people didn't starve when they had brothers. What are you going to do for me?'

M. Octave felt something of the same indignation as an Austrian general at the insolence of Napoleonic strategy. But he answered all the more gently:

'I am quite prepared to help you, Elie. Only I find it a little *unfair*[1] when you could easily sort your problems out yourself.'

'Sorry, don't understand English. Explain.'

'You have nine thousand francs a year. By investing your capital in a life annuity, at your age you would triple your income.'

M. Elie's plan was simple: to force his brother to give him an allowance by threatening to go and live with Léa Meyer, or even marry her. These threats were only a means to an end; he was as determined not to put either of them into execution as he was convinced that Octave would give in at the first word. The solution proposed by his brother both flummoxed and attracted him. He said he did not know what a life annuity was, and M. Octave explained it to him at length. When he understood it he was distrustful. Such a source of riches frightened him because his brother had suggested it. He preferred his brother's money.

[1] In English in the original.

'What if the insurance company goes bankrupt?' he growled. 'What if there's a war or a revolution? Or the state takes over insurance? No, I won't play. Not such a fool.'

It was useless for M. Octave to explain how childish his reasons were; he was adamant. The more the baron recommended the life annuity, the more M. Elie dug his toes in, confirmed in his suspicions—'He wants to do me down.' They argued for some time, then Elie said:

'Don't bother to go on. Throw three hundred thousand francs down the drain! If you don't want to give me enough to live decently on, I'm not worried about what to do. I know where to go.'

'Where will you go?' the baron asked, vaguely uneasy.

'Women are better than men. There are women who for twenty-five years . . .'

'Elie, you wouldn't do that!'

'Why not?'

Need we go into all the details of their discussion, and M. Elie's bilious grievances? ('Who will ever know? Does anyone know I exist! The family! . . . I'm supposed to take the opinion of the family into account, when I've never meant anything to them!') It was a classic scene; the familiar phrases come flocking to one's pen. M. Octave was beaten in advance. His brother! An old Jewish whore! His anxiety was now concentrated on the question: how much is he going to fleece me of? M. Elie asked for ten thousand a year. He already had nine; with nineteen thousand he could live 'without disgracing the family'. The baron breathed again, not without a pang. Elie might have asked double. But what was to prevent him from raising his price tomorrow? He offered eight thousand, which Elie accepted.

'Not a word of this to Léon de Coantré, you understand?' said the baron. His brother gave a snigger: 'I should think not!'

M. Octave, who hated gushing, nevertheless thought his brother's thanks a bit curt.

Having obtained what he wanted, M. Elie, glowing with contentment, had a violent desire to smoke (the cigarette on coming out of Mlle G's flat . . .). His brother had a phobia about tobacco, or rather had developed one out of affectation, and M. Elie never smoked in his house. But this time, to smoke there was like putting his foot on the chest of his fallen adversary.

'Can I smoke?' he asked. The blow struck home. An hour earlier M. Octave would have answered: 'Can't you wait until you're outside?' But now his brother had the whip hand over him and knew it, and wanted to show that he knew it; this little smoking episode was the first visible sign that the situation was reversed.

'If it's absolutely necessary,' said the baron with a grimace.

M. Elie gave a grin. 'Yes, it is absolutely necessary.'

Naturally there was no ash-tray. M. Octave had to fold a sheet of paper, into which his brother dropped his cigarette ash. Some of it fell on the carpet. The expression on M. Octave's face on seeing the smoke in his room (*his* room! . . .) and the ash on his carpet (*his* carpet! . . .) was worthy of the theatre. But when M. Elie, having thrown away his cigarette, proceeded to light another one out of bravado, M. Octave reached the zenith of martyrdom and M. Elie the nadir of despicable enjoyment. 'This is what the future will be like,' the baron said to himself. 'At least I'm being warned in good time.'

The baron also noticed the sarcastic look on M. Elie's face as he glanced at a small six-pound dumb-bell lying in a corner of the room, which M. Octave used to lift three or four times every morning. Sensing that his brother despised him, he did not react. And still M. Elie, for a variety of reasons (he enjoyed teasing Octave . . . he did not know how to leave . . . he was making a point of not leaving too soon after getting what he wanted) did not budge. Determined to talk about something or other, he talked about himself. Nevertheless silences crept in, when he could think of nothing to say, even about himself. 'Now's the time!' M. Octave thought to himself, meaning, 'to show him the door'; but he did not dare. And he was too proud to go and tell Papon to announce a visitor. Chum up with the servants against a Coëtquidan—never! Under the strain of all that was happening to him, M. Octave was overcome with a sort of torpor, an agonizing drowsiness, like a man falling asleep on horseback at dawn. In the depths of his somnolence, only one feeling still remained alive: a desire to eat some excellent muscat grapes which had been sent to him and were now in his cupboard. But he thought his brother might turn sour again—'You're a lucky one, you are! They look after you all right!'—and preferred to forgo his grapes. His lethargy was so overwhelming that he reached the point of no longer trying to hide it. He yawned. M. Elie began to yawn too, but he did not go. It went on like this for an hour and a half: these two men, one incapable of leaving, the other incapable of making him leave; between them, silence gradually encroaching; and behind them, their sordid bargain.

M. Elie left at last. For a long time, sitting in his armchair, the baron kept that beautiful, grave expression—presenting, almost, the illusion of thoughtfulness—which men get when they have just lost money. Then he sighed. Newfoundland dogs often have a little moisture oozing from the corner of their eyes, as though they were crying. What makes Newfoundland dogs cry? The knowledge that they have been fooled.

Back from his nocturnal escapade, M. de Coantré had explained at Arago that on arriving home at midnight he had discovered that his key was missing. Not wanting to wake M. Elie by ringing, he had spent the night at a hotel. This went down beautifully. Innocents are good liars.

The escapade remained in his memory as something he was glad to have experienced, as long as that was the end of it for ever; it was one of those trials which become blessings if one can speak of them in the past tense. He had had nothing, but was as satisfied as if he had had what he had sought. He had no regrets.

August passed uneventfully. Léon went on packing, gardening, sleeping. He watched his money dwindling in his drawer, like a man watching a gauge showing the amount of oxygen in his room, but he watched it fairly calmly. Indeed, the prospect of soon being reduced to nothing at all produced something of that secret euphoria which extreme circumstances provoke in certain people, provided always that Brother Ass, the body, does not feel itself in danger. When he was reduced to *nothing* they would be forced to look after him, they wouldn't leave a Coantré in the gutter. Quite shamelessly he was relying on their pity, staking everything on it. He could see himself quite happily begging from people. For ten years he had heard his mother sigh, 'Oh, to be able to live in a hotel! No more servants! No more meals to order!' For him, the prospect of total destitution seemed as inviting as the prospect of prison or hospital seems to some poor devils: no more decisions to be taken, no more responsibilities.

He no longer received any mail, not even replies to letters he had written. He saw in front of him, as one sees a physical object, this simple fact: that he counted for nothing. And the people with whom he counted for nothing did not even know one another, had exchanged no secret password. It really was something *in him* that made them feel like this.

The baron spent the month of August at a watering-place. On September 1st he returned home, and Léon courted him with renewed zeal, keeping him informed and asking his advice about everything, snorting with excitement when he repeated to him that on October 15th he would be as naked as St John the Baptist. M. Octave floated on a cloud of optimistic generalities: to expect the worst is a policy contradicted by the facts, etc etc. From which Léon inferred that his uncle had there and then decided to come to his rescue.

The truth was quite otherwise. The baron had indeed made a decision, the decision to help his brother, and was now under the impression that for the time being the family was catered for. But what, it may be asked, was he waiting for in regard to his nephew? Well, he was waiting for it to be too late.

He was immovable. Often he would deny Léon's plight, telling himself, for example, that he remembered Léon saying, 'I can carry on like this until August 1st' and so he would triumphantly exclaim: 'Well, it's now September 10th, and the little beggar's still alive! With highly-strung people it's always the same. Nothing but words!' At Vichy, he had received a letter from Léon on writing-paper engraved with a count's coronet. It was clear from the yellow-ish tint of the paper that it was an old sheet, fifteen or twenty years old, which Léon had dug out, and his using it was surely a sign of economy. Nevertheless, this coronet was the chemical particle that sufficed to disintegrate any remote inclinations M. Octave might have had to do something for his nephew. He turned to his sister:

'He hasn't a bean, yet he uses embossed writing-paper! A coronet! In the first place, the Coantrés' title would need to be pretty closely examined—if one attached any importance to such tomfooleries. *I* don't even have my address printed on my writing-paper, I write it myself. And I'm expected to make him an allowance for life . . . Léon de Coantré has nothing to do, nothing to worry about: he'll bury us all. Ah yes! these people who have no money certainly know how to get their own back—by bothering those who have. Just because my brother and my nephew have ruined their lives by their idleness and their eccentricity and incompetence, I, who have worked like a slave and done something with mine by the sweat of my brow, I'm supposed to deprive myself for them! I shouldn't be taking this holiday!' Mme Emilie gave a groan. 'Yes, yes! The minute I come to Vichy, thanks to the money I've earned honestly, while they *can't* go, I'm made to feel guilty. The family! What's the use of a family? Simply to ask you for money, that's all. "Family feeling"—I've never heard anyone use the expression except when they wanted to get some money out of me for some creature who isn't worth the slightest interest. The exploitation of the rich by the poor; there's an unmentionable disease for you! It's always everything for the poor! When three-quarters of the poor are only poor because they ask for it!'

The sense of vast social injustice lent a note of pathos to the baron's words. In her gentle voice Mme Emilie observed:

'Yes, but you forget that Léon is not like everyone else.'

Time and again M. Octave had said that Léon was a half-wit. But his passion for contradicting his sister made him retort:

'Léon de Coantré is no more stupid than the rest of us. I don't know how he got that reputation. He's like all people of good family.'

There was a silence, broken at last by Mme Emilie.

'Ah! my poor Octave!' she concluded, as though it was M. Octave who was ready for the doss-house.

On September 15th M. Elie received a letter from his brother postmarked Fréville. This was the country house—some would have called it a château—which the baron had bought near Le Havre when, to the scandalized amazement of the family, his 'modernism' had made him sell the ancestral home on the death of old Coëtquidan. This letter had a distinct flavour of absurdity, having been typed by the baron himself, who liked to play with a typewriter—which he even took with him to the country—as his brother played with his cane, his stamps, etc. Only the concluding words, 'Your affectionate brother', and the signature were in handwriting. The whole thing was imitation American, which is to say that it was typical of present-day France, since for quite some time now the national genius has largely consisted in copying.

M. Octave informed his brother that he had gone to Fréville and would be back at the beginning of October. Both our heroes, though they said nothing, found this behaviour rather off-hand. At the approach of this historic day, October 15th, which was to alter their fate, they would have preferred to have M. Octave nearer at hand. However, they did not lose heart. Léon had another cause for anxiety, which was that his uncle showed no sign of preparing for the move. Several times he sounded him on the subject, but the old man answered, 'There's plenty of time,' or 'I've begun.' He had not begun at all, as Léon ascertained in the course of some thorough investigations in his uncle's room while he was out, investigations that never came to an end, now that he had given up buying cigarettes, without his stealing a few good pinches of tobacco from the game-bag.

On October 2nd, M. Elie received another typescript from the baron, announcing quite simply that he felt 'a bit off-colour' and wouldn't be back until the beginning of November. He would meet them on the 2nd at his sister's grave. 'Have you found yourself a boarding-house? I hope to find you settled in when I get back.'

'He can go to blazes,' thought M. Elie. But he was on velvet. On the 15th, he would move into a hotel and send the bill to Octave when he arrived back. At the slightest demur, he would produce the Léa Meyer bogy. As for Léon, he was utterly crushed. Where was he to go between October 15th and November 2nd? Why had M. Octave written to his brother and not him? How selfish of him to go off like this, leaving them to shift for themselves! What a give-away it was! Perhaps he ought not to rely on Uncle Octave any more? He felt his heart beating, he gulped for air, and, suddenly aware of all his inner anguish, he realized what it must be like to fall ill from such a blow, what it must be like to die of it.

Next day—M. Octave, always sensitive to shades of distinction, had been anxious to underline the order of precedence—Léon received the same letter with slight variations: 'Have you found a job at last? What are you going to do on the 15th? Keep in touch.'

That morning Léon felt a tiny pain, something like the bite of an invisible insect, in his eye-lids and round about his eyes, the sort of pain that for days had never left him during the worst moments of the Lebeau affair. Another thing tormented him. Ten days before the date of departure, M. Elie had still not even begun to sort out the contents of his room. And Léon felt again the fear he had had when he first announced that they would have to leave Arago: the fear that M. Elie would quite simply refuse, saying 'I'm not going. So there!' This fear was all the greater because, when he asked him about his plans with his usual tact and deference, M. Elie remained vague. For a long time Léon hesitated to speak more firmly to his uncle. He had none of the determination which his mother sometimes showed, as when, for example, driven to extremes in spite of her sweet temper, she seized Elie's squalid old straw hat which for years he had refused to replace, flung it on the ground and put her heel through it. 'There, now you'll have to buy a new one!' Finally Léon took it on himself to offer to help M. Elie to pack, conjuring up a hair-raising picture of the old man's belongings being thrown out of the window on the morning of the 15th. He expected a refusal, and could have fallen on M. de Coëtquidan's neck when he accepted. It must be said, however, that the old man had been waiting for such an offer—partly out of laziness, partly because no one was as clumsy with his hands as he was, and partly because he was glad to see his nephew doing a menial job on his behalf.

Léon certainly needed to roll up his sleeves! The whole room was in an appalling state. The charwoman had orders to touch nothing in it, because if the slightest thing was moved, and he could not find it at once, M. de Coëtquidan flew into a rage. The result of this was that there was so much dust that the old man's handkerchief was always black and his sticky black hands left marks on everything he touched. Here and there on the floor the dust had formed into bits of fluff, which danced around whenever the door was opened, much to M. Elie's amusement. Cheap fag-ends and little piles of cigarette ash lay scattered about all over the place—the disgusting traces which the male leaves behind him. The sheets, too, were full of cigarette burns. Anywhere else but at home, M. de Coëtquidan would have preferred to sleep on the naked floor rather than lay his head on a pillow-case as greasy as his own—which was greasy to the point of transparency. But if he ever happened to be struck by the smell of his own filth, he adored it because it was something that belonged to him. Even in the height of summer, the window was never open for more than an hour or two, because 'open windows are an American fad' (an allusion to M. Octave, who, on principle, lived in a perpetual draught), so that the sickly smell of eau-de-Cologne and glycerine pervaded the whole of his part of the house.

M. Elie pleaded rheumatic pains as an excuse for not helping Léon, who spent three days sorting out his uncle's belongings and packing them in four trunks.

M. Elie sat in his armchair handing out instructions. 'I say, if you've nothing better to do, you might amuse yourself by giving these togs a going over with. . . .' 'Amuse yourself' was a gem, for the job consisted in spraying the 'togs' with an anti-moth solution, an hour and a half's work, plus an hour for brushing them. They were clothes which the old man could no longer wear, not because he thought they were too soiled but because he had developed a paunch since the armistice (no more rationing!). Two or three tailors had refused to make the prodigious alterations M. Elie demanded, but he could not make up his mind either to sell the clothes at the ridiculous price he would have been offered for them or to give them away, because it broke his heart to give. Overflowing from the crowded wardrobe, they lay piled several feet high on chairs, awaiting the Day of Judgment, covered with a white layer of dust against which the moth-stains showed whiter still. While Léon toiled away, M. Elie from to time made as if to lend a hand, but immediately gripped his back with a groan of pain. When the old man's room had been transformed into a miraculous void occupied solely by trunks and furniture, Léon turned to him beaming and said, 'Thank you, uncle, for lending yourself to this irksome job with such good grace. And thank you especially for letting me rummage like that among your belongings. You have shown a trust in me that I deeply appreciate. You know, I may not appear to be very demonstrative, but I *feel things* . . .' And M. de Coantré sincerely meant all this.

He also offered to find lodgings for his uncle, and went round the neighbouring boarding-houses asking prices. M. Elie threw the cards he brought back into the waste-paper basket, and finally told him that his brother and sister had promised to look after him. He intended to go to a hotel until their return. This was also Léon's intention. But when Léon noticed by chance a placard advertising a double furnished room with a loft, they decided to save money by moving in there until the baron settled their future.

Two days before the move a scene took place which, though irrelevant to our narrative, is enjoyable to relate.

Characteristically, M. de Coantré had made it a point of honour to hand over the property in a state of perfect cleanliness. Two days before their departure he was still raking and weeding when, through the garden gate giving on to the boulevard, there entered an old lady of distinguished appearance, who came up to him and asked:

'Is Count de Coantré at home?'

'No, madame, he is out of Paris at present,' said Léon. It was not the first time that, dressed as he was, a visitor had taken him for the gardener or an odd-job man, and it amused him enormously.

'Oh, how annoying!' said the old lady in a high, fluting voice and an accent that was too good to be true—a voice and accent which alone would have betrayed her as a member of the highest society.

She asked when M. de Coantré would be back. But now she was scrutinizing Léon with a black and beady eye. He thought he had been spotted, and, in his good-natured way, could not help smiling. At which she said:

'But . . . but . . . surely it's . . .'

'Yes, madame, I am Léon de Coantré. But you see what I'm doing, and the clothes I'm wearing. That is why my first impulse . . .'

'I recognized you by your eyes! You have the eyes of the Coantrés!' cried the old lady in a voice like a fog-horn (for the true society woman is a creature of extremes: either she emits the most tenuous whispers, or she utters the most excruciating bellows). 'I am the Marquise de Vauthiers-Béthancourt, an old friend of your dear mama. Probably you do not know me; I live almost all the time in my little cottage in Sologne (it was in fact a magnificent historical château). And yet, the times I've been to see your dear Mama here! (She had been once, fifteen years before.) And I also knew your dear papa—such a charming man. . . .'

Léon, having established that it was indeed him that Mme de Vauthiers wanted to see, offered the old lady one of the rusty garden chairs, and sat down beside her, his blue apron only half concealing his old, patched corduroys and his feet scarcely touching the ground, so stubby was he.

'Yes,' said Mme de Vauthiers, 'it was you I was after. I am Vice-President of the Royalist Ladies of the nth *arrondissement*. We decided we ought to get our men to rally round, and I thought of you, remembering that your dear papa was a staunch supporter of the White Carnation. And as I had to come to this neighbourhood today . . . But now I'm afraid I may have been mistaken. You must find society repellent.'

With the utmost simplicity, Léon gave her an outline of his tastes and of the life he had led for the past twenty years. He put all the delicacy at his command into saying 'After the war, mama didn't have a sou,' returning to it again and again. Mme de Vauthier's mind was wandering a thousand miles away, but her face expressed a passionate interest and attention, as though it were her own son describing the life he had led during a long absence. Her black eyes were aflame, and when Léon had finished, she cried out in a voice so piercing and loud that people driving past along the boulevard must have heard every word:

'Ah, my dear sir, you have chosen the better part. A simple, healthy life, far away from the cares of our accursed civilization, amid natural surroundings and family affections. What a perfect place for a rest-cure! Such a charming house! And so tastefully adorned!' She eyed three drooping ivy plants. 'One might be a hundred miles from Paris. I've always longed to have a real country house in the middle of Paris, but this dog's life of mine has decided otherwise. I have to live in that frightful Boulevard Latour-Maubourg.' ('Dog's life' was not bad from a person with an income of eight hundred thousand francs a year and never a care in the world. But Mme de Vauthiers always said precisely what convention dictated, and it is the convention—in every social milieu—to say that our world is a vale of tears, which, God knows, it is very far from being. In addition to this, assuming that Léon was unhappy, Mme de Vauthiers wanted out of courtesy to have him believe that she was unhappy too.)

'Your dear mama was really spoilt, having this ravishing retreat (Mme de Vauthiers would have described the *Critique of Pure Reason* as 'ravishing') and your tender care to protect her old age. The last time I saw her she was telling me you were the consolation of her life . . .'

M. de Coantré felt as if he were in a hammock being rocked by this ancient blue-veined hand—such a charming hand! Though dressed like a tramp, and despite his phobia for visitors, he had no desire to see Mme de Vauthiers go, and felt a stab of regret when she rose. Besides, he was always a little distressed when anyone—however boring—said good-bye to him first, surprised that the person did not take more pleasure in his company.

'How delighted I am, my dear sir, to have been able to get to know you a little! And if you only knew what a comfort it is to me to see a man of our world with enough character to keep away from the grimaces of the salons, from all those stupid society people!' (We have already seen M. Octave, Mme Emilie and Mme Angèle putting on the record entitled *Stupidity of Society People*. It is a sort of password among society people to say that society people are stupid. In fact, society people are like the rest of us.) 'I shall say no more about my plan for the Royalist committee. It would be a *crime* to divert you from a life which is true and satisfying. I shall not say good-bye, but "au revoir". I am just off to Sologne' (the marquise was always just off to Sologne, which was an excuse for dodging anything which bored her) 'but when I come back, it would be so nice if you could come to lunch at my house one day. My daughter would be so happy to meet you!'

Léon, bowing and scraping and obviously in his element—'Yes, ma'am . . . Certainly, ma'am . . .'—escorted Mme de Vauthiers to the garden gate, kissed her hand, and watched her disappear into a motor-car that was not sumptuous but something much better than sumptuous: a motor-car that exuded rank. The moment Mme de Vauthiers left Léon, the cheerful, almost ecstatic expression she had improvized vanished as abruptly as an electric light going out. Her features fell, her face lengthened, and her expression became cold and hard. But some time after the car had moved off, as though it had taken her that long to recover her spirits, she burst into a shrill laugh and went on repeating to herself aloud, 'Goodness, what a scream! . . . Goodness, what a scream! . . .'

Meanwhile M. de Coantré stood dreamily in the garden as though under the influence of a spell such as certain holy men leave in their wake; she had revealed to him, or rather recalled, that there existed a higher order of being. Moreover, he was thrilled at having so easily risen to the occasion, so easily shown himself a man of rank, and he said to himself, 'After all, there is something in being from the same stock!' He felt that, after all, he could have arranged his life otherwise, could have kept in touch with the people of 'our sort' of whom, from a distance, he had made a bugbear but who were probably in many cases as easy to get on with as Mme de Vauthiers. And in thinking all this, M. de Coantré was right. He could quite easily have had a normal, dignified and satisfying life, if he had agreed to the small effort needed to keep his position. What he was paying for now was very little, but it was everything: he was paying for having let himself go, for what one might call (to coin a dubious but expressive phrase) 'the snowball of indiscipline'. Mothers, let this be a warning to your sons. Nevertheless, at this moment he regretted nothing, for the old Circe had engendered in him a happy image of himself. All that evening, he genuinely believed that he had made the right choice, that the Marquise de Vauthiers-Béthancourt really envied him for having cut himself off from society etc. Thinking about the 'ravishing' house, he even went so far as to feel a twinge of regret at the idea of leaving Arago. Next morning, the effect of the philtre had worn off. 'She had me all right, that old bag! But never mind, she has a way with her.'

On the 15th, the furniture removers transported the contents of Arago to the shed Mlle de Bauret had hired. They also transported to the Rue de la Glacière the belongings of M. Elie de Coëtquidan, consisting of four trunks—three small and one large—and the belongings of M. le Comte de Coantré, consisting of one small trunk and one large suitcase. All this was put in the loft. The gentlemen had sold their furniture to a local second-hand dealer at the price he offered them.

There had been a great scene with Mélanie, who was giving up service for good. M. de Coantré had embraced her. We have refrained, during the course of this narrative, from expatiating upon the relationship between M. de Coantré and Mélanie, since it was the traditional relationship between master and servant in a society devoid of authority and order, in which the first impulse of either when anything happens is to forget his place. M. de Coantré quailed before this beady-eyed slut, never dared to criticize her, surrounded her with the same extravagant attentions as he surrounded his uncle, —and when one thinks of the harshness with which he treated his mother one must regard this difference as shameful. At the slightest provocation Mélanie would threaten to leave, and M. de Coantré would panic and give in. As we have said, such sordid behaviour is traditional, and has been described a thousand times. And yet M. de

Coantré regarded Mélanie as perfection itself. However much, for the past thirteen years, Mélanie had openly taken advantage of her position (though not in the matter of honesty, for she was *really* honest); however much, since time immemorial, M. de Coantré had seen servants repay the family's inexpressible kindness with sudden departure, insult, theft, calumny and blackmail—he nevertheless continued to proclaim, and even to believe, that only the common people have hearts and that compared to them the upper classes are regular monsters of unkindness. Similarly, for all that Mélanie would nearly faint at the slightest twinge in her stomach, would spend three whole days in bed because of a headache, or howl like a dog if she had a boil; and for all that most of the menservants the family had had, whether from North or South, had proved to be the most unbelievable mollycoddles, always on the verge of collapse, exhausted by the slightest effort, blaming fate on every occasion when nothing but their own will or moral resilience was at fault ('What has to be will be . . .'), it remained clear to M. de Coantré—as he had heard it repeated *ad nauseam* by 'people of our kind'—that it is only among the people that you find any backbone. The masochism of class is a splendid thing! Dear people, you would be foolish indeed not to take advantage of it! And a class in which, for a century and a half, it is eternally August 4th, certainly deserves no better.

M. de Coëtquidan decided to take his meals in town, at a restaurant where there was an adorable cat which he had fallen for. It was an expensive cat, for the restaurant was some distance away and he had to change buses to get there. Léon unearthed a cheap eating-house, but on arriving there the first day at half past twelve, he found it so full, and with such people, that he decided to return an hour later, when the people would have gone. During this hour he walked frantically. In any other neighbourhood, he would have sat down on a bench, but here, where he was known, he did not dare; for there is a certain class of people who believe that a man who sits on public benches must be a down-and-out; the next thing will be the drinking-fountain. At the restaurant he was asked if he wanted a napkin, and was afraid to say no; but, weighing up the minimal pleasure his napkin procured him against the extra franc a day it would cost him, he was overcome with gloom. He ate hurriedly, in order to reduce the risk of being seen in such a place, and without raising his eyes, as though the fact of not seeing others might prevent them from seeing him. In order not to waste anything, he ate the heads of his fried smelt, stuffed himself with bread, and ordered cheese instead of the orange he would have preferred, because cheese is more nourishing. Before leaving, he slipped the remains of the bread into his pocket.

On November 1st, in the car which was bringing them back from Fréville to Paris, Mme Emilie said to her brother (who, at over seventy years of age, was wearing plus-fours, so smart and dressy was he):

'I have an idea for poor Léon. You ought to send him to Fréville.'

'To Fréville! And have him dirty everything! You must be mad!'

'Not the house. Picot's cottage (Picot was the keeper). He could eat at Finance's. You could tell him you were offering him Picot's house for preference because you know how much he likes simple, rustic things.'

The keeper had died three weeks before; they had not found a replacement, and his cottage was empty. M. Octave considered the idea, which had taken him unawares. Obviously it could not be a permanent solution. But it would solve the immediate problem, and above all, for a time at least, relieve him of Léon's visits. They talked it over, thought about it, and finally decided on it.

Next day, M. Octave and his sister met the two gentlemen at Mme de Coantré's grave in the Montparnasse cemetery. On the way out, M. Octave took Elie aside and told him to come and see him that afternoon. Then he communicated his project to Léon.

Léon was in the seventh heaven. Nature! The countryside! And not a place where he would feel lost, but Fréville, under the Coët-quidans' wing, a place where he would be known as the nephew of the Marquis de Carabas! And at once! He could leave tomorrow if he wished! Ah, it was not in vain that he had put his trust in the family. Without a moment's hesitation, he told M. Octave that this decision, which was being transmitted to him on All Souls' Day, must have been inspired by the soul of Mme de Coantré, and M. Octave, although he did not believe in God, was obliging enough to infer that this was not impossible. M. Octave then took Léon to the Boulevard Haussmann in order to give him a letter of introduction to Finance, the café proprietor at Fréville. And as it was mid-day, he invited him to stay to lunch, a thing he had not done for some fifteen years; knowing that his nephew was leaving, he felt he could afford to. Léon was on his best behaviour, though occasionally annoyed by M. Octave telling him that he ate too fast and so on, as though he were a ten-year-old. M. Octave gave him another five hundred francs, but it was when he handed him the keys of the keeper's house that Léon felt he had grown ten feet taller. Fréville keys! How they trusted him! He was the son of the house! When he had gone, Mme Emilie observed that he had behaved very well and that no one would ever have thought he was a fool.

On leaving his uncle's house, Léon was in the same state of happiness and warm emotion as four months before when he had wandered along the Boulevard Haussmann towards the haunts of perdition. He decided to leave the day after tomorrow. In the Boulevard Arago, he lingered for a time around the old house. Gardeners were cutting down the ivy from the façade and painters were repainting the railings. With a sudden impulse of forgiveness, he gave the house absolution.

M. Elie spent the following afternoon in the company of his sister, visiting boarding-houses in M. Octave's motor-car. As he wanted to return to the haunts of his youth, they searched in the neighbourhood of the Rue de Lisbonne. In order to emphasize that he was starting a new life, Léon went to the hairdresser's and after his haircut ordered a shampoo. He had abandoned all the hairdressers in the district one after the other, because he had to fight every time to stop them giving him a shampoo, and he was ashamed of having to fight; for he felt sure that they did not believe him when he told them he hated getting his hair wet, and guessed that it was a question of money.

That evening, Léon and his uncle sat up late in their shabby room with its two beds side by side, like the beds of two over-grown children. They had lived for forty years under the same roof, and this was their last night together. Both were moved, especially Léon. They had so many memories in common, so many impressions, habits, mannerisms, ways of speech, words and phrases invented by the family and which could only be understood by themselves and their nearest relations. That night, they were sharply aware of all these special ties, which seemed to them to constitute a rich treasure. Léon forgot his feelings of resentment against M. Elie. M. Elie forgot that he had written an anonymous letter—oh, a long time ago—to some prospective in-laws of Léon's to tell them (it was pure calumny) that Léon had some illegitimate children. These two troglodytes looked towards the future with a sense of security, because they knew that they would remain within the framework, and as it were the aura, of the family. And yet each of them felt that he was going to miss the other.

All this time M. Elie was kneading a lump of bread which he had brought back from the restaurant and which his saliva and his dirty fingers had made as black and shiny as a lump of tar. Suddenly, in the middle of a piece of sentimental reminiscence, he stopped dead and began ferreting under the furniture with a wild look in his eyes.

'What is it, Uncle?' asked Léon anxiously.

'I've lost my pellet,' said the old man with a look of desperation. Léon got down on his knees and searched with him. When he saw it, he hesitated for a moment; then he remembered that it was his last evening with his uncle, and in the name of the past, the family, and his mother's memory, he picked up the ignoble little object and gave it back to him.

M. de Coantré was due to leave at one o'clock. In the morning, he had a sudden impulse to pay a last visit to the house in the Boulevard Arago. He pretended he had left some secateurs in the entrance to the cellar and wanted to recover them. Opening the garden gate, he was startled to find a tennis court under construction where the lawn had been; much good it had been to look after his lawn so carefully! But all the windows were closed, and neither at the front door nor at the back was his ring answered. As he opened the gate on his way out, he must have been deeply upset, for his head began to swim and he had to hold on to the railing as he undid his collar stud and took off his hat to cool his head. But it did not last long, and by the time he set off towards the Rue de la Glacière he was quite himself again.

9

To CATCH the one o'clock train, M. de Coantré arrived at the Gare St Lazare at 12.15. As there had been a great farewell scene with M. Octave two days earlier, he felt certain his uncle would not come to see him off. This filled him with a mixture of slight bitterness (the distance between the Boulevard Haussmann and the station was so short that it was almost insulting not to make the journey on such an occasion) and immense relief: the greatest proof of friendship one can show to a nervous person is not to accompany him to the station, where one's unsettling presence is bound to fluster him, perhaps to the point of disaster—lost luggage, missed trains, or, at the very least, the worst seat in the compartment.

Having registered his trunk—an old, battered trunk with one of its two locks broken—but keeping his suitcase with him, he bought a ticket, choosing third class not only out of economy but because he would be among humble people. Sweating with anxiety, he was looking for his train when he saw Georges, his uncle's chauffeur, coming towards him.

'Monsieur has already bought his ticket? Monsieur le baron sent me to look after Monsieur. And first of all, here is the *Daily Mail* for Monsieur to read in the train.'

Georges handed M. de Coantré a copy of the *Daily Mail* (he pronounced *Mail* as one pronounces it, for example, in *l'Orme du Mail*) and at the same time forcibly removed his suitcase from him. M. de Coantré saw the ten franc note he would have to give him as a tip flying away like a red balloon. 'Oh! for these few steps it's quite unnecessary. We're already at the platform.' And he pointed to the barrier, where a man was punching the tickets. 'But I have a platform ticket,' said Georges.

So Georges was going to notice that M. de Coantré was travelling third! Léon could have settled in a second-class compartment, and then moved to a third when the chauffeur had gone. But this operation seemed to him positively Himalayan, for not a minute had passed since his arrival at the station when he did not think the train was going to leave the very next minute: it was obviously impossible, for lack of time. Then he made a heroic decision.

'I've lost my ticket,' he said, searching through his pockets 'I'll have to buy another.'

'I'll go,' said Georges, 'if Monsieur will wait here.'

'No, no!' cried the count, who wanted to change his third-class ticket for a second, whereas Georges would have to pay the full price for a second.

'Monsieur will only have to wait a moment. First class?'

'No, second. But I'll go myself, I'd rather. Please!'

'So Monsieur doesn't trust me!'

'Of course I trust you,' M. de Coantré stammered out, getting more and more agitated and not daring to say another word now that he was being taken like this. 'All right, go ahead, but for God's sake be quick!' He gave him a hundred francs.

He waited by the ticket-barrier with his suitcase at his feet, in a state of extreme annoyance. So, thanks to this creature—and his dear uncle—he would have to pay for two tickets, a second and a third! Worse still, Georges seemed to be taking a long time: the train was going to leave! And he had his ticket in his pocket, and had only to settle into his seat—but Georges would be sure to track him down! It was all so frightful that one hasn't the heart to describe it. At last Georges returned, and M. de Coantré, in a state of nerves bordering on frenzy, felt he could not give him less than a twenty franc tip.

Throughout the whole journey, which lasted five hours, M. de Coantré failed to recover his spirits. M. Octave's gesture had cost him sixty-six francs (forty-six francs for the second-class ticket and twenty for Georges). He could have wept. He had decided that, as soon as the train started, he would take his first puff at a pipe he had bought the day before, a 'Jacob' clay pipe, the stem of which he had bound with string, which he intended to season carefully, and which was to be the symbol of his new life—a new life and, as it were, a new youth, for he had smoked 'Jacobs' throughout his stay at Chatenay, but not since. And now he was in such a bad humour that he had no wish to christen this pipe, and perhaps could not have done so without being sick. He had thrown the *Daily Mail* under the seat unopened. After a time, having decided that this punishment was too mild, he picked the paper up and took it to the w.c. where he left it in full view on top of the sanitary bin.

The journey was one long string of anxieties: anxiety in the train, in case it was late and missed the bus, or the bus was full, or they forgot his luggage; anxiety in the bus, in case the man Finance was supposed to be sending with a wheelbarrow to the place where M. de Coantré was to get off failed to turn up. What would become of him then, waiting alone at the side of the road after dark, with his suitcase and his trunk, two kilometres from the château? When he thought of it his mouth went dry. And he went on repeating to himself, 'As if old Octave couldn't have lent me his car!' When you do someone a favour you must never do it by half measures; you must go the whole hog or not at all, otherwise you will make an enemy.

At the bus-stop, the man was waiting by the roadside. Oh conscientious fellow, to arrive at the rendezvous at the appointed time! Oh noble specimen of a vanished species, I lift my hat to you! The man put the trunk and suitcase on his wheelbarrow, and they set off through the forest.

Suddenly M. de Coantré was transformed. A forest is a healing place—or so it would appear. Léon absorbed the aroma of Nature as one absorbs the aroma of a church, so compact and powerful was the scent of the forest—a scent of sugary moisture—on this St Martin's summer day. The scent of the forest! It was the scent of Chatenay once more. Was it possible that this wonderfully precious thing, Nature, could go on existing all the time while one ignored it and felt obliged to live away from it instead of gorging oneself on it to the exclusion of everything else! He became steeped in this smell like a sponge swollen with water. It seemed to him as though the leaves of the trees were smoothing the wrinkles on his forehead. He would have liked to grasp the air in the palms of his hands and press it to his face. He pulled back his shoulders, as proud as if he were showing off a brand new apple-green suit. His gait was that of a clockwork toy, or of a drunken man—unbelievably different from what it was in Paris. Oh new-found youth! Oh thrilling metamorphosis! The certainty that he could still be happy shone forth in this ageing man, the conviction that he possessed at last what he had always desired and what had been destined for him from time immemorial.

They walked on for two kilometres. The man was an agricultural labourer. M. de Coantré wanted to dazzle him with his woodland knowledge: with childish pride he named the different species of trees, talked of trees being 'rolled' by the wind, from which one can extract the pith like lead from a pencil, criticized the administration of the forest: ill-kept cutting lines, 'premature' plants which were devouring their neighbours and which should have been cut down, etc . . . And he trotted steadily along on his little legs, having difficulty in keeping up with the labourer in spite of his loaded wheelbarrow, but eager to show him that he was no soft Parisian but a hard-baked countryman.

At last they reached the château, an indifferent building to which M. de Coantré took an instant dislike because it reminded him of wealth. They deposited his luggage in the keeper's cottage, not without a complicated rigmarole from M. de Coantré explaining that it was he himself who had chosen to live there rather than in the château, out of love for simple, natural things: he all but quoted Jean-Jacques Rousseau. The man was to escort him to Fréville, and not wanting to keep him waiting (that courtesy of his!) Léon merely glanced inside the house, which consisted of one big room, a kitchen, and a lumber-room. It had been built to M. Octave's own specifications, and he himself, to show his esteem for manual labour, had insisted on lending a hand with it. Disguised as a bricklayer and mixing with the workers—to their great inconvenience—he played at being a manual labourer for several hours on two or three occasions, not forgetting to have himself photographed in this get-up. (The pictures showed him looking fifteen years older, an elderly man exhausted by a physical effort well beyond his age and strength.) M. Octave adored, at smart dinner parties, to remark casually to his gorgeous neighbour: 'When I was a bricklayer . . .' Raised eyebrows. 'But yes, madame, I myself built my keeper's cottage.' And then he would extemporize on one of his favourite themes, the dignity of manual labour.

M. de Coantré and his guide went off to Fréville, which was six or seven hundred yards from the château.

There is something so splendid about the grasping proprietor of a cheap eating-house being called Finance that it would be regarded as absurd if it happened in a novel, reminding one of those simple-minded novelists who think they can bring a bailiff to life by calling him Graball or an avaricious peasant by calling him Graspgrain— puerile and hackneyed conventions which will last as long as the French novel. So in the course of these pages we shall call Finance by his wife's maiden name, Chandelier.

Chandelier gave M. de Coantré a warm welcome. It was 'M. le Comte' this and 'M. le Comte' that. The men at the tables stopped chattering and silently contemplated this preposterous count. Chandelier was a man of about forty-five, fattish, blond, with a full, pink face, who adopted a forced heartiness when he spoke to M. de Coantré, and suddenly a hard expression when he addressed his wife or the waitress. On the whole he looked like a wild boar, but one which was mainly fattened pig. It was agreed that while the weather remained fine, M. de Coantré would eat at the inn. Later on, if it was necessary, the waitress's son would take the meals to the château. 'We'll manage somehow.'

Léon had dinner. Chandelier came and chatted to him, about his family and his 'worries' (for a self-respecting man *must* have 'worries'). Léon talked again about 'rolled' and 'premature' trees, not forgetting the 'cutting lines'. He was bathed in happiness: the substantial meal had raised his new-found self-esteem even higher. Chandelier asked if he might offer him a glass of brandy out of friendship.

Next morning Léon, hungry for the forest, dressed himself up like a tramp and spent the day among the trees. He had first of all looked for a suitable branch and cut himself a stick. Like the 'Jacob' pipe, a stick was indispensable as a symbol of his new life, and he would have suffered if he had not had one straight away.

A painter could have depicted the landscape with two colours only, green and brown. M. de Coantré walked on a thick carpet of dead leaves, whose brownish-yellow hue turned almost pink in the distance, and through withered bracken. The tall forest pines, all leaning away from the sea wind, swayed slowly like submarine plants. Here and there a tree-trunk lay on the ground with its branches sticking up like the horns of a dead buffalo. No sound could be heard but the cawing of an occasional crow or the cry of some little tree-creeper as it climbed. But the faint, distant murmur of traffic on the main road brought to this solitude a reminder of humanity, like land glimpsed from the open sea.

The next day was also spent in the forest, in a similar state of euphoria. Léon wrote in lyrical vein to his two uncles, to Pinpin and to Mélanie. The day after that it rained, and the disadvantage of having to go down to the village to lunch made itself felt. In the evening the waitress's son brought in the meal, which had to be heated up. 'Of course old Octave didn't think about this problem of meals. It's always the same. He isn't practical!' And you, dear count, do *you* happen to be *practical* by any chance?

The following day, there was more rain and lunch was brought up, but it was appreciably less good than at the inn. It had been agreed that the boy should do the house every other day. He was a greyish-yellow child, with grimy hands and knees and teeth rotted by cider. Since he knew and understood nothing, Léon guessed that the only thing he would get from this so-called help would be the ruinous fatigue which an untrained servant causes.

In the afternoon he could think of nothing to do. Now that his worries had been dissipated he lacked a solid base. It was like the rather sinister silence of a motor-boat when the engine breaks down at sea. And then, in an old den like Arago where nothing was ever thrown away in case it was needed, there was always something to be done. As there was no armchair in the keeper's house ('The rural life is all very nice, but it has its limitations . . .'), he spent the whole day lying on the bed waiting for dinner-time, his head unbelievably empty, cursing the log fire which, on the first day, had so delighted him (gramophone record: *The Poetry of the Log Fire*: 'A living presence! A companion! Something better than those trashy modern inventions! . . .') but which now forced him to get up every five minutes to re-arrange something in the fire-place.

At half past seven the boy, who was supposed to bring the dinner at seven, had still not arrived. At eight o'clock, still no one. No doubt they had not sent him because of the rain. This off-hand behaviour shattered Léon. He weighed up the pros and cons of going out in the rain or going to bed without any dinner, and finally went to bed, his heart full of bitterness. Chandelier! Another guardian angel whose wings had begun to moult.

Next day Chandelier excused himself. The boy could no longer 'come up': his mother needed him at meal-times. For the house-work, M. de Coantré might come to some arrangement with old mother Poublanc's daughter.

'But, if I may say so, it's no kind of life for monsieur to be leading up there in winter in such conditions. Monsieur is his own master, of course; but if monsieur wants to live an open-air life and at the same time be looked after properly, why not take a room in the village? Even here, if monsieur liked, we could clear the daughter's room, which we've been using as a store-room ever since she got married. We could make a fine room for him!'

'I should be only too delighted,' said M. de Coantré guilelessly, 'but you see—I don't know whether M. de Coëtquidan told you—I'm absolutely penniless. I can't afford any extra expense if I can avoid it.'

Country people do not take the trouble to hide their feelings. Within a second—like characters in a play—a sort of mask came over the faces of the two Chandeliers; their jaws dropped, the light went out of their eyes; and as if they were choking, they said not a word. No sound could be heard but the powerful, majestic, insistent tick-tock of the clock on the wall. An atmosphere of calamity invaded the room, as sharp and as cold as if the windows had suddenly been flung wide open.

That day the weather was cold and dry. Léon, in the forest,

literally no longer *saw* the scenery: he was too preoccupied—'drawing up plans'. He decided to buy tinned food and eat at home, and to do his own housework.

That evening after dinner Chandelier presented him with the bill. Léon had only been there a week, but, alarmed by his admission that morning, the man wanted to make sure. Léon paid the bill without checking it. When he looked at it afterwards, he saw that Chandelier had included the brandy he had 'stood' him on the first day.

He said he was going to do his own housework, that he had been advised to take exercise. He noticed that Chandelier no longer spoke to him in the third person. On the first day it had been 'Monsieur le Comte' at every turn, so much so that Léon, conscious of the absurdity of the title being applied to a poor devil in his situation, had begged the innkeeper to refrain from using it. Then it had been the third person without the title, which Léon, humble as he was, considered *proper*. Now it was 'you'.

M. Octave, in writing to Chandelier, had told him that Léon wanted a 'rest cure', and that he was by nature 'a little eccentric'. He had said not a word about his penury, assuming that the innkeeper would soon find out for himself. Chandelier, for his part, had got used to the idea that all noblemen were half-mad. He had seen M. Octave alternating stinginess and extravagance; he had heard about the eccentricities of old Coëtquidan, and once or twice he had caught a glimpse of the scarecrow figure of M. Elie. That the nobility were all half-mad was something that he not only believed in all sincerity, it was also an idea that he cherished. He had, indeed, a deep-dyed hatred for them, and considered that they had not sufficiently atoned. Although, in France, the record on this subject proclaims that as the aristocracy no longer exists as a class, being strictly null both in what it is and what it has, no one can hate it, because one cannot hate what does not exist, nevertheless this hatred remains. Once upon a time a girl-friend of Léon's, who had taken a long time to reach the stage of being confiding and amenable with him, had finally confessed, 'You see, it put me off, your being a viscount.' Chandelier went so far as to envy and hate titles which he knew to be false, like that of a local squire whose grandfather was well known to have been a draper. For it was the title not the person that he always concentrated on, forgetting, as the masses always do, that there are as many (or almost as many) noblemen without titles as there are commoners with.

That same evening M. de Coantré bought some condensed milk, some tins of food and a pot of jam, which he took home in his haversack. He made the best of a bad job, telling himself that it was healthier to eat a light meal at night. He had expected to find this shopping painful, because it might be a source of rumours, but it turned out not to be.

On the other hand, two new facts *were* painful. One was the recognition that the countryside no longer interested him. Just as, in his conversations on the first day with the wheelbarrow man and the innkeeper, he had given a firework display of all his country knowledge, and now had no fireworks left because he had said all he had to say, in the same way he had used up during the first two days all his reserves of feeling in regard to Nature. Forced to admit he was no longer the same man as he had been at Chatenay, he looked at himself with the expression worn by cows when they watch a train go by and by men when they discover the meaning of the term 'integrated personality'.

What also pained him, unsociable though he was, was the feeling of having been deserted, a feeling that was now stronger than ever. He acknowledged it with comical surprise; it gave him the look of a girl at a ball who has had few invitations to dance, and it hurt him even more than his lack of money. M. Octave replied to his lyrical letter with a message congratulating himself on his nephew's happiness at Fréville. These congratulations arrived just when Léon was beginning to be unhappy. But neither Mlle de Bauret nor Elie nor Mélanie answered him. And when he arrived at Chandelier's, where he had his mail addressed, and was told once more that there was nothing for him, his eyelids twitched and his throat went dry. It was Mélanie's silence which hurt him most of all.

The coarseness of the people among whom he had to eat at Chandelier's, which had delighted him at first ('Simple people! The good, natural life!') he now found hard to bear.

'Come on, I'll stand you a noggin if you can prove there's a God.'

'If only I'd drunk when I was young! But I've only been boozing for the past eighteen years. What about you, how much d'you drink a day?'

'Well, I'd say about six litres, like everyone else.'

He was tired of hearing such remarks. He felt as isolated as though he were alone on an island. His thoughts now wandered back to the house in the Boulevard Arago. Arago! There was Uncle Elie there, who after all was one of the family, his mother's brother, who could be obliging enough when he chose, and was almost touching when he volunteered to deliver by hand (so that he could remove the stamp) a letter he had been asked to post. With Uncle Elie he could always go and gossip when he was too bored—he remembered the day he had asked him to help with a division sum which he could not work out because of the decimal point (and the old man had failed too). At Arago, too, there was Uncle Octave, eternally helpful. And there was Mélanie, a temperamental, peevish, insufferable old bird, but reliable and devoted. All of them people who had known his mother (how important this fact had suddenly become for him!), all of them from the same cell, and most of them congealed together, as it were, by having lived together so long. Arago meant 'security' (his mind continually fastened on this word). Arago meant *home*— he discovered this new word. And the Arago days were gone for ever!

At last he received a note from Mélanie, trivial and brief. She said, with a touch of sourness, that M. Elie was pleased with his boarding-house. He realized she was jealous, and was glad. The idea of persuading Mélanie to come and live at Fréville crossed his mind. Then it faded. But for a moment it had shone.

After a few days, Chandelier informed Léon that the boy could bring him his meals again. The innkeeper had pretended he was not available in order to sicken M. de Coantré with the keeper's house and force him to take a room at the inn. His plot having failed, he now regretted the profits he was losing through Léon's eating at home. Léon saw through the manoeuvre, and would have liked to refuse: now that he had grown used to tinned food, he appreciated its convenience and especially its cheapness. But he was afraid to incur Chandelier's resentment. It was the first time it had struck him quite so forcibly that he was at the mercy of this brute, and he realized the drawbacks of the country, where there is no choice of people as in a city, and you have to come to terms with everybody. He agreed to have the boy back, but held out for doing the house-work himself.

Often he would take out his wallet to see how much money he had left. But having done so, he was afraid to count the notes, and left it open beside him before pocketing it again. At last he made up his mind. Expecting to find three hundred francs, he found two hundred and twenty. What would he do when they were spent? Appeal to Uncle Octave once more? The latter knew perfectly well, after all, when he gave him five hundred francs, that such a pittance would soon run out! Why hadn't he set him up properly, if only to be rid of him for a while? (Léon envisaged quite calmly the most humiliating possibilities.) He was turning all this over in his mind when he began to feel unwell, mildly at first, then with agonizing sharpness. His fingers were cold, and so, too, was the upper surface of his thighs. Like a drowning man searching desperately for something to cling on to, he wanted to concentrate on some action or other; so he snatched up some nail-clippers and cut his nails. Feeling worse, he went to the lavatory, although he felt no need to do so. But it seemed to him that any change which occurred in his body might bring him some relief. . . .

The feeling eventually disappeared, leaving him with that sensation of weakness and heaviness combined which he had already experienced more than once—during his night in Montmartre, for example. It was the combined weakness and heaviness of his flabby, drooping body, that succession of thick and thin strokes—the big head and the narrow chest, the bulging stomach and the skinny legs. He sat there limp and shrivelled in his chair, thinking of the old familiar Arago sounds: the squeaking of the rats, the crack of a splintered lamp-glass, the falling of the coal in the stove, the voice of M. Elie giving orders to the cats. Had he been at Arago now,

Mélanie would have plied him with her own special medicines and M. Elie would have said in an avuncular way: 'Mustn't stay like that, my boy. Oh no, that won't do at all,' and gone off to fetch the doctor—for he adored going to fetch the doctor because it made him feel important and at the same time gave him something to do. Suddenly the clock chimed. Léon gave a sudden, violent start. The chiming of the clock made him want to cry.

He thought he must have grown weaker through going short of food.

He went to look at himself in the mirror, convinced that it must show in his face that he was a sick man. But he could see nothing abnormal in his face. He simply found it ludicrous.

However, less perhaps from concern for his health as from the need for some human contact which would cleanse him of the atmosphere of the inn, he decided to pay a visit that afternoon to Dr Gibout, general practitioner at Saint-Pierre-du-Buquet, a market-town which could be reached in half an hour's walk and a twenty minute bus-ride. M. Octave had told him, 'You'll have two people to rely on at Fréville: Chandelier and Gibout. You'll see Gibout for yourself—he's a real countryman, a big, round fellow, father of four, and an excellent doctor. He could have been a Deputy ten times over, but he prefers to do his job, and *he makes money*[1] hand over fist.

Mme de Coantré had made a cult of illness. She had a little cupboard entirely devoted to prescriptions (all of which were kept, sometimes for as long as twenty years), to those marvellous advertisements for patent remedies which one has only to read to feel cured, and to phials and bottles of medicine, which sacred economy forbade one to throw away as long as some of the mixture remained. Even though the mixture must long ago have gone bad, it was still kept and it was not until the day it was needed that its sinister colours would prompt the decision to throw it out. Léon's relations with doctors had always been strange. Whoever was looking after him, Léon alternated sharply between the notion that this doctor knowingly and deliberately was killing him and the notion that the

[1] In English in the original.

163

mere presence of this doctor in his neighbourhood was enough to prevent his dying. According to the mood of the moment, Léon would either defy the doctor's orders not to smoke, for example, and deliberately smoke a great deal; or, on the other hand, he would be pusillanimity itself and could be seen standing in the middle of a crowd on the edge of the pavement absorbed in a mysterious occupation which they could not understand: he was feeling his pulse. Sometimes, to the suspension of all other business, he would go back to see the doctor to check up on some minor point—whether a tablet should be chewed or swallowed—and at other times it was terrifying to see him, having mislaid the spoon, swigging his potion from the bottle. All this was the height of incoherence, though not so very different as one might think from the behaviour of a normal man towards doctors and medicine.

If M. Octave had not sung the praises of Gibout, M. de Coantré might not have been able to bring himself to cross the doctor's threshold that afternoon. This poor man would have refused to put his life in the hands of a man who gave the appearance of poverty—which may perhaps justify the Chandeliers' stricken faces and the atmosphere of catastrophe that had pervaded the room at the inn when the count had revealed that he had no money. This wretched little garden, this dusty, threadbare door-mat, these dull, greenish door brasses, this broken bell-push, this slattern who opened the door, this smelly little hall . . . And yet, as M. Octave had said, the doctor was rolling in money and dealt on terms of equality with all the nobs in the *département*. M. de Coantré wrote 'Count de Coantré, nephew of Baron de Coëtquidan' on a piece of paper and sent it in to the doctor. Then he went into the waiting-room, which was already occupied by a lady whose mourning clothes gave her an air of superficial dignity.

He had just sat down, and had not yet had time to give way to his uneasiness about the welcome he would receive from the great man, when the door into the consulting-room opened and Gibout walked in. He came up to him and asked if he would mind waiting while he dealt with the lady, and they whinnied politely in one another's faces. Gibout recalled Chandelier in age and appearance:

he was indeed a 'rustic', whom one could visualize in a blue peasant's smock; ill-shaven, florid, with short, thick curls like the fringe on an ox's forehead. His trousers, worn too low, left a gap below the waistcoat revealing his leather belt and even an expanse of shirt.

After a quarter of an hour he reappeared and led Léon into his consulting-room.

'So you're M. de Coëtquidan's nephew! I see, so your mother was his sister? . . . Quite so. And therefore you must be related to the Champagnys?'

'I call Mme de Champagny "cousin", but I couldn't tell you exactly how we're related . . .'

'Your cousin! Well, how very interesting! Tell me, then, is it true that she's a first cousin of the de la Naves?'

'Goodness! I haven't the least idea.'

'You see, in my spare time I collect documents about the families in the neighbourhood. I suppose you're only here for a short stay, but if ever you had a moment I should be delighted to show them to you and ask your advice.'

'Alas! I don't know much about it. As you see, although the Champagnys are my cousins, I should be incapable of explaining how,' said M. de Coantré who had come for medical treatment.

'What a pity! Your uncle told me more or less the same thing. But with him it's a fad. You know what he told me? That all the gentry were fools, and the only intelligent ones were those who had married Jewesses, because they then acquire something of the Jewish intelligence. Ah! it's a great pity the nobility don't take more trouble to get to know one another better and form a united front. But still it's something, by Jove, to have been on top for four hundred years! You can always tell a gentleman, you know. I've met them in Morocco, for example, settlers in the *bled* dressed like highway robbers. Well, one look at them and I could see they had that something that gave them the right at certain moments to sneer at the rest of us.'

'I can't say I've ever noticed that something,' said M. de Coantré, making a wry face.

He looked at this grubby man, reeking with vulgarity, this slovenly peasant with his passion for the nobility. He longed to talk to him about his health, but he felt it might be tactless, that he would be regarded as a spoil-sport. It was Gibout who came to his rescue.

'Enough of this gossip! I haven't yet asked you what brings you here. Nothing serious, I'm sure,' he said jovially. And having dismissed this tiresome possibility, he leapt on to his hobby horse and was back in the clouds once more. 'Still, I should have liked to show you first of all the château of Champagny. I've got a photo of it here which the baron gave me himself. It isn't on sale, which is why I'm so keen on it.'

'I know Champagny well,' said Léon. 'I stayed there when I was a young man.'

It was no good. Gibout was determined to show him his château. He searched for the photograph. M. de Coantré wondered if there were suffering patients next door waiting with bated breath to be told if they were going to die or not. He wondered if Gibout would ever be able to recover enough detachment of mind to examine him seriously. Finally the doctor produced a green cardboard box full of envelopes, each of which contained a postcard. The envelopes were annotated and each of them bore a coat of arms drawn in pen and ink.

'Here we are, this is Champagny,' said Gibout, as if Léon had not told him that he had been a guest at the château. 'And here's the Macé de Thianville's. You must know them, they're also cousins of yours.'

'I don't think so,' said Léon in the accents of truth.

'Yes, yes. They are your cousins. Mme Macé de Thianville was a des Mureaux, not the des Mureaux of the Aveyronnais, the branch which . . .' (he recited a pedigree). 'Well, well! I must say it's a bit thick that I should have to tell you who your relations are! But here we are, the proof. . . .'

He opened a file which was bursting with clippings from the society columns of the *Figaro*.

'Yes,' he said, 'I keep in touch. You have to!' And he showed him a des Mureaux in the wedding procession of a Macé de Thian-

166

ville—which led to a long rigmarole. All these titled people from the society pages, whom he had never seen in his life and who, if the occasion arose, would have given him a glass of red wine in the kitchen like the plumber—or very nearly—were extraordinarily alive to him, almost familiar companions.

At last he came down from the clouds.

'However, enough of this. We can talk about it another time. Let's have a look at this health of yours.'

Now that it was no longer a question of trivialities but of the serious business that had brought him there, M. de Coantré suddenly felt that he was a fool, or must look a fool, and began to jabber incoherently. His forehead became moist with sweat. Any examining magistrate who had heard him would immediately have judged him guilty. He explained about his tiredness, and the attacks he had had that morning and when he had gone to pay his final visit to the house in the Boulevard Arago. Examining him with a stethoscope, Gibout stuck his greasy, dandruff-spattered head under his nose, exuding a powerful odour of ill-kept male. Then he made Léon breathe in and out, and took his blood pressure.

'Everything in perfect order, Monsieur de Coantré,' he said at last. 'There's *nothing* wrong with you. I can give you an ab-so-lutely clean bill of health.'

'Nothing?'

'Let's say a bit of nervous hyperaesthesia, just to please you. . . .'

M. de Coantré, if not exactly disappointed, was at least put out. That very moment, he had an intense and powerful conviction that Gibout was mistaken; *he* could feel that alien presence inside himself, that terrible presence of illness. But thinking that his supposed good health must make him seem in Gibout's eyes a simpleton or an alarmist, he began to complain of imaginary ailments in order to justify his visit, as a young penitent in the confessional will confess imaginary sins if he finds that his authentic ones are not interesting enough to be taken seriously. But to everything Gibout replied: 'Excellent! . . . absolutely normal . . .'

'He's made up his mind,' the count said to himself, 'he's determined to contradict me. Nothing will make him let go. Fancy being

167

ill with a doctor who *won't hear* of your being ill! I'm in a fine mess!
I can understand a military doctor automatically assuming that
there's nothing wrong with you, since you're not paying him. But a
doctor whom you're paying—that's a bit stiff!'

'So you won't give me a prescription?' he asked gloomily.

There are doctors who dazzle their patients by prescribing all
sorts of complicated things. Gibout dazzled them by prescribing
nothing. And it is true that this is more subtle.

'No drugs, Monsieur de Coantré! No drugs! But every day,
before dinner, a nice warm bath. Nothing more. You're lucky M.
de Coëtquidan has had a bathroom installed at Fréville . . .'

M. de Coantré realized that Gibout was under the impression he
was staying in the château. He was too ashamed to undeceive him.
Instead he asked him, in that flat tone of voice with which one asks a
doctor for details of a treatment he has prescribed and which one
has no intention of following:

'You couldn't tell me what temperature, more or less?'

'I said a *nice, warm* bath. In fact, everything you do for the next
fortnight at least should be pleasant and enjoyable. Above all, no
worries!'

M. de Coantré looked at Gibout as he had often looked at M.
Octave when M. Octave was wandering happily in the sphere in
which rich people move. But there is another sphere, in which
healthy people move, and it is in this sphere that doctors move.

'By the way, before you go,' said Gibout, 'I'll show you something that will interest you. The D'Hozier of 1738, with an account
of the Coëtquidans. Imagine, the last time your uncle came to see
me, a fortnight ago, I said to him: "M. de Coëtquidan, here's a tip
from the horse's mouth. There's an odd copy of this volume now on
sale at Champions—I've just seen it in the catalogue. And for next to
nothing, two hundred francs. Only be quick about it." And do you
know what he said? "If you think I'd ever waste two hundred francs
on an old book!" And this same man who haggles over two hundred francs gives eight thousand francs to a charity he's never even
heard of!'

'He gave eight thousand francs to a charity?'

'Didn't he tell you? Well I never, that's real modesty for you! He said to me: "I can't understand this sudden desire to do good which came over me a fortnight ago. You haven't any pills against that? When it happened, I looked through my sister's list of charities and said to myself I'd send eight thousand francs to the one I came across when I opened the book at random. The one I hit upon was called *L'Oeuvre des Berceaux Abandonnés,* which is quite obviously a vast swindle like the rest of them. And I sent the eight thousand francs." And he added: "I know it's not a very French way to behave. More American really . . ."'

'But . . . when did he do this? M. de Coantré asked in a faint voice.

'He was here about a fortnight ago, and it was quite recent, because he said he'd had an answer from them the week before.'

'Forgive me,' said M. de Coantré, 'I don't feel well. . . .'

He had leaned forward in his chair, like someone trying to get a change of air.

'What's wrong?'

' . . . I'm sorry to be a nuisance . . . but . . . I think I'm going to faint. . . .'

Seeing the dead pale face, Gibout leapt to his feet and said: 'Lie down on the sofa.' At the same moment, M. de Coantré stood up, twisted round a little, murmuring in a weak voice:

'I'm sorry . . . I'm sorry . . .' and Gibout caught him in his arms.

═══ 10 ═══

M. DE COANTRÉ was shattered by the doctor's disclosure. M. Octave's action in throwing eight thousand francs out of the window when his nephew was destitute seemed to him monstrous and inexcusable. He was quite incapable of understanding the secret reasons for it, and if he had understood them he would not have accepted them; for they were too wounding to him. Nor was he the sort of man who would say: 'However unkind he has been to me, I've been equally unkind to lots of other people. And yet I'm not a bad sort. Therefore old Octave is probably a good man.' Such insights do not occur to average people: they must keep their illusions. Between M. de Coantré and M. de Coëtquidan something finally snapped. And so this long exercise in equilibrium—for any relationship between two human beings is a precarious balancing act—had broken down at last! And so the infinite pains that Léon had taken to maintain this balance had been a waste of effort! Shaving before going to visit Uncle Octave, remembering not to wear brown boots with his black suit, although his black boots hurt him and his brown ones did not—everything he had done of this kind had been in vain, and regret at having put himself out for nothing recurred insistently amongst all his other feelings, occasionally overriding them all. He felt in addition a genuine heartache, for the cupboard love he professed for his uncle included an element of real affection. We understand nothing of life until we have understood that it is one vast confusion.

'It's all too much for me,' he said to himself humbly. 'Yes, it's all too much for someone who is not too strong in the head.' Up to then he hadn't understood. 'Are they going to let me starve? After all, they won't let me starve.' Now he knew. They would let him starve.

In a single day he grew older and uglier. His face remained plump and youthful enough, but the dull, lack-lustre look in his eyes, with their dark circles and heavy pouches, made them look as if they did not belong to his face, like two holes made by a rat in an otherwise healthy cheese.

He had decided not to ask M. Octave for any more money. If M. Octave sent him some he would accept it; but he would not ask for any more. He had one hundred and ninety francs left. Remembering Mlle de Bauret's remark: 'If ever you need anything . . .', he wrote to her (in his more and more proconsular handwriting, firm, forceful, grandiloquent). But his only real hope lay with Mélanie. As we have seen, he had been brought up under the 'genteel' delusion that the people can always be relied on, that they are far more worthy of respect than the propertied classes. He imagined some sort of association with Mélanie—without (for very good reasons) going into any details—but at any rate cohabitation of a kind. But, since he could live nowhere more cheaply than at Fréville, he would have to stay there a little longer, at least until he received the money from his niece. Moreover, having told Chandelier that he would stay for a month, to leave now would be to run the risk of a row. The innkeeper might even insist on being paid for the full month. 'He doesn't like me, and I believe he's capable of anything,' he thought to himself, and fear made his eyelids twitch. 'I must do my utmost to keep on good terms with him until the end.'

'No mail?' he inquired in a scarcely audible voice as he arrived at the inn for dinner.

'No.'

Within a few seconds he had begun to tremble all over. It was grief that made him tremble. But once he began to eat the trembling ceased.

As he ate, he felt more sharply than ever that he was surrounded by a circle of contempt and hatred and surreptitious looks. Because he was poor, because he was noble, because he was poor *and* noble, because he was a townsman, because he was different. A mystery to all, and therefore an affront. Irremediably apart. As remote from his fellow-countrymen as if he were in the depths of Amazonia. And yet there was one thing they had in common with him, mediocrity; they ought to have liked him, but the difference prevailed. He could feel, he could *see*, the insolence on the tips of their tongues, ready to spurt out at the slightest word or gesture on his part which might be misinterpreted, and he felt trapped. As in his war-time hospital, he was afraid to raise his eyes, and he smoked between courses to keep his courage up. He could not understand how everything had gone so well at Chatenay; but there was nothing to understand except that people and circumstances and he himself had changed (the basic difference was that at Chatenay he had had money, or could have had it). And again he thought of the contrast with Paris, where nobody took any notice of him. Clearly, Paris was the only place where one could be poor with impunity. In the country you had to be the master, the lord of the manor, or merely a bird of passage.

Passing through the village on the way home, he hunched his shoulders and kept his eyes lowered. Again this phobia about being *watched*!

On his return from Saint-Pierre he had put back in his suitcase and trunk everything he had taken out of them—except what he needed for current use—as if to keep himself constantly reminded that he would soon be leaving. Besides, he was gratified in his feeble-minded way at having all his possessions collected together, capable of being taken in at a single glance; this unity assuaged him.

He had taken once more to his habit of spending the whole of the afternoon stretched out on his bed—gradually he was trying to resume all his Arago habits. But his rest was continually disturbed by the log fire: time and again he had to get up because a log rolled on to the floor, because sparks flew out, because the fire was going down or because it was blazing up too fiercely; or else the chimney was smoking, and no sooner had the room become pleasantly warm than the window had to be thrown wide open to get rid of the smoke. Ah! the rural life is dearly bought! Even in an old den like Arago he had worked out a day-to-day system whereby everything was in order. As he lay on the bed, his eyes remained glued to his suitcase and trunk, the symbols of departure. For all that M. Octave's 'wicked action' had yesterday cast a shadow over the whole Arago period, in his desperate need for something to look forward to he dreamed of his departure from Fréville for Paris, as long ago in the army, he had dreamed of leaving the army, as at Arago he had dreamed of leaving Arago, and even as at Chatenay, he had dreamed of leaving Chatenay, though this he would never have admitted. Such are the ways of men.

Two days after his visit to Gibout, he received at Chandelier's a letter post-marked Saint-Pierre-du-Buquet. Gibout! He imagined that the doctor must have had an attack of remorse, must have decided to take him seriously after his fainting fit, was writing to inquire about his health and prescribe some treatment. It was like a ray of sunlight. He opened the envelope and drew out an enormous piece of paper—two big sheets stuck together with glue. It was the genealogical tree of the Macé de Thianville family, which the doctor had entirely copied out by hand.

Next day he had another attack. Sitting in his chair as on the previous occasion, he stared all round him with a hunted look, his mouth open, like those shell-shocked soldiers who say to you: 'Take my hand'. As on the previous occasion, the need to do something, no matter what, drove him to get up and go and look for some eau-de-Cologne. He stood there sniffing the eau-de-Cologne and fanning himself with a piece of blotting-paper, thinking he was going to die any moment and accepting the idea without the slightest emotion. His pulse was imperceptible. His anguish became so intense that he put down the eau-de-Cologne and the blotting-paper. Now he did nothing but press his hands together—cracked and shrivelled like dead leaves—and stare at them; they had become the centre of his world. After a time he felt released, and stopped looking at his hands.

A phrase came into his head, which from then on haunted him: '. . . no more joking'. For some buffoon of stage or literature to react to a warning of tragedy with a 'Joke over' is understandable. But why M. de Coantré?

He made up his mind to go back to Gibout. His emotion seemed to him irresistible. This time he would be able to convince the doctor that he deserved attention.

At Chandelier's, he could not eat; the food would not go down. Sitting at the end of the room with his greatcoat over his shoulders (he was always cold) and his felt hat on his head (to distinguish himself less from his neighbours by being as plebeian as they), he watched these coarse yokels at the counter, with their shouts, their frightful healthiness, their paunches one longed to stick a knife into, their teeth which were so green they looked like so many rows of vegetables. The world became divided for him into two spheres: his own, and that of healthy people. He was so cold (his calves especially were cold) that he drank three small glasses of rum.

Chandelier disliked M. de Coantré even more now that he was sick, but this is too natural an impulse for us to condemn him on that score.

'Seems he's a count!' he would explain to customers. 'As soon as I saw him arrive I said to the old man: "He's a bad hat. Look at the bags he's got under his eyes. That's a sure sign, you know." Something tells me that he's been up to no good. Right from the start he tried to worm his way in. But we didn't let him.'

Chandelier's 'soul' was made up of three attributes, exactly three: avarice, dishonesty, and envy. In this Chandelier was a fair specimen of his kind.

Six people, male and female, were waiting in Gibout's ante-room when Léon arrived. He sat down and went over in his mind what he would say to the doctor, 'You know, I think the time has come to take it firmly in hand.' In order to ingratiate himself, he intended to promise him some sensational information about the relations of the Champagnys in the Nivernais.

Time passed. Léon studiously refrained from touching the books and illustrated papers laid out on the table; in common with all the other patients, his mind was a blank—he developed to the utmost the impressive power he had of taking no interest in anything. After twenty-five minutes, no one having yet been ushered into the consulting-room, abusive thoughts crossed M. de Coantré's mind: 'Gibout is making love to his wife,' or 'He's reading his newspaper and has left us mouldering here simply in order to create an impression of being overloaded with work,' or 'He's engaged in genealogical investigations aimed at discovering which of the two is marrying beneath it in the marriage of the carp and the rabbit.' He realized that he felt nothing but ill-will and contempt for this man in whose hands he was placing his life. He could not forgive him for not having taken him seriously; nor, perhaps, could he forgive him his health, his children, his money. The silence of a baccarat salon reigned in the waiting-room, and on the faces there was a bovine brutishness. No one, it seemed, resented this long wait, as though the present prostration of these people was little different from their normal state. At last, after forty-five minutes, Gibout opened the door and made a sign with his head: 'First please'. An old woman got up and went in. During this short instant Gibout gave M. de Coantré a smile.

A quarter of an hour went by. Léon had been faintly surprised to see that Gibout did not signal to him to go in first. 'After all, I am the Count de Coantré, nephew of the Baron de Coëtquidan. Is he going to let half a dozen peasants and their wives go in front of me? Perhaps he has had a note from old Octave since the other day leaving him in no doubt about my social standing.' It was certainly something new for Léon to be sensitive about what was due to him. M. de Coantré on his high horse—that was a sight! He had waited hours in Lebeau's waiting-room and been quite happy. Perhaps this fit of ill-humour arose partly from his physical weakness, partly from the extreme of moral wretchedness to which recent events had brought him. He had reached the end of his tether, and now must pass into an entirely different state. He had been beaten like a piece of red-hot iron, and was now becoming solid.

When Gibout opened the door again Léon glared at him. Gibout gave him a friendly look and said, 'Can you wait just a moment?' to which he replied with good grace, 'Yes of course.'

His ill-humour had vanished, melted by a smile from Gibout. But as the visit dragged on, his anger rose again and swelled within him, and the blood rose to his cheeks. A mad idea crossed his mind and stayed there just long enough to be rejected: the idea of making a sensational exit. He realised the folly of it: cutting himself off from the only man here who could do something for him! He went on waiting.

No one who had seen him then would have recognized either the good-natured expression of the Coantré of Arago or the agonized face of the poor wretch emerging that morning from his attack. This sudden insistence on being treated with respect, together with his impatience at not being so treated, gave him an unusual, an almost unbelievable expression of hardness. At that moment he really hated Gibout, and he gave himself up to this hatred with a feeling of profound release. It did him good, made him feel a new man, as though he had just taken a swig of strong alcohol. For the first time in years his back was no longer bent: whatever the components of this feeling—anger, hatred, pride, malevolence—it was certainly a vigorous affirmation of life. He was sharply aware that he would be unable to avoid being rude to Gibout when the doctor received him, and that moreover he would make no effort not to be. Every other minute he looked at his watch. Once more the idea of leaving swept over him. He *knew* that the moment would come when there would be nothing left inside him to resist it. . . .

Suddenly he got up, went to the door and exclaimed in a biting voice, but without looking anyone in the face: 'If *you* don't mind being kept hanging around by a quack!' He opened the door. He could hear someone getting up in the next-door room. The maid appeared.

'Will you tell your master that I'm not the sort of man who waits for an hour and a half outside a village doctor's door.'

He went out. The night had fallen. His anger had all the characteristics of drunkenness: it gave him the courage and the pleasure that drunkenness gives. This feeling is not peculiar to the weak: 'Anger is sweet as honey,' Achilles said. He had gone no more than a few yards when he saw the bus, which had just stopped. He got on to it.

There were only three passengers in the bus, which flew along between two rows of phantoms (the white-painted trunks of the trees bordering the road), its speed matching the rhythm of his feelings. 'Now I understand,' he kept repeating to himself. What had he understood? In what way had his life been changed? The abyss still yawned in front of it. But something *had* changed, and that was his own opinion of himself. Just as the slats of certain shutters open at the slightest touch, turning a dark room into a sunlit fairyland, so a simple change of attitude—recalcitrance instead of acquiescence—transformed his inner world from shadow to sunlight.

He got off at the stopping-place and started down the forest path. The forest was empty of noise, scent and colour. Under the sky heavy with snow, great cold clouds sped by. The moon, blurred like a young girl's face after a night of love, was giving its habitual performance—now above a roof, now among the branches, now running into a cloud like a rabbit into its burrow—the whole thing devoid of the slightest pretension to poetry, the despair of the literary man. The pines formed a screen against the sea wind, their trunks silhouetted against the pale sky, tall, vertical rods that suggested a clump of huge tapers. But when M. de Coantré passed through a clearing the wind hurled itself at him and the trees swayed and knocked against each other like drunken men. Within sight of Picot's house he stopped to look at some wild geese migrating. The formation was the shape of a long ribbon flying very low—six hundred feet perhaps—sinuous and all of a piece like some flying carpet from the Arabian Nights or a monstrous serpent of the air. The geese—some fifty of them—were flying straight into the wind, a calm and vigorous flight, without passion or pretence. When the leader changed direction all the rest followed him with such speed and unanimity that the formation, from one end to the other, seemed to be revolving on a hinge; and the whole line, revealing their chests and bellies instead of their coats, changed from grey-brown to ash-grey. Motionless, M. de Coantré watched them until they had disappeared. *They* were free! *They* had no money troubles! *They* were going to the sunlit lands! And he remained lost in thought, struck by the impression of will, of cohesion, of mystery, of something brought from afar, which the flight left behind it, like the trail of a dream across the empty sky.

The fire in the house had gone out. He relit it. Going outside to fetch some more sticks, he heard the cry of the geese, their migratory call, so different from their call at normal times (both feminine calls, more tuneful than the call of the wild duck). He searched the sky but could not pick out the new flock: they were flying too high. And there was something disquieting about these signs of a life that could not be seen, these cries that seemed to have been uttered by the sky itself. M. de Coantré remained there for as long as he thought he could hear them still. When he went in, the fire had again gone out, and again he relit it.

He settled down and, keeping his greatcoat and his hat on, dined off tinned food. He ate little, having found few provisions in the cupboard. If he had eaten a lot his feelings during the hours that followed would have been different. If he had had a few drinks, they would have been different still. Which shows how little importance these feelings had; chance made them what they were; all feelings are like that.

'Now I understand,' he kept repeating to himself as he ate. He had understood the prescription that could cure him of his misery: this prescription was pride. 'Why didn't I think of it before?' Through pride he had broken with the man who could have saved his life. Through pride he had broken with the man who could have given him money. And all his misfortunes passed automatically from a sordid to a lofty plane, where they no longer hurt him.

Meanwhile the fire had again gone out. This struggle with the fire was exhausting. He wondered whether to relight it, and then with a weary shrug, 'Ah well, since it doesn't want to,' he tucked himself fully clothed between the sheets. He lay there quite still, his eyes wide open staring at the wall, watching the steam from his breath which seemed to fill the room with a sort of alien presence. He tried to distinguish in the silence the cries of other migrants. But he could hear nothing, except from time to time a piece of furniture cracking with the wild force of a man or a beast. If he had heard the geese he would have dragged himself from the warmth and gone out, so moved had he been by the first flight. Thus do secluded invalids put worlds of nostalgia into the contemplation of a corner of blue sky or the evocation of a landscape. And there are simple and even coarse people who are overcome by a mysterious poetic emotion, like nothing they have ever experienced in their lives—to the point of beginning to write verse—when the hand of death is upon them.

He put out the light. The cold seemed to him more intense, and he pulled the sheet over his head as he used to in the days of Mariette when he wanted to think of her more vividly. He had a poignant impression—was it partly an effect of the darkness?—that his new-found strength was leaving him, was returning to the atmosphere, like an intoxication wearing off, or the heat and glow draining away from an electric fire that has just been put out (his eyes themselves were going out). And yet this strength did not leave him quite as it had found him. He had been carried to the extremity of his being, and then beyond, into a region that was almost unknown to him, by a long ground-swell, and now, withdrawing, it left him alone, remote, detached from himself and from everything else. 'No one! no one!' he repeated inside himself. Under the sheet a smile, which was the final flower of his sadness, took shape on his features and stayed there, and he shook his head slightly as if to say, 'Incredible! It's incredible!' When he had already sunk into sleep, this mysterious smile was still on his lips.

Outside, the uneventful night went on. The whole forest crackled with the wind and the cold. The sleeping toads throbbed in the undergrowth, shaken by their too-powerful hearts. The foxes slept in their dens, snouts resting on one another's spines, thrilled by their stench, and the wild boars in their lairs dreamed of the star-cracked ice they had licked in the evening light. In newly-formed puddles the water congealed once more, and all around the mud hardened on the trunks of the trees against which hinds and stags had rubbed themselves. But in the depths of the clear sky, above the crouching stillness, the wild geese were still passing, their feet tucked under their bellies, borne by the wind among the myriad insects of the upper regions, along the great migratory route, like those invisible ocean routes for ships or the routes followed by the stars. These new flocks were flying in V-formation, each bird almost touching the next except for three which flew alone for no apparent reason. The unbelievable power of their flight created up there the whirlwind noise of a group of cyclists on a racing track. Sometimes the V broke up, and the fragments continued in the same direction. Then they joined up again, drawn towards one another by a sort of magnetic attraction, while another current of attraction drew the whole flight towards the south like the needle of a compass or a magician's wand. But still the three dissenters, strange and self-willed, flew on alone as though deep in thought.

Having slept a little, M de Coantré woke up to find himself equipped with a plan he had vaguely considered during the summer and which now reappeared in the shape of a definite decision: the very next day he would go into hospital in Le Havre. He had no doubts about being accepted there: either they would regard him as indigent, and he would be taken in without having to pay, or they would bank on his family doing the necessary when the time came. He had relapsed into a state in which he felt he had no rights but, as before, still counted on pity and charity. As for his illness, whatever it was, although he did not know whether it was serious or not, he was quite capable of passing himself off as more unwell than in fact he was: even in this solemn hour his little subterfuges had not deserted him. No matter how little good they had done him, no matter how many warnings fate had given him, he received not a glimmer of light, and what he was he would remain to the end. And in the low houses of the hamlet, as in the lairs of the forest, the same inner darkness enclosed both beasts and men, fraternal puppets, in their sleep that was scarcely less conscious than their waking hours.

The prospect of the hospital gave him almost as much of a fillip as he had received from his outburst at the doctor's. In hospital he would be warm without having to look after a fire; he would have the pleasant sensation of feeling his bare legs under the sheet without having to keep on his trousers, or even his underpants, as he had always had to here. Oh, there was no longer any question of pride. For a moment pride had held him upright like a steel corset; the corset once loosened, the body had gone limp again. Above all, his departure for the hospital gave him a precise aim for the following day, providing an escape from the sinister, the hellish idleness which awaited him. As soon as he got up in the morning he planned to give his body a bit of a wash, and then to strap up his trunk and suitcase. The very thought of this made him quiver with joy; he felt brave enough to face up to Chandelier, to find, without anyone's help in this hostile or seemingly hostile village, a man who would cart his luggage to the bus-stop . . . Through the shutters, the glow of the night penetrated the room, and as he thought of the wild geese winging their way towards the warmth and the light, his own hopes merged with that other hope flying high up in the skies.

They had foregathered two days earlier in solemn tumult, flapping their wings and chattering, driven by a divine impulse—their desire to be happy. For some time already they had been practising long flights to assuage their restless longing to be off. What they wanted was to give themselves a long holiday of love and pleasure in the sun, after which, for the nesting season, the season of worries and chores, they could return to the duller regions. They knew what a hard and exhausting journey lay ahead of them, they knew how many of them would come down on a pond for a rest and be killed by a shot from a wildfowler, how many would fall in the sea to the delight of the sharks, how many would be devoured by the sinister peregrine falcons which followed them in their flight. But none of this discouraged them, any more than the night, the wind, the rain, the mist, the absence of landmarks. Beyond were the Pyrenean passes, where the rain and the mist would cease abruptly as though an aerial partition blocked their way; beyond was the fragrance of Spain, and the green and the blue waters of Gibraltar, lying side by side without merging, and blue-breasted Tangier, a turtle-dove on the shoulder of Africa; and further still the warm, pink ponds sunk in their blazing torpor. And they set off, not wanting to stop, stopping just long enough to drink and preen themselves in a pool, hurrying, hurrying on as though they knew only too well that one can die for wasting a single minute on something other than happiness.

At this hour, too, there were men everywhere arriving in sight of death. Those who had been governed by principles and those who had feebly abandoned themselves to chance, those who had tortured themselves for nothing and those who had had no thought but to enjoy themselves, those who had done wrong and those who had not—all, when they arrived in sight of the Great Wall, acquired a mutual resemblance that was a kind of admission. It was hard to see how they differed and had differed from one another. It was even harder to see what use it had been to them to try to be different, to try to excel, to want this rather than that, to believe this rather than that. Everything, in the last resort, came to the same thing; it had all been, for every one of them, a way of passing the time, and now these men who had lived scattered and hostile were drawing together, like a group of men who are obliged to pass through the same door. M. de Coantré was among them, somewhere, more or less identical with each one of them (since they all had more or less the same face), not much higher than the base and the criminal, not much lower than the heroic and the renowned.

Suddenly he awoke with a start. It was no longer either the proud-souled Coantré, or the timidly hopeful Coantré, but yet another Coantré who raised himself up with a jerk, clutching the sheet with both fists, and sat there bolt upright, quite still, his eyes dilated, like a bat clinging to a wall. His soul, in its last convulsion, sucked in the skin of his face, hollowing his cheeks and eye-sockets until he was quite disfigured. Cold hands already grasped his hands, but he no longer felt them now; he had gone beyond all that. Then he let go of the sheet, and his hands went up to the iron bed-posts.

Suddenly he cried out in a terrible voice, 'Madame Mélanie, stay with me! I don't want to die alone!' His right hand, gripping the bed-post with the strength of a gorilla, twisted it like a rope, and then, with a great gasp, he fell back on the pillow.

II

Two DAYS having gone by without any sign of M. de Coantré, Chandelier was seized with a double anxiety—at the thought of displeasing the baron by having displeased his nephew, and at the thought that something might have happened—and went to knock on the door of Picot's house. It was closed, as also were the shutters, and there was no answer. He thought M. de Coantré might have gone back to Paris, but finding this odd, he wrote to the baron.

Ninety-nine times out of a hundred our presentiments turn out to be false, but the hundredth time they prove right and then we wag our heads and talk about 'the mysteries of life'. When M. Octave received Chandelier's letter he had a really extraordinary premonition that Léon was dead. And in the same instant burst from him, with the force of a rocket, the hope that he was.

He sent Papon to Fréville by the next train. And he thought to himself, 'If he were dead, what a miraculous solution it would be! Enough to make one believe in Providence!'

It was now four days since Léon had appeared. Papon and Chandelier went to see the mayor, who decided to have the door opened by a locksmith.

They found M. de Coantré stretched out on the bed, dead. There was nothing unusual about the corpse. Gibout, who was called, pronounced it a typical case of cerebral congestion, and the mayor gave permission for burial.

On receipt of Papon's telegram, M. Octave wired him some money with orders to get things done decently but without unnecessary expense and to have the body buried in the cemetery at Fréville. There was no question of his going there himself.

He had had a moment of uneasiness on hearing of Léon's death. Then he said to himself, 'Even admitting that I've been at fault—

which is by no means certain, one would have to look into it, examine the whole thing in detail—what's the use of torturing myself? Where he is now, he won't blame me. It's utterly pointless to worry about whether I behaved badly or not. It's all over and done with.'

Mme Emilie seemed much moved. She had thought of everything in regard to Léon except that he was mortal. 'And yet, God knows, we did everything we could for him!' After a moment devoted to reminiscence, and to groans about the necessity of bringing people from Le Havre to disinfect the keeper's house when it had already been done six weeks before, after the keeper had died, she withdrew to her room and, kneeling on her *prie-dieu*, prayed for Léon.

M. Elie received the news by express letter in the boarding-house M. Octave had found him—a boarding-house kept by a widow of respectable antecedents who had begun by letting one of her rooms to an American officer during the war and thereafter had slipped into taking lodgers, without diminishing herself in the eyes of her family by this 'business', justified as it was by its patriotic origin (another small item to add to the French debt to the United States). M. Elie, holding the letter in his hand, stood for a long time as though struck dumb, his pale eyes gazing into space, and thinking 'That's what is coming to me.'

Mélanie, who was informed by letter, felt her legs give under her and asked her concierge for a chair, into which she collapsed with a deathly look. She had to be given a glass of water etc. Among the things she said was one remarkable phrase: 'Poor M. de Coantré! He died because he had no one left to "declare himself to".' She meant, 'to confide in'.

Mlle de Bauret had been in Cannes, where she was busily pursuing an extremely attractive young Pole, when she received M. de Coantré's letter explaining his situation. She had had a twinge of impatience. 'After all, it's only a question of a few sous, whereas I've got to get hold of a man!' But she had sent off by return of post a five hundred franc postal order, which arrived after Léon's death. M. Octave's telegram announcing the news also reached her in Cannes. Without a moment's hesitation she decided that, even if it meant breaking with the entire family (but she knew very well there was no question of breaking with anyone over Léon), she would not, at any price, put herself out either for the funeral or for anything else. As she had warned everyone that she would be travelling about where the spirit moved her, she lay low for a week, and then, calculating that the funeral would already have taken place, asked a friend who was holidaying in Corsica to send the following telegram to the baron in her name: 'Only just received news, wire having followed me from town to town. Deeply regret too late etc.' Through the same channel she wrote M. Octave a 'perfect' letter.

Gibout wrote the baron a letter which was also considered 'perfect'. He explained how science is sometimes incapable of foreseeing a sudden quirk of nature. He spoke of Léon in 'perfect' terms. 'He enjoyed coming to see me because he could talk genealogy.'

At first everyone was much affected by the dramatic character of the affair, but afterwards they were pleased both for the sake of Léon, who would have dragged out a pretty miserable existence, whereas now he had rejoined his mother, and also for the sake of M. Octave, who had honourably extricated himself from a situation in which he had always had the *beau rôle* but which in the long run might have proved a burden. He was looked on with something of the tenderness people feel for a survivor from an accident. It is an elementary mistake to be surprised at people's indifference to the death of a member of their family. Not one of these people we are speaking of had loved M. de Coantré. How then could his death have aroused in them anything else but indifference? Fortunately it came as a nervous shock, which enabled them to make the appropriate faces.

At Fréville, Papon's heart throbbed with self-importance. Long live Death, for making people important! Papon was a capable man. He had been working for M. Octave for seventeen years and robbing him for only three, increasing the monthly food bill by a regular four hundred francs. He was devoted to him, and touched as

185

he was by the role he had been given in this affair, defended his interests with the utmost strictness. Thus he chose the cheapest wood for the coffin, deeming it unnecessary, like the good valet he was, to go to expense for something nobody will see.

As soon as the door of Picot's house was opened, and while the preliminary investigations were being made, Papon, confident that no one could have counted the money before him, stole eight francs from a cup in which M. de Coantré, in his bachelor way, feeling it necessary always to have small change at hand, had collected thirty francs' worth of small coins. But that of course was not the real joy which Papon received from this death. Even heirs who are genuinely grieved by the death of the 'dear departed' are nearly always consoled by the enjoyment they get from rummaging through the deceased's belongings, violating his most intimate secrets, hoping to discover something scandalous in the thick deposit which encumbers any dead person's room (letters, files, odds and ends), the sort of secretion every man produces day by day and in the midst of which he makes his nest. Society gives individuals a powerful satisfaction when it allows them in certain cases to do what they like with the complicity of the law—heirs who can rob legally, policemen who can beat people up legally, judges who can legally dispense injustice, colonial settlers who can legally murder a native whose face they do not like. Rummaging through M. de Coantré's belongings with the delicious feeling of taking part in a police inspection, Papon experienced one of the most exquisite pleasures he had ever experienced in his life. He opened a packet of letters addressed years ago by Mme de Coantré to her son and tied up with a shoe-lace. He read a few of them, but they were so innocent that they bored him and he stopped at that. He slipped Léon's diary into his pocket to read in the train on the way home (he would put it in the suitcase on arrival). He was infuriated by a sealed packet which bore the inscription: *To be burned unread after my death*. He could have read it and then thrown it away, but he did not dare. Having sorted everything out, he dined at Chandelier's and ate enough for four—for the lugubrious and the sublime induce hunger.

Much of the ill that might have been said of Léon at Fréville remained unsaid because Papon and Chandelier only spoke to one another in official circumstances, mutually regarding one another as a 'peasant' and a 'flunkey'.

M. Octave could not for a moment consider making the journey to Fréville for the funeral: the weather was too cold and his chest would not stand up to it. Still less could Mme Emilie, with her extremely delicate health. M. Elie said he was no longer of an age to catch trains at seven o'clock in the morning in winter; he would not do it for anyone, not even his brother. M. Octave was kind enough not to offer him his car and so deprive him of his excuse. The whole family had been informed, but not one of them went to Fréville. Gibout excused himself on the ground that he had a consultation at Le Havre. The only person to follow M. de Coantré's coffin was his uncle's valet.

Papon brought back M. de Coantré's little trunk: it was all that remained of the house of Coantré, like a trunk washed up on a beach, the sole remains of a sunken ship. The baron found in it some small household objects, a crucifix, a box of tools. In the address book were some cuttings of newspaper articles on the subject of longevity, which tends to prove that however bitter M. de Coantré's life may appear to some, he hoped it would not end too soon.

Papon handed over to M. Octave the bills he had incurred at Fréville. Among them was the bill for Léon's meals at Chandelier's. M. Octave considered that Léon had eaten a great deal for a man with no money. But he grew cross when he read '2 rums, 1 fr. 50', then the next day, 3 rums, 2 fr. 25', and then '1 bottle of rum, 15 francs'. This consumption of liquor was all the more impressive because Chandelier had doubled Léon's bills by adding food and drink he had not had. 'So he drank!' the baron thought. 'That explains a great many things.' And he fell into a long reverie.

One of the classic instincts of the human idiot is to reconstruct a whole animal from a single bone, but, unlike Cuvier, to do it on a false premise, the bone in question belonging to another species. If a young woman of means rejects two or three suitors simply because she suspects it was not for herself that they wanted her, how delightful to be able to explain it by saying she is a Lesbian. Why didn't we spot it before! That explains everything! What it is to have an emancipated mind! On the basis of these grubby bits of paper which showed M. de Coantré swallowing in the space of a few days a fairly considerable quantity of spirits, half of it the pure invention of a rascally café proprietor and the other half consumed only by a reflex of self-defence on the part of a poor wretch who felt the need to warm himself, frozen as he already was by the cold hands of death —on the basis of these bits of paper M. Octave reconstructed everything, understood everything: *et nunc reges intelligite*. The fact that Léon drank—a fact that was now 'established'—explained as clear as daylight the failure of the enlargers, the eccentricity of his life, his taste for 'the people'; and there it was, it was the key to everything! Even to his 'emotionalism'. 'When he was moved, and wanted to kiss me, he must have had a drop.' M. Elie having called to see his brother shortly after this great discovery, M. Octave asked him 'Did he drink?' 'I never noticed it at table,' M. Elie replied. 'But he could do what he liked in his room.' Hats off to M. Elie for this reply which contained a glimmer of honesty. It is a great mistake to put unlimited trust in the malice of men: they seldom do us all the harm they might.

Léon's supposed taste for the bottle enabled M. Octave to look upon himself as the personification of delicacy when he decided to keep his melancholy discovery from Mme Emilie. It also enabled him to believe that he had been shrewd in mistrusting his nephew, that he had been right not to help him more, and that it was more and more providential that he should have been whisked away at the required moment. Considering all the gratifications it brought, it would have been more meritorious had this established fact not been established.

Going through Léon's trunk, M. Octave came across the sealed packet inscribed *To be burned unread after my death*. He duly burnt it, with an extremely lively sense of the noble deed he was performing in not apprising himself of its contents. He could scarcely have felt prouder if, to attest some faith or other, he had roasted *himself*. M. Octave put aside Mme de Coantré's letters to her son, to be read at leisure some day, and whole bundles of files which were Mme de

Coantré's accounts, the forest of figures in which this penniless person had lived. On the other hand, he read carefully through Léon's diary, though it was of no interest, consisting mainly of humdrum household facts. However, when he arrived at the entry: 'Sentimental session with old Oct. We shall see!' he smiled to himself, without acrimony. This did not in any way alter his opinion of Léon, and everything he thought about it was summed up in the remark he made to himself, 'That's not at all bad!'

M. Octave gave Léon's tools to the chauffeur. He thought of offering some of his old clothes to the *curé* at La Trinité for the poor. But Papon's respectful hesitation when he mentioned it to him gave him to understand that it would be indecent to give away clothes in such a state of dirt and shabbiness (so much so, as Papon remarked in the kitchen, 'that they would run to the tub by themselves if they could move'). Annoyed at having allowed himself to be taught a lesson by his servant (it happened only too frequently), M. Octave would not even allow the clothes to be thrown into the dustbin for fear that the concierge might open the parcel and by a process of elimination work out where they came from. Papon tied M. de Coantré's clothes up in copies of the *Daily Mail* and threw them away after dark in some bushes in the Place de la Trinité.

M. de Coantré, always a Jonah, nearly brought off a remarkable achievement: a rift in the almost fifty-year-old friendship between the baron and M. Héquelin du Page. The baron learned through a third person that his friend considered he had not behaved very well towards his nephew. He was cut to the quick. If the world was mistaken, so be it! But that his old friend, who knew all his thoughts (except those he concealed from him), should adopt such a false view of the realities of the case and pass so unjust a judgment was really too bad. Léon himself would have reacted similarly if someone had told him that he had behaved badly towards his mother. M. Octave, deeply upset, was beginning to explain to his friend how he had done more than his duty in regard to Léon when M. Héquelin du Page interrupted him and said that this assurance was enough, that he did not want to hear another word. This short scene had an element of the sublime.

As the years go by, M. Octave shows more and more solicitude for Léon's memory. Contrary to what he had expected, his nephew's death caused him no trouble of a material kind, and he is grateful to Léon for apparently ignoring the many and various ways in which the dead can inconvenience the living. The baron has made a financial arrangement with Chandelier to ensure that his nephew's grave is decently looked after: it is a point of honour with him that the tomb of his sister's son should not appear neglected. In fact, three years ago when the stone was cracked by frost, M. de Cöetquidan had the whole thing remade in a better quality material and had engraved thereon the arms and the coronet of a count, though without abandoning any of his reservations as to the right of the deceased to this coronet (one can be generous towards the dead since they will get no pleasure from it). Whenever M. Octave and his sister are at Fréville, the grave of Léon de Coantré is covered with fresh flowers.